St. Helena Libr.
1492 Library Lane
St. Helena, CA 94574
(707) 963-5244

A Gift From
ST. HELENA PUBLIC LIBRARY
FRIENDS&FOUNDATION

Praise for *The Low Desert*

"The wild west is alive in *The Low Desert*, a collection of stories as brutal and compelling as the landscape itself."　　—Brad Meltzer

"The first Tod Goldberg short story I ever read was 'Goon Number Four,' which he wrote for my anthology, *The Darkling Halls of Ivy*. I loved that story so much that I was eager to read his new collection, *The Low Desert*, and guess what? It's engaging and supremely satisfying from the first page to the last."　　—Lawrence Block

"I'm a huge fan of Tod Goldberg, and these stories showcase all that I love best about his work—the wicked sense of humor, the razor sharp attention to detail and character, and the riveting momentum of a born storyteller. *The Low Desert* is a master class in how to write great Noir."　　—Dan Chaon, author of *Ill Will*

"There is something inherently violent about living in the California desert, about the imposition of human will—swimming pools and lush green lawns, air-conditioned palaces, and rolling golf courses—on an inhospitable, rust red, hard-as-stone landscape that otherwise seems indifferent to your suffering—be it from the punishing heat or the grifters and gangsters who've been drawn to the desert for generations. Tod Goldberg understands this and has written a collection of stories that are keenly observed, wryly funny, and heart-wrenching in equal measure. If wisdom can be gleaned from taking a sharp look at the human impulse toward violence, then Tod Goldberg is one of this nation's sagest storytellers."　　—Attica Locke, author of *Heaven, My Home*

"*The Low Desert* is a powerhouse. Each story is finely crafted and flawlessly executed—gripping, surprising, and satisfying. Goldberg finds humanity in what others overlook, beauty in what many ignore. He seamlessly marries violence and grace to understand both the root and the aftermath of crime. And in doing so he tells a damn fine tale over and again." —Ivy Pochoda, author of *These Women*

"Tod Goldberg's stories are full of humor, pathos, and sharp knife-twists of plot and insight. Featuring best laid plans that have gone horribly awry, and heartbreakingly authentic characters broken by violence, longing, and hope, *The Low Desert* packs a heady, emotional wallop. More of this, please." —Paul Tremblay, author of *A Head Full of Ghosts* and *The Little Sleep*

"*The Low Desert* blew me away. It's an astonishingly rich collection of stories—harrowing and hopeful, gritty and funny, elegiac and electrifying, and always, always, deeply human. Tod Goldberg has written a book that's impossible to put down and impossible to forget."
—Lou Berney, Edgar Award–winning author of *November Road* and *The Long and Faraway Gone*

"Tod Goldberg is a terrific writer, and *The Low Desert* is a smart, surprising page turner." —Don Winslow

"Like Mario Puzo, Goldberg understands that the way to write about organized crime is to write about the people who live in that world. Yes, they are criminals, but most of them aren't villains. A sterling collection that showcases the author's gifts as a storyteller."
—*Booklist*

THE LOW DESERT

ALSO BY TOD GOLDBERG

Gangster Nation
Gangsterland
Living Dead Girl

THE
LOW
DESERT

GANGSTER STORIES

TOD GOLDBERG

COUNTERPOINT
BERKELEY, CALIFORNIA

THE LOW DESERT

Copyright © 2021 by Tod Goldberg
First hardcover edition: 2021

This book is a work of fiction. Names, characters, places,
and incidents are the product of the author's imagination
or are used fictitiously. Any resemblance to actual events is
unintended and entirely coincidental.

Library of Congress Cataloging-in-Publication Data
Names: Goldberg, Tod, author.
Title: The low desert : gangster stories / Tod Goldberg.
Description: First hardcover edition. | Berkeley, California :
Counterpoint, 2021.
Identifiers: LCCN 2020021014 | ISBN 9781640093362 (hardcover) |
ISBN 9781640093379 (ebook)
Classification: LCC PS3557.O35836 A6 2021 | DDC 813/.54—dc23
LC record available at https://lccn.loc.gov/2020021014

Jacket design by Brian Lemus
Book design by Wah-Ming Chang

COUNTERPOINT
2560 Ninth Street, Suite 318
Berkeley, CA 94710
www.counterpointpress.com

Printed in the United States of America

1 3 5 7 9 10 8 6 4 2

For Wendy,
who is the good inside all of these bad people

A prisoner cannot free himself.

THE TALMUD

CONTENTS

THE LOW DESERT

THE ROYAL CALIFORNIAN

Three hours out of the hospital, his left foot too swollen for a shoe, Shane's car breaks down. It's July, a trillion degrees outside, Interstate 10 a gray ribbon of shit unspooling east out of Palm Springs toward Arizona. Not exactly where he wanted to go, but who the fuck wants to go to Arizona? It's what was on the other side of Arizona that mattered to Shane, the chance that there might be another life in that direction. He never liked being on the coast. The one time he ever tried to swim in the Pacific—during a vacation with his dad, so, over twenty years ago, half his lifetime now—he was gripped with the ungodly realization that unlike a pool, there were no sides. You were always in the deep end.

It was a feeling that stuck with him, even when he was in one of those towns in the San Fernando Valley that sounded like an escape route from an old Western: North Hills ... West Hills ... Hidden Hills ...

The Honda was the one damn thing Shane thought he could depend on. But as soon as he pulled out of the parking lot at Centinela Hospital in Inglewood, the check-engine light flashed on. A hundred thousand miles he'd put on that fucking car and not a single problem and the one time he really needed it, it was telling him to fuck off. He didn't have the time—or the money—to swing by the mechanic considering he'd left the hospital before the nurse had filled out the paperwork for the cops, which was a problem. Not as big a problem as staying would have been. It wasn't the kind of thing that would have the cops trawling the city for him, especially since the wound did look self-inflected, since it was . . . someone else holding his fucking hand while he shot himself with his own damn gun.

SHANE COULDN'T REMEMBER if he still had AAA, but he called anyway.

"Looks like you canceled your account six months ago," the customer-service agent predictably said.

Rachel must have done it after she moved out. Like how she canceled their credit cards. Or how she took their dog Manny to get his teeth cleaned on the same morning she kicked him out of the house, knowing full well Shane wouldn't have the cash to pick the dog up.

God, he loved that dog. Probably more than he loved Rachel. Not *probably*. *Actually*. If he got out of this fucked-up situation, he was going to buy another dog that looked like Manny and name him Manny, too.

"How much is it to re-up?" Shane asked.

"Sixty-eight dollars, which gets you seven miles of towing service."

"What if I need to go farther?" Shane asked, thinking, *What the hell, maybe I'll have AAA tow me to Arizona, give me someone to talk to.* Or maybe he'd just steal the tow truck. He could do that. He was capable of anything now.

"You'd need the premier membership for that," the customer-service agent said, and then he began to tell Shane the particulars of how amazing the premier membership was, going on about all the times you could get your car towed a hundred miles, the discounts you can get at resorts nationwide, Shane thinking that the only people who could afford this fucking service were the people least likely to need it. He had $274 in cash in his pocket; Gold Mike, the fucker who shot him in the foot, gave it to him as a parting gift after he'd asked him to stop by their storage unit by the Forum, Shane thinking it was to plan the night's job, Gold Mike with other ideas.

"It's not working out," Gold Mike told him. The storage unit was half empty already, Gold Mike's van filled with their DJ and Karaoke equipment, all their locksmith materials, plus their three industrial-sized lockboxes filled with pills. They'd been coming up light lately, but for a while, it was a good living. Black-tie weddings in the Palisades, bar mitzvahs in Calabasas, retirement parties in Bel-Air. How it worked: one of them would be inside at the wedding, singing or DJing, and the other would be parking cars and collecting addresses off of insurance cards and registrations. Three-hour wedding meant they could get as many keys made as they wanted. Spend the next couple days casing a house, go in and steal all the pills, which wasn't a crime any cop gave a shit about, particularly when there was no evidence of breaking and entering. Plus, it was a victimless crime, Shane not feeling too bad about taking a cancer patient's Klonopin, knowing full well CVS would hook them back up in thirty minutes, maybe less. They didn't steal jewelry or TVs or cars or any of that shit. Just pills.

Then this whole opiate crisis started getting on the news right when weed got legalized, so people in California started loading up on edibles and vape pens instead of Percocet and benzos.

"It's just an ebb," Shane said.

"I'm moving my operating base," Gold Mike said. "Got a friend in Reno. Says it's jumping off there. Everyone's hooked on something. He can get me into the hotels. That's next-level."

"Cool," Shane said. "I'm down to relocate." His only steady, legal gigs were running karaoke at Forrest's Bar in Culver City and a honky-tonk in Thousand Oaks called Denim & Diamonds, across the street from a bar where a guy went fucking nuts and murdered a dozen people.

"You're not hearing me," Gold Mike said. "You can't hit the high notes anymore. If you can't sing, this whole operation is moot." *Moot.* Where the fuck had he learned that word? "Don't make it weird, all right? We had a good run."

"Who needs a high note? You think Mick can hit a high note?"

"Who the fuck is Mick?"

"From the Rolling Stones. Mick Jagger."

"Bro," Gold Mike said, "I don't even like music."

"So that's it? No severance?"

"You think you're getting COBRA up in this bitch? Come on, man."

"Manny's chemo put me back ten grand," Shane said. Manny had a tumor on his ear that turned out to be a treatable cancer, in the sense that the dog could get treatment and still die, but he hadn't yet, as far as Shane knew. "I've been upside-down ever since."

"That was like eighteen months ago." Gold Mike took out his wallet, thumbed out a few fifties, put them on an empty shelf next to a broken turntable.

"Couple hundred bucks?" Shane said. "How about you give me 50 percent of everything or I walk into a police station. How about that?" And then Shane pulled out his gun, which had actually been a gift from Gold Mike. A .380. He'd given it to him after a robbery went sideways: a Vietnam War vet came home and found Shane in his bathroom, beat the fucking shit out of him with a golf club, Gold Mike coming in at the last minute and knocking the fucker out with a Taser.

You pull out your gun, you gotta be ready to use it, no talking shit, no hands up, nothing, just pop-pop-pop. That's what cops are always saying; it's what Gold Mike had taught Shane, too. Which is how he also had all of Gold Mike's credit cards and his driver's license, in addition to $274.

"Seven miles is fine," Shane said to the customer-service agent and gave his location on the 10, half a mile from the Monroe exit, according to the GPS on his phone, which it occurred to him he'd need to ditch. Shane examined all the main street names in either direction—Washington, Adams, Jefferson, Madison, Monroe, Jackson, Calhoun, Van Buren—trying to find a street that sounded friendly, a place he could tell the customer-service dude to find a room for him, but the dead presidents were giving him bad juju. He wasn't going anywhere near that fucking asshole Andrew Jackson. "There any motels near Jefferson Street?" he asked, thinking Jefferson seemed about 65 percent decent, relative to our other slave-owning asshole Founding Fathers. "I need a place with a ka-raoke bar, if possible." He had a hustle he liked to do where he'd bet people that he could make them cry and then he'd bust out "Brick" by Ben Folds Five and every girl who ever had an abortion would be in a puddle. It didn't make him proud, but he had bills to pay.

"Let's see what we have here." The agent made a whistling sound. "Well, the Royal Californian is 6.7 miles from where you are," the agent said, "and located between Jefferson and Monroe on Highway 111." He paused and Shane could hear him clicking away on his computer. "They have free HBO and free wi-fi, a pool, and a sports bar with karaoke. If that works, shall I charge it to your existing credit card and get the truck to you?"

"How about I give the driver cash," Shane said. He needed as little paper trail as possible.

"I'll need to check with my manager," the agent said, and put Shane on hold.

He was parked beneath a billboard that advertised *The Wonder of Waterfront Living in the Desert!* and showed a happy couple of indeterminate race walking into what appeared to be an Italian lakeside villa surrounded by palm trees. He looked to the west and could make out the obvious signs of civilization: the sign for a Starbucks, an RV park called The Long Run, a billboard touting an upcoming concert by Rick Springfield at the Fantasy Springs Casino. That fucking guy.

"We'll have a tow truck to you in about twenty minutes," the agent said. "May we get anything else for you?"

He looked down. His foot wept blood, the gauze packed around the wound a deep red. Shit. He'd need something to dull the pain, soon. And then stop the sepsis. Which was a thing he didn't worry about, usually, but this was not a usual day.

"Iodine? Anyone carry that?"

"Uh. No, sir, I don't think so."

It was worth a shot. Shane hung up. It was nearly four o'clock. He was supposed to be singing "Come On Eileen" in a couple hours, always his first song over at Forrest's, everyone always losing their shit when he did that "toora loora toora loo rye aye" bit, like it was 1982 and they were thirteen at the eighth-grade dance.

That fucking song.

More trouble than it was worth, that was for sure.

He couldn't think about that now.

He needed to get Gold Mike's body out of the trunk.

Or, well . . . parts of Gold Mike's body.

IT'S 2009 AND Shane's working the Black Angus in Northridge. They've got something they call the "Fun Bar," a relic from the disco years, lit-up floor, big dark booths, great sound system, but no one dancing. Just frat boys over from the college drinking vodka and cranberry, like they all have UTIs. At first, he's just doing karaoke like anybody does karaoke, stands up there and lets some drunk come up and sing "American Pie," helps him out when he realizes the song is eight minutes long and he doesn't have the wind. Flirts with the bartender, maybe gets a handjob in the dry storage. Woman or man. He didn't give a fuck. Handjob was a handjob, Shane equal-opportunity back then, because of all the coke and a profound lack of giving a fuck. Love is love, friction is friction.

Maybe a little guilt now, thinking about it, thinking about how he did Rachel wrong, staring at the ceiling fan twirling in his room at the Royal Californian, 11 p.m., still a hundred degrees outside, giant flying roaches committing suicide against his window every couple minutes, Shane dying for a fucking Percocet, a million of them still in Gold Mike's van, Shane could hit himself for being so stupid, not thinking this all through, his foot throbbing, sweat sticking his shirt to his chest.

His own fault. Rachel, that is. A lot of lying. *Fuck it* had been his point of view back when he worked at the Angus. Go home with a hundred bucks for the night and an empty load? *Fuck it.* Problem was, he'd kept that point of view long into his relationship with Rachel and she was not a *Fuck it* kind of person, so he pretended it was just how performers were, though by the time Rachel came along, he wasn't a performer anymore.

"Baby," he'd tell her, "you gotta just say 'fuck it' when you're in this business, otherwise every night would crush your spirit."

And Rachel, she'd say, "Then you should get another way to earn a living."

And so he had.

Kind of.

Thing was, Shane could really sing. All this other shit was ephemeral. His talent, man, that was in his genetic code. His dad played in the Catskills back in the day, singing in cover bands, even came out to California that one time he brought Shane with him, doing a night at Melvyn's in Palm Springs. Typically, Dad would come back home the first week of September with a roll of cash, and for a month everything would be good between him and Shane's mom. Dinners out. New clothes. Shane's mom falling in love all over again, talking about how maybe this year they'd get married, maybe she'd go to college, then maybe law school, Shane's mother always talking about how she was going to be a lawyer, but by the time she died, she'd spent twenty-five years as the lunch lady at Rensselaer Point Elementary down in Troy. She'd had Shane when she was fifteen. Dead by fifty-one. Got diagnosed with early onset Alzheimer's and put a fucking noose around her neck two hours later, Shane's dad saying, *Maybe she didn't really have the old-timer's, because wouldn't she have forgotten?* His dad was still alive, that was the irony, doing what Shane thought of as the Dead Man's Tour: Buddy Holly and Elvis tribute shows at Indian casinos in Connecticut, Shane keeping track of him on the Internet, that fucker doing pretty well.

But the Angus.

In comes Gold Mike. Sits at a table right by Shane's kit, nurses a Diet Coke. Really gets into it when Shane sings. Tapping his foot. Bobbing his head. When Shane hits his full register during "Come On Eileen," Gold Mike stands up and whoops.

When he goes on break fifteen minutes later, Gold Mike follows him outside, where Shane is having a smoke and watching the traffic on Corbin Avenue.

"You got a nice presence," Gold Mike says.

"Thanks, man," Shane says.

"Wasting it out here, if you want my opinion," Gold Mike says.

"Just waiting to be discovered."

"That's not ever gonna happen," Gold Mike says, like he knows. He's maybe twenty-seven, but he's one of those guys who talks like he's been around the world fifty times. Shane's seen Gold Mike on the circuit. Weber's in Reseda. Sagebrush Cantina out in Calabasas. Shutters in Santa Monica. Gold Mike fingers a diamond-encrusted *V* that hangs around his neck. Shane counts twenty-five little diamonds.

"Whatever," Shane says. He takes one more drag from his cigarette, then puts it out on the bottom of his shoe, like it's a thing he does all the time, which it isn't.

"Whatever?" Gold Mike says. "I insult you and you say, 'Whatever.' Passivity, man, that's an illness."

"You want me to hit you or something?"

Gold Mike laughs hard. He's one of those Armenian dudes who shaves his head just to look tough, Shane making out the outline of a full head of stubble. Shane isn't much of a fighter. He's the kind of person who will stab a guy, though. Put a screwdriver in someone's eye. You're either a pussy or you're not. Shane probably is one, but he's not squeamish around blood and that helps.

"I like you," Gold Mike says. "You a child molester or anything?"

"What kind of fucking question is that?"

"I been watching you," Gold Mike says. "You put your dick in anything. Just need to be clear what I don't get down with."

"How long have you been watching me?"

"A couple weeks," Gold Mike says, like it's perfectly normal. "You ever do any time?"

"*You* ever do any time?"

"A couple days here and there," Gold Mike says.

"That must impress some people."

Gold Mike laughs again but doesn't respond.

"What's the V stand for?" Shane points at Gold Mike's neck.

"My last name is Voski," Gold Mike says.

"Okay."

"It means 'gold' in Armenian."

That's lucky, Shane thinks, then says, "You speak Armenian?" because there's no way Gold Mike wasn't born in Reseda.

"Fuck no," Gold Mike says. "It's a dead language." He points over his shoulder. "I went to CSUN and everyone always wanted me to join the Armenian Student Union, bunch of assholes named Gabarian talking about getting the genocide recognized. Not my game. I'm multinational. Speak Spanish, French, got a little Russian, enough I could probably get by at Odessa. You ever been there? The OG Russian restaurant in Las Vegas?"

"No," Shane said. "I don't *get down* with the Russians. Not since *Fiddler on the Roof.*"

Gold Mike raised his eyebrows in mild amusement. Shane didn't make him for a fan of musical theater, but then he said, "What's your last name?"

"Solomon," Shane says.

"Does that mean something?"

"Peace," Shane says.

"Yeah?"

"That's what my mother told me," he says. "It's from the Hebrew word *shalom.*"

"You speak Hebrew?"

"Enough to DJ a bar mitzvah."

Gold Mike leans forward, motions Shane to lean in, too.

"You want to make some real money, Shalom?"

SHANE FINALLY FELL asleep after 1 a.m. but woke up again at 5:47 a.m., sunrise filling his room on the second floor of the Royal Californian with orange light, his foot like an anvil at the bottom of his leg. He unwrapped the gauze and examined the wound. His foot had swollen to twice its normal size, at least, even though the wound wasn't that big. An inch around. The nurse told him yesterday that the bullet shattered two of his cuneiform bones, that he'd need surgery to stabilize his foot, a couple pins would be inserted, and then he'd be in a hard cast for six to eight weeks. But he was going to need to speak to the police before any of that happened.

That wasn't going to work.

Not with 66 percent of Gold Mike rotting in his storage unit, the other 33 percent in the Honda's trunk, Shane thinking 1 percent was probably drying on the floor, blood and viscera and whatnot. He'd chopped Gold Mike's head off using the fire-hose hatchet, then cut the head up into smaller pieces to make it easier to shuttle around, then took off Gold Mike's hands and feet, too, because he thought that would make it harder to identify him, but with DNA, fuck, it probably didn't matter, but Shane hadn't been thinking too straight.

He'd taken the battery out of Gold Mike's van and poured acid over the rest of the body, but that was just cosmetic. For sure Shane's DNA was in the unit and the van and on Gold Mike's body, but then his DNA was all over everything regardless. They were business partners. That was easy enough to explain. Plus, he had no *legitimate* reason to kill Gold Mike. Anyone who saw them together knew they were a team. The only proof that it was Shane who'd plugged him an excessive number of times was probably the hole in Shane's fucking foot and the gun itself, which Shane had tucked under his mattress.

Well, and Gold Mike's head and all that, which was now in his hotel room's safe, zipped up inside a Whole Foods freezer bag filled with ice.

Shane stepped out onto his second-story balcony—which was just wide enough to hurl yourself over—and lit up his second-to-last cigarette. He'd given up smoking when Manny got cancer, truth be told he sort of blamed himself for that whole thing, but it was the only drug he had on his person and he needed about ten minutes of mental clarity to figure out how he was going to get himself out of this situation.

He needed to get rid of Gold Mike's parts.

He needed to get rid of the gun.

He needed to get himself an alibi . . . or he needed to change his identity, which didn't seem like a plausible turn of events, but he was open to whatever presented itself to him.

He needed to go across the street to the Circle K and get some disposable phones.

He also was in a fuck ton of pain and under normal circumstances might go find a dispensary and get some edibles, but he wasn't showing anyone his ID. He'd get some ice and soak his foot in the tub; that should bring down the swelling. He'd get some bleach from housecleaning, put a couple drops in the water, maybe that would disinfect the wound? Then he needed to get a new car.

The Royal Californian sat on a stretch of Highway 111 in Indio that could have been Carson City or Bakersfield or Van Nuys or anywhere else where someone had the wise idea to plant a palm tree and then surround it with cement. This wasn't the part of greater Palm Springs where people came to visit—it was nowhere near the

leafy garden hotel he'd stayed in with his dad, the Ingleside Inn—
unless they were going to court or bailing someone out, since the
hotel was a block west of the Larson Justice Center, the county
courthouse and jail. He hadn't realized it at first, not until he was
checking in and the clerk gave him a brochure of local amenities.
Page one had dining options. Page two was local entertainment and
information about how to get to the polo fields a mile south, where
Coachella was held every year. As close as Shane was ever going to
get to *that*. And then page three was all bail bonds, attorneys, and
AA meetings.

Made sense, then, when the clerk didn't seem bothered by his
bloody foot and that he didn't have ID when he gave him Gold
Mike's Visa to check in.

He'd given the AAA driver an extra fifteen dollars to park his
car just down the block, in a neighborhood of taupe houses called
the Sandpiper Estates, the word *estate* apparently one of those
words whose meaning had been lost to insincerity, since all Shane
saw were a lot of children standing by themselves on front lawns
made of rock, staring into their phones. Shane left the keys in the
ignition and the doors unlocked. Best-case scenario, the car would
be stripped clean in a few days. Worst case, it would get towed to
some county yard and there it would stay, forever.

Shane counted seven cars in the Royal Californian's parking lot.
A van with a "Save Mono Lake" sticker faded on the bumper. A
white pickup truck missing the tailgate. Two Hondas that looked
just like his dead Accord. A red Buick Regal, probably a rental, no
one bought fucking Buicks. An SUV. Another SUV. He tried to
imagine who owned each car, and what their favorite song might
be, Shane always interested if people picked a sad song or a happy
one. You could tell a lot about a person based on their pick, could

imagine what they thought was going to happen to them in their life, or could better understand their situation.

Rachel's favorite song was "American Girl" by Tom Petty. His mom's favorite song was "Suspicious Minds" by Elvis. Shane? He didn't have a favorite. Not anymore. Songs stopped having meaning for him.

A man of about seventy walked out of his ground-floor room and into the parking lot, wearing blue boxer shorts, a white V-neck undershirt, and a pair of black sandals, keys in his hand. A Sinatra guy, Shane thought. Probably "My Way" or "Come Fly with Me." Shane made him for the red Buick Regal. It was backed into a space, always the sign of an asshole. Instead, the old man looked up and down the block, which was deserted, then crossed the street to a one-story office building with storefront-style signs advertising a law office—"Terry Kales; Criminal Defense/DUI/Divorce/Immigration"—accounting offices, a Mexican bakery, a notary, and a place where you could get your cell phone fixed.

Not Sinatra.

Neil Diamond.

He went inside the law office, came out a few minutes later holding a manila envelope, unlocked a silver Mercedes using his key fob, the lights blinking twice, disappeared inside, started it up, rolled back across the street to the parking lot. A woman came walking out of the old man's hotel room—she looked young, maybe sixteen—met the old guy in the parking lot, got in the passenger side of the car, and it pulled away. Five minutes later, the Benz was parked in Royal Californian's lot and the old man was headed back into the hotel, which is when he spotted Shane up on his perch.

"You always stand around at dawn, watching people?"

"Just having a smoke," Shane said, "while I contemplate which car to steal."

"Why not just get an Uber?"

Shane pointed at the man's Benz. "German engineering has always appealed to me," he said, "but as a Jew, it feels shameful. So you're safe." Shane telling him he was a Jew to put him at ease, no one ever felt scared of Jews, but also just to see how he reacted, Kales seeming like a Jewish last name. Shane flicked his cigarette butt over the balcony. It landed, still smoking, a few feet away from the man. "You mind stepping on that for me?" Shane pointed at his own foot. "I'm down a limb."

The old man scratched his stomach absently but didn't make a move to the cigarette. "You here for a court date?"

"No," Shane said. "Not today."

"You need a lawyer," he said, "I'm right across the street."

"How much for a murder defense?" Shane asked, but he laughed, a big joke, two guys at dawn, bullshitting.

"Less than you'd think." Terry walked over to the butt, stepped on it, cocked his head sideways to get a better look at Shane's foot up above him. "Looks like self-defense to me."

"I'll keep that in mind," Shane said.

"My AC is broken, so I keep office hours at Cactus Pete's." He pointed at the bar attached to the Royal Californian. "Be there until at least 6:30. I'll buy you a drink, we can talk about your case."

"I'm innocent."

"Yeah," Terry said. "That's what we'll tell 'em."

SHANE COULDN'T TELL if Cactus Pete's had a kitschy design aesthetic or if it was just a leftover from the seventies. He'd never been in a bar with shag carpeting. The VIP area, set off from the tiny dance floor and DJ booth by a red-velvet rope, had high-backed booths that reminded Shane fondly of the Angus, Terry Kales sitting in the biggest one, sipping on a glass of something brown, papers spread out in front of him, a cell phone to his ear, another cell phone and his car keys keeping his papers from blowing away, the overhead fans working overtime to keep the room cool. He didn't look up when Shane walked in, at least as far as Shane could tell, which was hard because Terry had on sunglasses, the bar's windows flooding the room with bright light.

It was just before three; tomorrow at this time, he'd be in the clear. That was the hoped-for result. He'd found a 99 Cent Store two blocks away, limped his ass over there, his foot on fire, picked up a change of clothes, some sunglasses, a Padres baseball cap. Went next door to the Circle K, got a disposable phone. He was about out of cash now, but he'd figure that out.

On the dance floor, a woman was setting up for karaoke, and for reasons Shane could not fathom, there was guy dressed as a clown sitting at the bar. Green hair. Red nose. Striped pants. Big red shoes. Stars-and-stripes shirt and vest. Back of the vest, embroidered in rhinestones, it said HERMIETHECLOWN.COM. He had a cup of coffee and the *Desert Sun*, reading the sports page. Shane sat down at the bar but kept a stool between himself and Hermie.

"Get you something?" the woman setting up the karaoke asked. She was younger than Terry, older than the clown, somewhere on the plus side of fifty. She had on a tank top that showed off her shoulders—muscular, but lean—and a full sleeve of tattoos down her right arm. Shane saw two names—Charlotte and Randy—amid flowers, sunsets, and spiderwebs. She had a nametag pinned above her left breast that said "Glory."

"Was wondering what time the show was," Shane said.

"Six," Glory said. "You sing?"

"Yeah."

"We have a lot of regulars, so sign up early."

"Truth is," Shane said, "I was wondering if I could warm up first."

When Glory didn't respond, he said, "I'm staying here."

"Room?"

"Number 204," he said. "On account of my foot. Gotta have surgery in the morning. Just trying to have a good night before I get the knife." He looked over at the clown. "Unless you've got first dibs."

"He don't speak," Glory said, "or sing." The clown nodded in the affirmative. Glory leaned over the bar and examined Shane's foot. So did the silent clown, who blew lightly on a whistle he kept around his neck. Shane slid off his flip-flop, wiggled his toes. "You can't be in here without shoes," Glory said.

"Just letting it breathe," Shane said.

Glory nodded solemnly, like they'd come to some agreement about life. "What's your song?"

"I mix it up," Shane said, and out of the corner of his eye, he saw Terry slide his sunglasses down his nose, "but mostly Neil Diamond."

SHANE WAS MIDWAY through "Girl, You'll Be a Woman Soon" when Terry came over and stood next to the clown, closed his eyes, mouthed the lyrics. Terry and the clown swayed back and forth together, Shane digging down deep for the end, giving it some soul, some real pathos.

"Again," Terry said, and tossed Shane a fifty, so he did it again, Terry had tears in his eyes this time, clearly going through some shit. When he finished, Terry said, "One more, your pick," and then went and sat back in his booth, the clown following him. Shane went with "Song Sung Blue." When he was finished, Terry motioned him over to his table.

"You really having surgery?" Terry asked once they were all comfortable in the sweaty, half-moon banquette, Terry's shit spread out everywhere, Shane eyeing his car keys, his plan coming into full focus, Hermie busy on his phone, answering texts. Popular fucking clown. "I heard you talking to Glory."

"Yeah," Shane said. "At the hospital up the street." He'd seen it in the brochure. It was named for John F. Kennedy, which Shane thought was yet another example of bad presidential juju. Whole town was lousy with it.

"Good hospital," Terry said. "All of my best clients have died there."

"Like the girl this morning?"

"That was my daughter."

"Really?" *Really.*

"Yeah," Terry said. "I've got limited visitation at the moment, so I take what I can get."

"Okay," Shane said, not sure if he believed him. "What about you, Hermie? Any kids?"

Hermie looked up from his phone, shook his head no.

Thank God.

"Can I give you some legal advice?" Terry said. "Jew to Jew."

"Mazel," Shane said.

"You've clearly been shot in the foot," Terry said. "In about two hours, when the courthouse closes? This bar is gonna fill up with off-duty cops, DAs, public defenders, judges. You should be gone by then."

"That is good advice," Shane said. "Why are you giving it to me?"

"When it all comes down," Terry said, and he pointed at a television above the bar, the sound off, running Fox News, "they'll take us both."

"Apart from that."

"You have the natural ability to make a person feel something, you know? That's special." Terry adjusted his sunglasses, Shane thinking maybe he was getting a little teary-eyed again, or maybe he just liked the Jim Jones vibe he was giving off. "Sometimes a song, sung by the right person, it'll touch you. You touched me up there just now. I don't know. Maybe I'm drunk."

Hermie nodded vigorously.

"You saw my daughter? Her mother," Terry said, "won't have me in the house, which is why I'm in this situation over here. 'Girl' was our wedding song. Seems dumb, no?"

"People pick terrible songs for their weddings," Shane said, and then he told Terry about his job working weddings, all the times he sang "Wild Horses" for newlyweds.

"No one *listens* anymore," Terry said. "Words used to mean something." He looked over at Hermie. "No offense."

Hermie shrugged.

"Anyway," Terry said. "You seem like a nice guy in a bad situation. So. Maybe I can help you. Do you want help?"

"I could use a friend," Shane said.

"I could be a friend." Terry reached into his back pocket and pulled out his wallet, slid a business card over to Shane. One side was in English, the other in Spanish, but both were for a dentist named Marco Degolado in Los Algodones, Baja California, right over the Mexican border, according to the thumbnail map printed on the card.

"You got any warrants?" Terry asked.

"No," Shane said.

"That's two hours from here," Terry said. "Two exits before Yuma. Easy in and out of Mexico, all the snowbirds go there for dental care. They're liberal with their opiates and antibiotics in Mexico." Shane nodded. "Dr. Degolado knows his way around minor surgery as well. He's a friend, too." Shane nodded again. His foot *was* killing him. "Let me make a call."

"You'd do that?"

"You walk into JFK with that," he said, "you won't walk out."

Shane looked over at Hermie, who gave an affirmative nod. What the fuck went on in *that* guy's fucking mind?

"All right," Shane said. "Set it for tomorrow afternoon?"

"What's your name?"

Shane thought for a moment. "My friends," he said, "call me Gold Mike."

"What do you want the doctor to call you?"

"Mike Voski," he said.

Terry picked up his cell phone. "Give me five minutes," he said and headed outside, which gave Shane a chance to snatch up Terry's car keys from the table. He turned and looked out the window to where Terry's Benz was parked, around the corner from where Terry stood, hit the unlock button, watched the car's lights blink twice, set the keys back down.

Hermie the Clown didn't say a word, so Shane said, "You a monk or something?"

Hermie stared at Shane for a few seconds, then said, out loud, "You ever meet a chatty clown?"

"Can't say I have."

"That's part of the game," he said. He reached over and picked up the car keys. Hit the button. Lights flashed again. Locked.

"How about I give you fifty bucks and we call it even?" Shane said.

Hermie said, "How about everything you've got in your wallet?"

Shane had his gun tucked under his shirt and could have, he supposed, shot Hermie, done him like Han Solo did Greedo, but Shane wasn't yet the unprovoked murdering type.

"Not gonna be much more than fifty," Shane said. He dug out his wallet, pulled out everything, set it on the table, sixty-seven bucks. Hermie took it all.

"Not personal, you understand," Hermie said.

"Just two guys doing business," Shane said.

Hermie stood up, gathered up all his belongings, then pulled out a business card, everyone in this fucking place the kings of Vistaprint, apparently. It said:

HERMIE THE CLOWN
Parties. Charity Events. Private Functions.
Restaurant & Bar PR.
NO KIDS 18+ ONLY
SEE WEBSITE FOR RATES/CELEBRITY PHOTOS
Hermietheclown.com
Phone: 760-CLOWN-69
Email: Hermie@Hermietheclown.com

"I'll be back in a few days," Hermie said. "If you're coming back."

"I'm coming back."

"You'd be good in the clown game," Hermie said. "You've got a nice presence."

"Thanks," Shane said.

"I got my teeth capped in Los Algodones," Hermie said. "Can't have janky teeth and be a clown. Freaks people out. Terry hooked me up."

Hermie was silent again, like he was trying to get Shane to ask him a question.

"And then what?" Shane finally said.

"I have to do Terry favors, periodically," he said. "Drop things off. Take out the garbage sometimes. Clean up his room. Favors. So if you're not willing to do that, I'd say keep moving, hoss."

There it was.

"He really Jewish?" Shane asked.

"His cousin was a rabbi," Hermie said.

"Was?"

"Died."

"Natural causes?"

"I didn't ask for an autopsy."

"Out here?"

"Las Vegas," Hermie said. "Everyone here is always trying to get to Las Vegas, everyone in Las Vegas is always trying to get somewhere else, no one happy to be any one place."

"You make a lot of sense, for a clown."

"You'd be surprised what a guy can learn staying quiet." He looked outside, where Terry was still on the phone. "My Uber is here," he said. Hermie stood there for a moment, shifting back and forth on his big red shoes. "He doesn't have a daughter," Hermie said, then closed a giant, exaggerated zipper across his mouth, locked it, tossed away the key, and left, into the heat of the day. Hermie bumped fists with Terry, got into a waiting Prius, and drove off.

Shane unlocked the Benz, again.

Terry came back in a few minutes later. "You're all set, Gold Mike," he said.

"What do I owe you?" Shane asked.

"Doctor will have a couple prescriptions for you to bring back."

"That all?"

"Well," Terry said, "you'll need to go back for a follow-up. In which case, I might have something for you to deliver. Could be you come to find you like Mexico."

"I'm gonna need wheels."

"You beam here?"

"No," Shane said. "Car broke down. It won't be fixed for a week, at least."

Terry tapped a pen against his lips. "Okay," he said. "How about I have Enterprise drop off a car for you. Nothing fancy, you understand. What do you have for collateral?"

Shane pondered this for a moment, then reached under his shirt and put his gun down on the table.

SHANE WAITED UNTIL Cactus Pete's was in full swing to make his move. Terry wasn't kidding about the clientele: a steady stream of men with brush cuts and tucked-in polo shirts were followed by men and women in business suits, mostly of the off-the-rack variety, not a lot of tailored sorts doing time in Indio's courthouse. Terry came out a couple times to take phone calls, cops and attorneys greeting him as they passed by, Shane watching from his hotel window as they all glad-handed one another, cops and robbers passing one another at the time clock.

Shane took Gold Mike's head, hands, and feet out of the safe, refilled the freezer bag with some fresh ice to help with the smell, zipped the bag back up, and headed downstairs. It was about seven, the sun still up, at least 105 degrees. Shane saw that there were now anthill mounds rising up through the cracks in the parking lot pavement. The lot was full, a dozen Ford F-150s with American flag and 1199 Foundation stickers in the windows, a couple Lexuses, a few BMWs, another five nebulous American cars, a surprising number of motorcycles, a couple Benzes. There was a kid, maybe six or seven, sitting on the tailgate of an F-150 parked next to Terry's Benz, eating a popsicle, playing on his phone. Shane's rental, a white Ford Fiesta, was parked next to it.

"You staying here?" Shane asked the kid.

"On the other side of the fairgrounds," the kid said, pointing beyond the courthouse and jail.

Shane looked down the block. There was, in fact, a giant county fairground right next to the jail and courts. Across the street was an A-frame Wienerschnitzel cut and pasted from the 1970s, a fire station, an Applebee's, a used-car lot. He tried to imagine what it would be like to grow up here. Figured it was like anywhere else. Either you lived in a happy home or you lived in a shitty one.

"You should go home," Shane said. "It's late."

"My dad works at the jail," the kid said.

"Oh yeah?"

"He's inside having a drink."

"What's he do there," Shane said, "at the jail?"

"Something with computers."

So probably not a cop. That's good. "You see anything weird here?"

The kid looked at Shane for a few seconds, like he couldn't be sure of his answer, then said, "I saw a clown. Like in that movie."

"What movie?"

"I didn't see it," the kid said. "But my cousin? He saw it and said it was fucked-up."

Shane looked around but didn't see Hermie. "Recently? The clown I mean."

"Couple minutes, I guess."

Odd.

"You do me a favor?" Shane asked.

"I'm not supposed to talk to anyone," the kid said, "cuz my dad says the East Valley is filled with criminals and pedos and losers and that's just who he works with."

"Yeah," Shane said, "that's smart." He pointed at his foot. He'd wrapped it in a towel and then taped his flip-flop to it, so he could walk around a bit better. It looked absurd. "Could you just run over and get me a bucket of ice from the front desk?"

The kid looked at Shane's foot. "What happened?"

"Stepped on a nail."

"Must have been pretty big."

"You do this for me or not?"

The kid slid off the back of the truck and headed to the hotel's lobby, which gave Shane the chance to pop open the unlocked trunk of Terry's Benz, drop the freezer bag in, and then close it.

SHANE GOT IN the Fiesta—it smelled weird inside, like vinegar and shoe leather and wet newspapers—started it up, turned left on Highway 111 out of the hotel, so he wouldn't pass Cactus Pete's, since he told Terry he wasn't leaving until the morning, then kept going, driving west into the setting sun, his left foot inside a bucket of ice. He rolled past the presidents—Monroe, Madison, Jefferson—then was in La Quinta—Adams, Washington—and into Indian Wells, then Palm Desert, just another snowbird in a rental car, could be anyone, so he opened the Fiesta's moonroof, let some air in, get that weird smell out. Then he was in Rancho Mirage, passing Bob Hope Drive, then rolling by Frank Sinatra Drive, Shane starting to feel like he'd gotten away with it, so he took out his burner, called the anonymous Crime Stoppers hotline, was patched through.

"This is going to sound crazy," Shane said, now in Cathedral City, passing Monty Hall Drive, a street named for a guy who spent his entire career disappointing people by giving them donkeys instead of cars, "but I swear I saw a man at the Royal Californian in Indio chopping up a human head. He put it all into a bag in the trunk of his Mercedes."

By the time he finished his story, Shane was in downtown Palm Springs, rolling north down Indian Avenue. His left foot was numb, but the rest of his body felt alive, sweat pouring down his face, his shirt and pants damp, even though the AC was cranked at full blast, the moonroof just cracked. He'd go back to LA tonight, get all the pills from the storage unit, then torch it, now that he was thinking straight. Then he'd turn around and go to Mexico, get his foot operated on, since he had an appointment already, and Terry was going to be in a jail cell for a good long time, maybe forever. And then he'd just keep rolling east, until he got back to upstate New York. Find his father at some Indian casino, see if he wanted to start a duo, figure out how to have a life together, Shane thinking, *Whoa, what? Am I high?* Shane thinking his foot was probably infected, that what he was feeling was something bad in his blood, sepsis most likely, and then he was passing the road to the Palm Springs Aerial Tramway, burning it out of town, the fields of windmills coming into view, Shane finally taking a moment to look in the rearview mirror, to make sure there weren't a hundred cop cars lined up behind him, and thinking, just for a moment, that he was really fucked-up, that he was really hallucinating some shit, that he needed to get some real meds, because sitting right there in the backseat, a gun in his hand, was a fucking clown.

THE LOW DESERT

It was before dawn, the Saturday after the Fourth of July, when I found Jim Connelly standing shirtless on the other side of my bedroom door. He'd walked in through the front door. I didn't bother with locks. You came in my house, you were either invited or you weren't.

"I'm sorry, Morris," he said. "I've been outside knocking for ten minutes. Can you put that pistol down?"

I looked behind me. My wife, Katharine, had the sheets pulled up under her chin. I closed the door and walked Jim into the family room, set my gun down on top of the TV console.

"The hell's going on?"

"Gloria and I were walking the beach," he said, "getting ready for the boat races this morning, and found something." Connelly was the marketing manager at Claxson Oil, the company that employed us both. He and his wife, Gloria, lived across the street in the Claxson Oil Executive Housing Unit—twenty-five prefabricated houses and a few bungalows for visiting Claxson bigwigs, all cut into the desert surrounding the banks of the Salton Sea—and in direct view of the oil derricks. I'd spent the last several months working as the project's head of security, which basically meant I was the law, the closest real cop sixty miles away in Palm Springs, which in 1962 meant we were in another world entirely. The Claxson 500, a speedboat race sponsored by the oil company, was set to start at ten that morning, launching from the northwest side of the Sea. Two hundred campers were already out at the recreation area just adjacent to the launch, and we expected another five hundred spectators to filter in by the end of the day. The race teams had been housed in trailers next to the marina the entire week, getting their swift boats ready.

"What kind of something?"

"A boy," Jim said. "I think. I couldn't tell, Morris, with all the . . ." He flapped his arms about, sputtering. "The body is pretty eaten up."

"Okay," I said. I'd fought in Korea, so death was something I knew how to work around. Tragedy was not as simple. Jim picked at something on his bare chest. "Where's your shirt?"

"Covering the body."

I WENT BACK into the bedroom, got dressed, told Katharine the news.

"Have you heard about any runaways?" she asked. "From the workers?"

"Negative."

The workers—a mixture of roughnecks brought in from Oklahoma and Texas, Mexicans up from the border, and a smattering of Indians from the various tribes between Palm Springs and Blythe—lived in makeshift barracks near the oil derricks along the North Shore, where we also kept office space, in addition to the digs encircling the 350 square miles of the Sea. If I showed up at any of the locations, it wasn't good news. I'd spoken with the county sheriff, Luther Ward, the day before about a fight between a migrant worker and one of our roughnecks, guy named Dixie Cooper, a first-rate scumbag, over at a bar in Bombay Beach. The worker ended up choking on his own teeth, was back in Mexicali, could go either way.

I sent Dixie back east on the train, told him to find a place where no one knew him and stay there. Or tried to, anyway. I ended up breaking both his wrists in the middle of the conversation. Which is to say: if one of the workers' children was missing, I might not ever find out.

"Maybe it's a camper," I said, "about to wake up with a problem."

Katharine nodded. We'd grown up, six years apart, in Granite City, Washington, where my father was the sheriff and where her father operated a fishing spot down the way on Granite Lake. This alien place in the middle of the desert was like nothing we'd ever imagined, a vast inland sea on top of an ancient salt plain; a mistake made in 1905 when the Colorado jumped its banks and flooded the region, unimpeded, for eighteen months. Except it wasn't really a mistake. There'd been plans going back to the late-1800s to re-wild the Salton Basin, the dreamland of developers, the United States government, your basic grifters, and now oil companies. Each had a plan to change what nature had already decided: that marine life in the middle of the desert was folly. If Claxson had its way, this would be the great inland riviera of California, oil just phase one of their plans. They would harvest beneath the earth, they would build on top of it, they would populate the shifting sands, and they would own the Salton Sea. They'd already built a luxury marina and yacht club; a million-dollar hotel was next. Jerry Lewis, so the talk went, was figuring out how to get a casino in these parts. Sinatra was going to play a show . . .

. . . provided a drop of oil showed up.

Company geologists assured everyone it was just one more inch away, every day.

We would all be rich.

So here Katharine and I were living in the middle of someone else's mistakes, though we didn't know that then. Our plan, unlike Claxson's, didn't seem foolish when we began. We'd live on the Salton Sea for a few years, accumulate our nest egg, start a family, find our way back to Granite City, or maybe Seattle, or Portland, and then live through it all, whatever all of it might be.

Katharine went into our bathroom, came out with two hand towels. "People drowned at Granite Lake all the time," she said. She sprayed her perfume on the towels. "Take these. Give one to Jim. He'll need it."

JIM'S WIFE, GLORIA, stood a few feet from the body, keeping the gulls away. She was five months pregnant and had the neck of her T-shirt pulled up over her nose and mouth, which caused the hem to reveal the bulge of her belly.

"Are you all right?" I asked.

"No," Gloria said. She let the shirt slip off her nose, the collar resting on her chin. She'd been crying.

"Kat's up," I said. "Why don't you go over to the house. We're gonna be here for a bit."

Gloria gave Jim a look. "Do you want me to stay?"

"I doubt it will do either of us any good," he said, towel pressed to his nose. I'd given him a denim work-shirt to wear, which he hadn't bothered to do up. Gloria came over and kissed Jim on the forehead, then buttoned his shirt, like he was an infant.

"You recognize him?" I asked Gloria.

"That age? Could be anyone."

Jim and I watched her walk back up the dune, until she was gone. "We lost a baby," Jim said. "Before we ever got out here."

"I know."

"You do?" Jim was a private guy. He didn't like to bullshit and he had a problem with people who didn't practice their faith, which was everyone out here. Jim's faith was Catholicism. But I liked him, and he liked me, I think, and for a time that was important.

"She told Kat."

"We never talk about it," he said. "It's this shadow over us." He shook his head. "Let's get to it."

The Salton Sea lapped at the boy's feet, and I could see where Jim had dragged the body from the water, toes leaving tracks in the sand. The body was facedown, left arm tucked under, right spread out wide, like it was directing traffic. I removed Jim's shirt from the head and torso and tipped the body on its side, so I could look for obvious signs of foul play. I saw no bullet holes, stab wounds, or ligature marks around his throat, though his body was covered with ragged cuts and abrasions, all of which looked postmortem. His eyes and tongue were gone, but it had been at least 110 every day since the start of July, so the Sea hovered between 85 and 90 degrees. With the salinity and the wildlife and the biting flies, anything soft was going to be devoured in just a few hours. Even the top of his scalp had been picked clean, revealing white bone at the crown, the gulls having had their way before Jim and Gloria found the body, a pile of hair not far down the beach.

Around the boy's right ankle, however, there was something odd.

A ring of missing flesh, a wound too uniform to have happened arbitrarily, not like the deep gouges in the boy's back where it looked like maybe the engine blade of a boat had gotten to him. I took out my penknife and pushed back the flaps of skin and found what I was looking for: a length of concertina wire tied down to the bone, slicing all the way through the boy's Achilles.

"Recognize him?" Jim asked. He was a few feet away, not watching too closely.

"I think it's Mr. East's boy," I said. I flipped the body over on to its back. "I met him for just a minute the other night. His name is Darren."

Jim stumbled backward a few steps. "Oh no," he said, and then retched into the sand.

Woodrow East was the vice president of Claxson Oil, the kind of guy who told you to call him Woody but didn't mean it. His bungalow, which he stayed in when he wasn't in Chicago, was two blocks away from my house. Only time I'd seen Darren was on the Fourth, running down the beach holding a sparkler in one hand, his mother, Brenda, skipping to keep up, bursts of silver burning past her, the golden hour behind them both. Kat and I pleasantly drunk, a cooler of beer between the lawn chairs we'd dragged to the shore.

Three nights ago.

Brenda introduced herself and Darren to us as we walked home, the last firework dying in the sky, told us we'd be seeing a lot more of one another, Kat remarking that she sure was nice.

Jim wiped his mouth. "I'm just . . . not adequately prepared for this."

A black speedboat roared across the water, setting a flock of egrets into the air, a flood of white splashed against the deep blue sky and the dawn sun. The boat was maybe two hundred yards away. Soon, the shore would be filled with people watching the race. "We need to get this boy off the beach."

"Should we call the police?"

Another speedboat, this one painted like the flag, shot by, followed in short order by a metallic red vessel. The racers were doing practice laps.

"They won't get out here for two hours," I said. "At least. Cancel the race; I'll stand here all day with the boy."

"That can't happen," Jim said. The race wasn't just a race. It was Claxson paying off about fifty different entities in order to do business in the region. Already there were vendors setting up inside the beer garden, the Cadillac dealership in Palm Springs had a giveaway going on, a new DeVille for a lucky guest, most of us sure that lucky guest would be one of the tribal leaders invited to sit with George Claxson himself to watch the finals. There was talk of Congressman Wilson showing up to hand out the trophies and award money. Lena Horne had rented a house. Rumor was Artie Shaw had, too. They'd been spotted water-skiing. "I'll take him to La Casita," he said. That was the hospital in Indio, forty minutes away. "What do I say?"

"The truth," I said. "That you found this body."

"Do I tell them his name?"

I thought about that for a moment. "No," I said. "Give them my contact information. Let me get the family on the horn first. Make sure."

"They'll John Doe him," Jim said.

"Not for long," I said. "It's fine. I'll handle it."

"Okay, Morris," Jim said. "It's your call."

"You ever had a conversation with Mr. East?"

"Nothing substantive," Jim said. "When he's in town, I try to avoid him." He looked down at the boy. "His face, Morris. Lord."

"Look," I said, "I can do this if you're not up for it." It occurred to me Jim might be in shock.

"Gloria worked at a vet's office before we moved out here," Jim said. "She's better with this stuff. I'll have her drive with me." We stood there for a moment, not speaking, a dead body between us. "Morris," Jim said, finally, "why hasn't anyone reported this boy missing?"

•

I PULLED UP in front of the Easts' and already their sprinklers were running, barely 7:30 a.m., the sun casting rainbows through the water. Woodrow East's bungalow had a lush green lawn from the road to the front door, full rose beds, and manicured box-hedges of flowering yellow lantana, even though he only spent about a week a month at the Salton Sea, overseeing production, and the rest of the time he was usually in the corporate offices in Chicago. And even though everyone else had a patch of rocks in the front of their house and a patch of dirt in the back.

I'd not seen Woodrow for at least ten days, his wife and the boy coming alone for the holiday.

I'd stopped at home first, showered, and changed into my uniform, put on my silly, meaningless badge. Still, I could smell Darren East on my hands when I knocked on the front door. There are times, even now, when I think I catch a whiff of him.

No one came to the door.

I tried the handle.

Locked.

On the driveway were three newspapers. I picked one up. It was from July 6.

I hopped the padlocked side gate and made my way into the backyard. There was an aboveground pool there—blue vinyl stretched tight over a steel frame. I climbed up the short ladder and looked inside. It was drained, an inch of drift sand spread across the bottom, along with palm fronds and dead date roaches. I climbed down, felt the ground. It was dry, but I dug an inch down with my hand and found a hint of moisture, brought up a handful of sand, smelled it, thought I caught a suggestion of chlorine.

There were two chaise lounges on the deck, both still with towels bunched up on them. One also had a paperback novel, *Hawaii* by

James Michener, beneath it, the pages yellow and brittle from being out in the sun. I flipped through it and a bookmark for O'Gara & Wilson Bookshop in Chicago fell out.

I stuffed the paperback into my back pocket.

I tried the sliding glass door into the house. Also locked. I peered into the Easts' kitchen. There were dishes on the counter—two glasses, a plate, a cereal bowl—and dishes in the sink. The *Desert Sun* newspaper was spread out on the small kitchen table. The front page had a photo of the Palm Springs Fourth of July parade down Palm Canyon. The lights were off, and when I pressed my ear to the door, I didn't hear the TV or radio. I didn't know if that was good or bad.

I went back to my car and got on the radio to the Claxson barracks, where my only quasi-deputy, Mark Sarvas, kept our office. He was at least twenty-five years older than me and had been a cop out in Springfield before he got fired for running over a man with his cruiser. An accident, he swore, but he'd been drunk. So now here he was, sober, but his addiction had been replaced by a kind of free-floating anger at everything. I only bothered him when I really needed him.

"You hear of any missing kids?" I asked.

"Negative," Sarvas said. "Something going on, Captain?"

"Had a floater this morning," I said.

"Indian?"

"No," I said.

"Only a Mexican or Indian would get in that water on their own. It's polluted as shit, in my opinion. I tell all our people to stay out of it, ones who speak the language anyway."

"You got Mr. East's home phone there? In Chicago?"

"Yeah, you better let him know," he said. When he came back, he said, "Just anecdotally, this boat race is bullshit, Morris. From a public-safety standpoint. This were in Springfield? It would never go down like this. Why they got a private security company doing crowd control is beyond me. I'm going on record here that if a boat flips into the crowd and kills a dozen people, you and me both will be out of a job."

"You got that number?" I said into the radio.

He gave it to me, then said, "How old was the kid?"

"Hard to tell. Maybe five."

"A little guy," Sarvas said. He whistled through his teeth. "The world is a shit can, Captain. You're still young enough to think otherwise, but it's a shit can."

"10-4," I said.

I CALLED WOODROW East from my den, where I had a company phone to handle corporate business. Claxson had offices all over the world, wherever there might be oil, from Texas to Iran, and calls came in at all hours. Which was fine. Having first been a Marine rifleman in Korea and then a police officer in Granite City, the idea of being cooped up behind a desk for any time longer than it might take to type up a report felt like solitary confinement, so I spent most of my days patrolling. Even though I wasn't the real law, my uniform, my car, and my gun eliminated any difference in most people's minds.

Katharine sat on the loveseat in the corner. "Be formal," she told me before I dialed, "but don't sound practiced. You can be practiced sometimes, when you're scared or worried. This is a moment when empathy is called for, Morris. Do you have something thoughtful prepared?"

"No," I said. What would I tell Woodrow East? That I'd found his son. That I was worried his wife might be dead. That I was prepared to contact the police but wanted to be the person to tell him first. "Something will come to me."

"Are you positive it was the boy we met on the beach?"

"Yes," I said.

"If he drowned," Katharine said, "could it be Brenda tried to save him?" I hadn't mentioned to Katharine the wire around Darren's ankle. "Could it be she'll wash up next?"

"Could be," I said. I started to dial. "You sure it's Brenda? Her name?" Katharine nodded. The phone rang twice and then was answered. By a woman. "Oh," I said. "Is this the East residence?"

"Yes," she said. "Who is this, please?"

"It's Morris Drew," I said. "From Claxson. Out in California. Sorry to be calling on Saturday, but there's a situation here at the Salton Sea project." I waved Katharine over. "Is Mr. East available?"

"Oh," she said, vaguely surprised. Katharine came around the desk and knelt beside me, so she could hear the call. "It's no problem. But Woody is away." *Woody.* "He's down in Corpus for the week. Do you need the number there?"

"No," I said. Katharine mouthed, *Go on.* "I have that number. I'm sorry. Is this . . . Mrs. East?"

"I have my own identity," she said. "But yes."

"We met on the Fourth," I said. "I'm the director of security? And my wife, Katharine? You and your son, we met on the beach, after the fireworks."

"I'm afraid not," she said, but something had crept into her voice. "I've never been down to the site. I can't imagine why I'd want to. And I don't have a son. Or a daughter." She paused. "What made you think we'd met?"

"I'm sorry," I said. "I must have made a mistake. Must have been another Claxson family staying in the bungalow Mr. East usually stays in. I'm terribly sorry. I've made a grave error, I'm afraid."

"No," she said. "It's fine. Don't worry. I just . . . did the person you met tell you they were Woody's family? You can tell me if they did." She paused. "It wouldn't be the first time."

"It wouldn't?"

"Have you met my husband?"

"I have," I said.

"I don't suppose that means you know him, does it?"

"I've only shaken his hand twice," I said.

"Morris Drew, is that what you said your name was?"

"Yes, ma'am."

"Morris, my name is Eliza. This woman you met. Did she have my name?"

"No," I said. "Her name was Brenda, I think."

"Brenda," she said. I heard a drawer close, and I heard what sounded like her scribbling something on paper. "That's a new one."

"Ma'am," I said, "I'm sure I've made a mistake. This certainly has nothing to do with you or Mr. East. I'm very sorry for bothering you this morning."

"Wait," she said. "Don't hang up." She cleared her throat. "My husband is a very important man at Claxson," she said. "I suppose you know that well enough. But he's just a man in a very nice suit. I know you're worried now that you have to cover for him, I can hear it in your voice. But you don't." I heard her light a cigarette and then blow smoke out above the receiver. "What happened? What's pulled you out of bed on Saturday?"

"Nothing to worry about," I said. There was a knock on our door. Through our thin Venetian blinds, I saw a long black Cadillac idling on the street. It looked to me like George Claxson's car. His daughter, Gretchen, had grown up across the street from Katharine, which is how we all ended up here together. I'd solved her disappearance—which is to say, her murder—two years ago. When George was in town, he always made a point of sending his assistant to drop off some fresh flowers or smoked salmon from Granite Lake. Sometimes George would just come to talk with Katharine about Gretchen, because Katharine had more memories of her than he did. As grief and time had compounded, the memories he did have were becoming more opaque in his mind. Her death had left him with a genetic ache that I've come to understand myself as the curse of growing old in good health.

Katharine went to the window, peered out. "Of all days," she muttered, and then she left me there in the den, closing the door behind her.

"So you're calling the vice president of Claxson Oil at—what time is it there? Nine o'clock? You're calling to tell him . . . nothing?"

"Mrs. East," I said, "what I meant is that it doesn't concern you. I don't want you to worry about something that isn't in your purview."

"In my *purview*," she said, and laughed. "Did the boy do something? Was that it?"

"Neighbors thought he might have untied a boat," I said.

"Well," she said, "listen. If someone needs to be paid for damages, just tell me. I'll send a check, okay? Whomever the child belongs to, if they needed to lie and say they were Woody's family, then they have bigger problems than this boat."

"Yes, ma'am," I said.

"How old are you, Morris?"

"Twenty-nine."

"Good god," she said, "we're the same age. Stop calling me ma'am. I'll send a check for $500. Do you think that will cover it?"

"You don't need to do that." Five hundred dollars in 1962 was more money than I made in a month.

"I'll put it in your name," she said. "Handle it as you see fit." Before I could respond, she'd hung up.

•

I FOUND KATHARINE in the kitchen, putting salmon into our freezer. "George sends his regards," she said.

"He come in?"

"No, it was his driver."

"Did you say anything?"

"No," she said.

"Mrs. East says that we didn't meet her. That she doesn't have children."

"I got that much."

"We met those people," I said. "Didn't we?"

"You need to speak to Mr. East."

"I called his number in Corpus Christi," I said. I walked over to our back door and locked it. "They said he's here." I showed Katharine the piece of paper I'd scribbled the information on, as if it were evidence. "Got into Palm Springs last night. Staying at the Riviera. Room 305." I put my gun belt back on. "I asked if he was in town for the races and they didn't know what I was talking about."

"Is that strange?"

"I don't know what goes on in Corpus," I said. I went to the front window and looked to see if Jim and Gloria were back yet. They weren't.

Katharine came and stood next to me. "We'd had a lot to drink on the Fourth. Maybe your memory is clouded."

"Even if I'm wrong," I said, "Mr. East has some explaining to do."

"To his wife," Katharine said. "He owes you nothing, if that boy isn't his."

"Soon as that woman and that boy showed up here and said they were his family," I said, "it became my business, too."

Katharine put a hand on my back. "What are you planning on doing?"

"I'm going to drive out to Palm Springs and have a conversation with Mr. East."

"Why don't you wait until he's here on the property?"

"Because on the property, he's my boss."

"You could call him," Katharine said.

"I could." I went back into my den, opened my desk, took out two more clips, stuffed them in my pocket. If I had to shoot someone two dozen times, I was now prepared. "Someone tied concertina wire around that boy's ankle. Which means they probably held him underwater using a gaff and then cut him loose when he was dead."

Katharine sat down, hard, on our sofa. "I could have lived the rest of my life without ever knowing that."

"People do terrible things, Kat." I came and sat beside her, took her hands, kissed them. "I want you to know that I love you," I said. "When Jim and Gloria get home, I want you to go stay with them. Do you understand?" She nodded. "Anyone comes to see me, don't let them in. And Katharine? Lock the door behind me."

THE RIVIERA HOTEL was located on the north end of Palm Springs, about an hour from the Salton Sea. It was the kind of hotel Elvis stayed in when he was visiting. The kind of hotel where you stayed so you could tell people you'd stayed there.

The hotel consisted of six two-story villas surrounding a serpentine pool, the hundred chaise lounges in perfect rows adjacent to the water mostly empty—I counted eleven people using them—the season in Palm Springs long over. It was already at least a hundred degrees, the sky half filled with high, white clouds, the air alive with the electric buzzing of desert cicadas. A sweating bellman dressed in black velvet directed me to the correct villa, and I climbed a narrow, carpeted staircase to room 305 and knocked on the door.

"You're not who I was expecting," the man who answered the door said. He was short, maybe five foot five, with red hair combed straight back. He had on swim trunks and a tank top, which stretched uncomfortably over his gut, and had a cigarette between his lips.

"I'm looking for Woodrow East," I said.

"Keep on looking," he said, and he went to close the door, so I slammed my sap in the jamb.

Red squinted at me, like he was trying to make sense of something. "You a cop?"

"You a criminal?"

This got Red to laugh. "You think a guy showing up with a gun in a holster intimidates me," he said, his accent straight from the bleachers at Wrigley Field, "you're knocking on the wrong door."

I looked around Red, which was easy since I had six inches on him. Room number 305 was a suite, with two sofas facing each other, a glass coffee table, a kitchenette, and bedrooms on either side. Straight behind Red, on the expansive balcony, I spotted a man on a chaise lounge, tanning shirtless between two women.

"I feel like we've started on the wrong foot," I said. I slid the sap back out. Smiled. Champion of courtesy. That was me. "You tell Mr. East that Morris Drew from Claxson is at the door. And if he doesn't want to see me, you can come back and tell me that."

"And then what?"

"And then you'll find out if I'm a cop or not."

He looked down at the sap in my hand. "You got a license for that?"

"Robert Kennedy hand-delivered it. You want his number?"

Red stared at me for a few seconds, a smile forming at the edge of his mouth. "You're a hard-ass," he said. "You want to make some real money?"

"I got a job."

"You work for Claxson," he said. "Funny thing is, George Claxson works for my family."

A man came walking up the stairs behind me in a white linen suit, shirt unbuttoned halfway down his chest, sweat pouring down his face. "This fucking town is too hot," the man said, and then he saw me and said, "Who the fuck is this?"

"Morris Drew," I said. "I'm the director of security for Claxson Oil."

"I like your policeman pajamas," the man said. He extended his hand to me. "Tommy Faraci, real estate mogul and philanthropist." This made Red laugh.

"You do me a favor, Mr. Faraci?" I said, still holding his hand.

"What's that?"

"You see Woodrow East on the balcony tanning? Tell him I'll be waiting for him in the coffee shop."

"And what should I tell him this is concerning?"

"The dead kid," I said, "I pulled out of the Salton Sea this morning."

WOODROW EAST SLID in across from me in the Riviera's coffee shop. He was in his late forties, stood over six feet tall, and was lean and sunburnt across his nose. He had on a pair of sand-colored slacks and a butter-yellow Penguin polo shirt, tucked in. He smelled like he'd just shaved. "I have fifteen minutes." He waived over the waitress, asked her for a glass of orange juice, freshly squeezed. "Have we met before?" he asked me.

"I'm in charge of security at the Salton Sea," I said.

"Right, right," he said. "You found George's daughter, is that right?"

"That's correct."

"I remember when that happened," he said. "I've known George twenty years, so I remember Gretchen when she was a toddler. Most inquisitive child I ever met." The waitress came and dropped off my plate—a New York steak and eggs—and another cup of coffee, then came back and slid a glass of orange juice in front of Woodrow. When the waitress was gone, he said, "What a terrible thing."

"I'm glad I found her." I cut into my steak and chewed it for a few moments, let Woodrow wait on me. "Do you know anything about the man who killed her?"

"No," he said.

"His name was Milton Stairs. They'd been dating for three months. Give or take. I'd gone to school with him. Kindergarten all the way up through high school, but he dropped out before graduating. We all thought he was down in Walla Walla working the wheat. That's what he told us when he came back to Granite City." I took a sip of my coffee. "Turns out, he was in the penitentiary there. Raped an itinerant farm girl, pled down to assault."

"Jesus," Woodrow said.

"Yeah. It was shocking. I'd lost touch with him, because I was fighting in Korea. And then I re-upped, twice. You must have served in Europe?"

"No," he said. "I'm colorblind."

"That got you out?"

"I wanted to serve," he said, and he left it at that.

"I was just happy to see my old friend. You must have grown up with some people who went away and then showed back up with a story that maybe wasn't altogether true?"

"I grew up in Chicago," Woodrow said. "It's not like that in a big city."

"You believe that? People in the big city are somehow different than small-town people?"

"I believe that the people I knew growing up," he said, "lied in less imaginative ways."

"I see what you're saying." I cut another bite of steak, watched Woodrow's eyes glance at the steak knife. "Mr. Claxson is a good judge of character. He took one look at Milton and didn't trust him. Looked into the guy, finds out he did time, gets Gretchen to dump him, straight away. Big family drama. *Romeo and Juliet.* That's what my wife says, because she was Gretchen's ear. Me, I'm the kind of person who thinks maybe you get out of prison, you can come back a better person. Assault, maybe you get drunk, hit a guy in a bar. We've all done that."

"I've never been in a fight," Woodrow said.

"Not even with your brother?"

"Only child."

"See, I got a younger brother. We'd get rough with each other. You know. Like how bears playfight. Not trying to kill each other. But letting the other one know it's possible. Showing our teeth. Getting our claws out." I took one last bite of steak. "Mr. Claxson didn't share my point of view."

"Turns out he was right," Woodrow said. While we'd been talking, three beads of sweat had formed on his upper lip, so he took a napkin and casually wiped off his face.

I broke off a piece of toast and dipped it in the yolk of my egg, chewed it. "The thing is, I should have known. I should have seen it in Milton. But I was so up in my own head after Korea that I was incapable of reading other people. I left something elemental out there. Something that gave me empathy, I think. And for a long time, I didn't know if I'd ever get that part of myself back. Does that make sense to you?"

"No."

"Well, the fact was, I knew Milton Stairs was a piece of shit. I'd known it since he was seven. I once saw him cut the head off a cat. Just for fun. Just to hear the noise the cat made. That's not normal."

"Evil exists," Woodrow said. "I believe that."

I drank down the rest of my coffee. Leaned back against the banquette. "So let me ask you something," I said. "I tell your friend Mr. Faraci that I'm here to talk to you about a dead kid, and you sit down across from me and you don't say a word about that. Doesn't that strike you as odd?"

"Why would it?"

"Lots of people show up with questions about dead kids while you're on vacation?"

"Number one," Woodrow said, "I'm not on vacation. I have business meetings with the mayor of Palm Springs tomorrow, talks with tribal leaders, and then I'm catching a plane from Los Angeles on Tuesday back to Corpus. Number two, I am the vice president of a major oil and development company. Terrible things happen at our locations around the world."

"And Tommy Faraci, he's what? Your chauffeur?"

"He's a business associate with interests in the region," he said. "We have many investors. I don't need to clear them with you." He dabbed at his damp face again. "Whatever has happened this morning with this boy, we'll make it right."

"How do you know I'm talking about a boy?" I said. Woodrow reached for his orange juice, but I put my hand over it, slid it, and my steak knife, away from him.

"You must have said something," he said.

"I didn't."

We sat there like that for ten seconds, staring at each other. I could have pulled out my gun and shot him. I could have cuffed him to the table and then called the sheriff. I could have done anything I wanted to Woodrow East right then, but I did nothing, just waited for him to speak.

"Where'd you find him?"

"He washed up on the south shore. Most of his face was gone, but I recognized him."

"As who?"

"As your son Darren, according to his mother, Brenda."

"I'm afraid those names aren't familiar to me."

"Brenda said she was your wife," I said, "and that Darren was your son. They were staying in your bungalow." I reached into my back pocket and took out the bookmark from the novel I found. "This was in the paperback Brenda was reading when they came to get her and Darren from your bungalow, best as I can figure out." I held it up to my nose. "Can still sort of smell her suntan lotion on it." I slid it across the table, but he didn't pick it up.

"My wife," he said. He tried to sound incredulous, but there was a tremor in his voice. "My wife is in Chicago. You should call her."

"I did," I said. "She offered me $500 to stay quiet, in fact."

"Do you hear how absurd this sounds?" He covered his mouth with his hand, shook his head. And then, he bit into the skin between his right thumb and index finger.

"Easy," I said. I reached across the table, but he snatched his hand from his mouth.

"You're fired," he said. "I will approve two months of severance."

"I can help you," I said.

"Six months," he said. "A year. Whatever you want."

"Someone is going to be looking for that boy, Mr. East."

"No one is going to be looking for him." He slapped his hand on the table. "Don't you understand?"

"I understand you're involved with some bad people," I said. "That they've done some things for you that you might regret."

"You're involved, too," he said. "We're all involved. Open your eyes." He cut his gaze out the window for a fraction of a second. "Do you see a white and black Oldsmobile Starfire idling in the parking lot?"

I looked out the window. Took my time. An Oldsmobile Starfire was parked facing the sun, so I couldn't see into it, but there it was. "Yeah."

"If I don't walk out of here in . . ." he looked at his watch, "nine minutes, they're going to drive out to the Salton Sea and murder your wife. Is that what you want?"

"No, they won't," I said.

"You don't know these kinds of people," he said.

"Woody," I said, "I am those kinds of people."

"Please," he said. "Please."

"There's a child in a refrigerator in Indio without a name. You need to tell me if his mother is going to show up next. *You're* not guilty of anything," I said.

"They'll kill my wife," he said. "My real wife."

"What did you do, Woody? What the fuck did you *do*?"

"I asked for a favor," Woodrow said. "I was involved in a . . . situation. I asked for a permanent solution to a temporary problem. I didn't understand the scope of their intentions. Of what I would owe them. My god. *These people.*"

"When did you learn their intentions?" I said.

"Now. Today."

"Just give me a name. I'll leave you out of it."

Woodrow East pushed himself out of the booth, took out his wallet, put a ten on the table. "What did you do to Milton Stairs when you caught him?" Woodrow asked.

"I beat him until I thought he was dead," I said. "I meant to kill him."

"You should do that to me," he said. He picked up the bookmark, smelled it, and then tore it in half.

"Be a decent man," I said. "You're still capable of that."

"I'm trying to do that," he said. "If I tell you that boy's name, your entire life will be upside-down. Everyone you know, every hope you've ever had, will be gone." He looked out the window. The Starfire pulled up by the front door of the diner, idled there. I made out Tommy Faraci in the passenger seat, Red behind the wheel. From where I was sitting, if I had my M18 rifle, I could kill them both before they put it back into drive. "Do me a favor, please. Leave me somewhere I won't be found."

I DIDN'T GET back to the Salton Sea until close to 4 p.m. I'd gone to the hospital in Indio, met with a representative from the coroner's office, and gave what verifiable information I had, which was nothing. I put in a call to the sheriff's office, let them know that we'd found a body, and the deputy on duty, Warren, told me the sheriff would get back to me on Monday or Tuesday . . . Friday at the latest. "We don't have any new missing-children reports," he told me. "Could be it's a Mexican, floated in from the New River." The New River ran north from Mexicali and met up with the Salton Sea just outside Westmorland.

"That happens?" I said.

"Every bad thing happens," Warren said. "It's no place to live."

Down on the shore, crews were cleaning up from the boat race. Three dozen fans milled around under a billowing white tent, but the intense afternoon heat—it was at least 115—had cleared out the VIP area and beer garden, save for Mark Sarvas standing guard over the giveaway Cadillac. He stood beneath a fixed umbrella. His uniform stuck to him like plastic wrap.

"Where is everyone?" I asked.

"Inside the yacht club, eating lobster and drinking gin," Sarvas said, "that would be my guess."

"Go home," I said.

"You'll be surprised to learn the private security company hired a bunch of yahoos who couldn't take the sun," Sarvas said. "So I'm on this spot until the Caddie dealership comes to lock up the car."

"Per who?"

"Per Jim Connelly," he said. "Who can fuck himself, if you don't mind me saying so. He's not my boss."

"Go home," I said again. "I'll cover it."

"You sure?"

"Before you have a stroke."

Mark began to walk off, then stopped. "Hey, anything on that kid?"

"Nothing good."

"Too bad," he said. "Was hoping . . . well, I don't know what I was hoping."

"When you were up in Springfield," I said, "you ever encounter anyone named Tommy Faraci?"

Mark Sarvas unbuttoned his uniform shirt, balled it up and dried his face, neck, and hair, then stood there in his sweat-matted undershirt, looking out at the water. "Why would you ask me that?" he said finally. The hand holding his shirt was shaking.

"I met a guy today," I said. "Two guys, actually. In Palm Springs. With Woodrow East."

Mark wiped at his face again. Stared at his uniform. "You planning to have children, Captain?" he said.

"I guess so," I said. "Why?"

"This job," Mark said, "it's about to be no good for you. You and your wife, in the morning, you should pack up and go back to wherever you're from. Forget Tommy Faraci. Don't bring that darkness close to you. Forget Woodrow East, too." He went over to the water station, filled up two Dixie cups, gulped down one, poured the other over his head, then dumped both cups, and his uniform, into the garbage. "The world's a shit can, Morris. I told you. Don't go kicking the can."

I CAME HOME and discovered Katharine in our backyard, sipping a beer, reading *Hawaii*. It was close to six, and a breeze had picked up from the west.

"I thought I told you to go to Jim and Gloria's when they came back," I said.

"You did," she said.

"And?"

"And you're not my father," she said.

I sat down beside her. She handed me her beer and I took a long drink. It was Rainier, from Seattle. "Where'd you get this?"

"George," she said. "He dropped it off with the salmon." I handed the bottle back to her. "You going to tell me what happened today?"

"I'm not sure," I said. "Do you think I'm a good man, Kat?"

"If I didn't," she said, "I wouldn't be sitting here."

"I met a man today," I said, "who had nothing left to lose."

"Why is that?"

"Got himself into trouble with the wrong people."

"Are there right people to get into trouble with?"

"If I told you every bad thing I'd ever done," I said, "I'd be sitting here alone."

"That's where you're wrong." She shook out a cigarette from a pack of Marlboros at her feet, lit it, blew smoke into the sunset. "You're not made up of your worst days, Morris," she said. "No one is."

I took the beer back from Katharine and finished it. "Keep reminding me of that," I said.

THAT NIGHT, AFTER Katharine went to sleep, I walked down to the shore of the Salton Sea. The breeze moved the clouds out, leaving the sky brilliant with stars, the moon half-full in the east, the Sea silver in its reflection. Campers had bonfires going, even with the heat, which gave the world a flickering, smoky glow, so that when Jim Connelly showed up beside me, he appeared like an apparition out of the darkness.

"Couldn't sleep?" I said.

"Didn't try." He had a bottle of Jameson with him and two shot glasses. He filled one and handed it to me. "Indulge?"

"You knew I'd be down here?" I took down the shot.

"I saw you walk out." He filled his glass, sipped at it while we watched the water. "Can I ask you an impolite question, Morris?" he said after a time.

"If you need to."

"Do you know, roughly, how many men you killed in Korea?"

"I didn't keep count," I said.

"A hundred?"

"I don't know, Jim," I said. "A lot."

"What did it feel like?"

"Like . . . nothing," I said.

"It didn't bother you?"

"No," I said. "I mean it felt like . . . *nothing*. Like an absence. A void. It's hard to explain." I paused. "But it opened up something in me that was always there. Something I'm not proud of."

"Did it make you worse?"

"No," I said. A man and woman came walking by us on the beach then, hand in hand. Tomorrow, the beach would fill up again with spectators, and the boy Darren East would still be dead. "I didn't hate myself for what I did," I said once the couple had passed. "If that's what you're wondering. It was either me or the other guy. A situation like that, you always choose the other guy." I poured myself another drink. "Fact is, Jim, I liked it. Wish I could say it was about justice or liberty or some such thing, but it wasn't. It was power."

"You kill refugees? Women? Children?"

"I aimed," I said, "and fired, for three years, Jim. The orders were to kill everyone. So I did."

I heard a splash. Down the beach, people were running, drunk, into the Sea.

"I need you to take care of something," Jim said. He dug a small plastic sandwich bag from his back pocket, handed it to me.

Inside was an eight-inch length of snipped concertina wire.

"What the hell did you do?" I said.

"I made a decision. For our families," Jim said. He sat down in the sand. "Do you know who we work for, Morris?"

"I'm trying not to." I took the wire out, turned it over in my hand.

"That boy is dead no matter how it happened. You did your part. Now we need to let it go."

"A good cop," I said, "is going to see the wound on that boy's leg and will investigate. With or without this wire."

"A good cop," Jim said. "Look around you. Look at this place."

"Is that what your book tells you, Jim?"

"My book tells me that boy is at the right hand of God now," Jim said. "He has the ultimate peace."

"What about us?" Nothing. "What about his *mother*?" Nothing. "If I had to guess," I said, "she's buried underneath the pool in Woodrow East's backyard. I don't suppose you have a backhoe?"

"Please," Jim said. "I don't want to know anymore. I can't, Morris. *I can't.*" He began to cry.

The concertina barbs were covered with tiny matted shards of fabric, hair, and skin. I picked the barbs clean, placing the bits of Darren East, or whatever his name was, back into the plastic bag, which I then topped off with a handful of sand and rocks and shells and hurled it all back into the Sea. I imagined the bag floating south, against the current, picking up the tributary of the Alamo River and getting swept down across the low desert riverbeds, through Baja California, and then out into the Pacific. I imagined the boy sinking to the bottom of the ocean, mixing with the silt, washing back up in the sand at my feet. Imagined him in the blister of wind, burnt into my skin by the sun, until he was everywhere and nowhere at once. And how, the wire balled inside my fist, tearing into my flesh, I wished right then that I could join him.

PALM SPRINGS

Used to be Tania hated taking the bus. She didn't want to become one of those people who brought the bus up in every conversation, as if it were part of her life and not just how she got from one place to another. Like her friend Jean, back when Tania was still living in Reno and working at the Cal-Neva. They'd sit in the smokeroom—back when they still had a smokeroom—and Jean would always have some story to tell about the bus. There was the time a guy had a heart attack in his seat and died before the bus could even come to a complete stop. There was the time a little girl fell off her seat and bit through her bottom lip and ended up bleeding on Jean's new shoes. There was the time Jean swore she saw Bill Cosby in the seat across from her and that he was just as sweet as could be and had asked for her phone number.

Tania wonders now, as she steps aboard the #14 that will take her from her apartment in Desert Hot Springs to the Chuyalla Indian Casino in downtown Palm Springs, whatever became of Jean. After Tania left Reno for Las Vegas in 1985, they exchanged letters for a few months, though Tania quickly realized she didn't have much to write about other than the weather or various personal calamities: a broken toe that kept her from cocktailing for a week, a winter heat wave that blew out her car's AC, her basset hound Lucy getting into an anthill. And so she just stopped writing, eventually tossing out Jean's letters unopened. Tania remembers a vague sense of guilt concerning this whole episode, but in retrospect it all seems petty. Just because you're friends with someone doesn't mean you have to stay friends with them. Sometimes it's just easier to go without.

And anyway, what would they have to talk about today? Yes, better all around.

Settling into her regular seat—third from the left—Tania can't help but think Jean would find Tania's present condition all very ironic, particularly since Tania used to tease her about "taking the limo" to work every day even when Tania offered to pick her up in her Honda. She loved that car: a black Honda Accord with leather seats, a cassette player with a detachable face, six speakers. She remembers how important it was that she have six speakers, how she obsessed over the sound quality in her car, how she rolled down the windows on even the hottest days so that passing strangers could hear her stereo. Twenty-three years old then and the thing she was most proud of was a set of goddamned speakers.

Tania closes her eyes when the bus leaves the curb. The ride from Desert Hot Springs to the casino takes between thirty-seven and forty-eight minutes, depending on whether or not the bus stops at all the benches along the way. It's a Sunday morning, so she figures she's only got thirty-seven today, seeing as the bus is stone-empty. She likes to close her eyes for the trip, though she never sleeps, because she knows it's the only time for the next nine hours she'll get to see darkness. Cocktailing in a casino isn't like what it used to be. Back in Reno, they kept it midnight inside the casino: black ceiling, purple carpet, bloodred walls. These days it's all bright lights and warm yellows everywhere. The young girls think it's soothing, but Tania finds it irritating, wonders why anyone would want to see so much. What she wouldn't give to have missed a few things.

Forty-seven years old now, Tania figures she could unsee ten, fifteen years and be happy about it.

Sometimes, when she's done looking for her adopted daughter Natalya on the Internet, or chatting about her with other mothers online, Tania tries to find her twenty-three-year-old self on the Ouija board she bought at Toys"R"Us. She figures if a Ouija board can talk to the dead or people living in other dimensions, it might very well have the ability to reach back in time, too. It hasn't worked yet, but Tania thinks that maybe she's just not asking the right questions, thinks that maybe all she needs to do is find someone else to do the Ouija with her, double up on the spirit power, you see. And when she finds herself, she'll tell her to sell that fucking car and concentrate on getting her shit right because the future is painted in bright colors, baby, and no one will notice you.

IN ALL HER years working at casinos in Reno, Las Vegas, and now Palm Springs, Tania has only hit it big once. It was 1995, nearly fourteen years ago now, back when everyone had money, and she was working at the Mirage in Las Vegas. After a particularly good night—Tania can't remember what that means anymore, but when she tells everyone about Las Vegas in the nineties, she tells them she pocketed between two and three grand on a weekend night, though that sounds absurd now, the truth probably a good 50 percent below that—she put $500 down on a hand of Caribbean Stud and flopped a Royal, and just like that she was $50,000 richer. Taxes took fifteen off the top, leaving Tania with thirty-five; still more than enough at the time to put a down payment on a house, something with a great room, a nice yard, room for a pool, maybe even something on a golf course if she really kept banking at her job. Plus, she still had good credit back then, unlike most of her friends who had to keep changing their phone numbers to stay a few months ahead of the collection agencies, and loved living in Las Vegas.

Five hours into her shift at the Chuyalla Indian Casino and with just thirty-seven dollars in tips, Tania can't imagine ever risking $500 on paper again, because, really, she thinks while making her tenth round this hour through the blackjack tables, that's all gambling is: placing hope in colored paper. She wonders sometimes if her life wouldn't have been better if, instead of betting $500 on cards, she'd taken that money to a stationary store and purchased reams of 25-weight linen resume paper. Maybe that investment would have forced her into a better life, one where success was predicated on having something to put on all that paper.

Tania drops off three White Russians, five beers, and a Tom Collins to a kid who is clearly underage, since no one under seventy would have the audacity to order a Tom Collins and no one over twenty-one would even consider uttering it around a pack of their friends. Not when they could order Courvoisier and pretend to be 2Pac. Did kids still listen to 2Pac? She supposed they did, but Tania remembered listening to him when he was alive, thinking he was just okay, just another guy with mommy issues, like half the men she'd hooked up with since high school. When she decided to adopt Natalya, she threw out her entire gangsta-rap CD collection, figuring it wouldn't be appropriate for her new role to be singing along to songs about hustling. Plus, she wanted to like what Natalya liked.

Tania winds back to the bar and hands the bartender Gordon her orders: four beers, a Sex on the Beach, two Johnnie Walkers, three more White Russians. A blackjack table full of Marines in from the base at Twentynine Palms erupts in a flood of loud obscenities, prompting half of the casino to turn and stare.

"Classy people out there today," Gordon says. "Barely noon and people are trashed."

"I hate Sundays," Tania says. "People should just go home. Watch TV. Read the Bible. Something. "

"It's algebra," Gordon says. "In order for other people to have a good time, we have to suffer their stupidity and then someone else will have to hose their puke off the parking lot. Altogether, we get off pretty good."

"I'll be lucky to walk with fifty," Tania says. "You know what fifty gets you? Nothing. It's not even worth it to come in for fifty. Once I pay for the bus, get lunch, pick up dinner on the way home, what have I got left? It's not worth it."

Gordon places the four beers on her tray and for a moment Tania considers downing one of them, maybe line up a couple shots, too, see how the day passes with a little less clarity on things. Back in Las Vegas you could rail a line and . . . well . . . no, Tania thinks, you just can't compare your life along some arbitrary timeline, can't think of yourself as a compare and contrast. The past was different. The present is ever changing. No, it has to be about what comes next. About staying focused. Keep yourself together. Gather resources. Find Natalya. Don't force an apology. Fix things. Buy Christmas presents. Move to the city, any city, but get out of casinos and hotels and bars.

"How long you lived in the desert?" Tania asks. Gordon is new—she's seen him a couple of times in the last month, but this is the first shift he's been on alone—so they haven't found that rhythm yet, only know each other enough to flirt a little, tell a joke or two. Nothing personal. But for some reason today Tania feels like talking and can't stand to listen to the other cocktail girls on the floor. They call her "Mom" and always want her to listen to their problems, Sundays inevitably taken up by whatever horror happened at the club the night previous, or whatever drama they have with their "baby daddies," a term Tania just can't wrap her mind around. When did people stop being "parents"? But Gordon seems nice, maybe even smart. Smarter than her other choices, anyway.

"Five years, plus or minus," Gordon says. "I used to come here when I was a kid, you know? I remember my dad once drove us right up to Bob Hope's front gate and we got chased off by dogs. Big old Dobermans. I'll never forget that."

"What did your dad do?"

"Low-level crook," he says. "Stole cars, kited checks, told everyone he was in the mob, but I don't think he was."

"Everyone in Las Vegas," Tania says, "knew a guy who knew a guy." Including herself.

Gordon pours himself a Sprite, adds a little grenadine, sips at it for a moment. "My dad was one of those guys who always had something cooking the next town over. One day he'd bring my mom a fur coat, next day he'd pawn it. Basically a professional liar." He takes another sip, then nods toward the floor. "Like half of these people. Everyone's on their bullshit."

"That's why I can't see myself living here much longer," Tania says. Gordon puts the rest of Tania's drinks down and then rechecks the order. No one ever does that, Tania thinks; no one else here gives a damn if they screw up her money.

"Oh," Gordon says, "you live here a while, it becomes like anywhere else. You find your shit, you know? This town, I can bartend until I'm sixty-five, seventy, and no one would think differently about me. Maybe along the way I find a rich old woman who wants to take care of a young stud like me, I hold her hand for a few years, take her to her Botox appointments, and then, one day, she dies in her sleep and I'm a millionaire." Gordon's laughing now, but Tania sees something sad in his face, like it's not just him joking around, like part of him believes this might be his best chance for a good life.

"You've got it figured out," Tania says.

"Presuming I don't blow my head off first," he says.

"You don't seem the suicide type," Tania says.

"They'd just prop me behind the bar. It wouldn't be much difference. But if you stick around until I get my millions," Gordon says, "I'll let you move into my guest house. We'll sit around the saltwater pool all day reading thrillers and sipping cognac."

"I see myself moving somewhere with a bit more character. Less tourists. All my life, I've been stuck with tourists."

"Like where?"

"Somewhere," Tania says.

"No way for me," Gordon says. "I'm California bred and spread." Another girl—Tania can never remember if her name is Cindy or Bonnie, so she just calls her "sweetie"—slams her order on the counter, prompting Gordon to glare at her. "To be continued," he says. "Don't pack your bags just yet."

Really, Tania was thinking about Russia—Tula, Russia, specifically—but telling Gordon that would mean she'd have to explain her situation and she just isn't prepared for that, at least not at work. Talking about Natalya here would make her seem trivial.

Natalya was eighteen when she disappeared. If she'd been a minor, if she hadn't been Russian, perhaps the police would have cared. But then 9/11 happened and that was the end of any real searching. That's what Tania felt, anyway, that a part of her life dragged behind her like a rusted chain. Eight years of waiting to hear from her daughter.

But still.

Maybe there was an email from Natalya waiting for Tania right this instant telling her to come back to Tula, that she was sorry, too, and that she'd love to see her mother.

Before she picked up Natalya in Tula, Tania imagined Russia would be a gray country filled with scary Communists, like the ones they used to show marching in Red Square, back when Ronald Reagan used to scare her, too. Everyone told her to be careful, tell people she was Canadian so they wouldn't kill her, be as inconspicuous as possible.

But when she finally arrived—she remembered the date exactly: February 22, 1996—after flying into Moscow and driving for two hours with an administrator from the orphanage, she couldn't get over how beautiful the country was, how pleasant the people she met seemed to be, how *substantial* everything felt. The administrator kept pointing out interesting landmarks between Moscow and Tula, talked about Peter the Great, discussed the rich mining history of the city. And what a city: Citadels from the sixteenth century. Lush green forests surrounding the Upa River. Museums honoring famous writers and warriors. It was nothing like Las Vegas, nothing like Reno, nothing like any place she'd ever visited. She wondered what it might be like to settle in Russia, to raise her child in her home country, to live in such a place! Yes, she'd come back here when Natalya was fully integrated as an American. Adopting a twelve-year-old would present problems, she knew that, but Tania thought that later in life they would travel back here together, maybe buy a little house. Tania was thirty-five then, just twenty-three years older than her new daughter. Young enough that they'd be like friends the older Natalya got, less like mother and daughter.

So foolish, Tania thinks, grabbing up her tray. All of it.

Adopting Natalya wasn't something Tania planned. It was the money that did it. Well, the money and loneliness. A few weeks after she hit the Royal, Tania's fifteen-year-old dog Lucy woke up one morning and urinated blood; three hours later Tania's vet quietly inserted a needle into her dog's right front paw to put her to sleep (a term Tania has never liked as the implication is that the dog will someday wake up and be just fine), and just like that, after fifteen years and three hours, she was alone.

She still had family and friends, people she had loved at some point. But when it all boiled away, she just didn't keep people very well. Her parents and older sister Justine still sent her Christmas and birthday gifts, invited her to their homes for Thanksgiving (they even offered money if she couldn't afford a plane ticket from Las Vegas, since her parents now lived in Spokane and her sister in San Francisco), called once a week.

She'd had a series of boyfriends, too. Most of them long-term affairs, actually, and at the time she had just broken up with a DJ at the Rio after he accepted a six-month gig on a cruise ship, but their relationship hadn't even been intimate. All things being equal, sitting on the sofa at home and talking to her dog was preferable most of the time anyway.

That night, though, her dog dead, her parents and sister filled with the kind of comfort people without pets usually provide—"What you should do tomorrow is go to a rescue and pick up an abused dog," her father said—she sat alone on her sofa and watched a documentary on HBO about the plight of children in Russian or-phanages. By the film's conclusion, Tania decided to put her Royal winnings to good use, give someone a chance at a better life, allow that money to be more than just a house she'd struggle to pay for night after night. She'd found the perfect place in Summerlin—a three-bedroom with a little lap pool out back, Corian counters throughout, a view of the Red Rock Mountains—and was preparing to make an offer, though she didn't even know what that meant. Either she'd buy or she wouldn't, and she hadn't.

No, she didn't need a house. Tania knew her life was disposable, as if someone could cut her head off and paste it on another girl's and the world wouldn't notice at all. She needed to *become*. She would adopt a child from Russia. She would look into dental hygienist school—several girls she'd worked with at the Mirage were studying at the community college during the day to become hygienists and it sounded like a good job, albeit one spent on your feet all day bent over people, which in concept sounded not much different than cocktailing.

She'd always had maternal instincts. Tania had been pregnant once, if only for a few weeks. Her boyfriend, a bouncer at the Wild Horse everyone called Slim Joe, got her pregnant—this was when she was thirty, though she told Slim Joe she was twenty-two— and Tania spent a long weekend off from work shopping for baby clothes at Walmart, rummaging through garage sales for baby carriages and strollers. It was too soon, she knew that, as she'd only just missed her period, but she'd taken an at-home test and had an appointment to see her gynecologist for the following week and felt a great desire to begin this new phase of her life, sure that being a mother wasn't so much a calling for her now as it was a station: a chance to be a better person. She was certain she'd need to move in order to get away from Joe, who, while he was a fun guy to waste time with, would be a terrible father. It wasn't that he'd ever hit her or been particularly cruel, only that he was stupid, and stupid would not do as a role model, plus he told everyone he was Bennie Savone's nephew, as if that was something to be proud of, the glory of being adjacent to some two-bit fake-ass Pacino.

She decided to move to Spokane with her child—who she

thought she'd name Corey no matter the sex—and her father could play that positive role until she found someone smart, someone who didn't work at a restaurant or bar. When she miscarried a few days later, she broke up with Slim Joe to pay penance for her own conceit; to bring a child into this world, when they couldn't even save the dolphins or blue whales or whatever, well, it was just silly. A dog would do. But even now, in the small storage locker she has in her building in Desert Hot Springs, there's a box marked "Corey" that she's hauled around across two states.

When she woke up the morning after seeing the documentary and couldn't get the idea of adopting a Russian child out of her mind, she knew she had to act. She had to learn to keep something, to not spontaneously rid herself of responsibility.

What Tania didn't realize was how long and arduous and pricey the whole experience would be. It took just under a year between the day her dog died and the exact moment she stepped off the airplane in Las Vegas with her daughter (*her daughter!*) by her side. She spent eleven months searching for the right child, filling out the paperwork, getting the approvals, paying the fees—it was $30,000 to the Russian agencies, another $5,000 for lawyers and paperwork stateside—until, in the end, she had to ask her parents if she could borrow another $5,000 just to get to Russia, where she'd need to stay for a month to attend adoption hearings and to get Natalya legal for her arrival in the U.S. Her parents ended up giving her $10,000, told her it wasn't a loan, that it was a gift, that they were so proud of her.

Natalya lived with Tania for five and half years. Five and a half good years, Tania thinks now, dropping off drinks in the slot aisles for nickel and quarter tips, though like everything else about the past, she's sure that's just the romantic version. She loved Natalya.

This Tania is sure of. And if Natalya never loved her, that's okay, too. She'd given Natalya the chance, and there was worth in that.

AFTER HER SHIFT ends at six, Tania walks down Palm Canyon Drive and looks into the shop windows, examining the silly T-shirts and bumper stickers ("What happens in Palm Springs stays in Palm Springs . . . usually in a timeshare"), the gaudy jewelry only a vacationer would find the impulse for, the fancy clothes she never sees inside the casino but assumes are worn somewhere. She's always reading about these gala charities and benefit balls held in Palm Springs but can't imagine the people who attend such things or where they buy their clothes. Surely none of them pile into the Mercedes and come to the tourist traps to do their shopping.

Tania pauses in front of Chico's and peers inside at the shoppers, all of whom look to be around her age, but infected with what she thinks of as Realtoritis: their hair about five years past the trend, their tans rubbed on, their heels inappropriately high. And yet they exude an air of success, as if by showing property they somehow glean personal value.

She wonders if she were a dental hygienist if people would be able to tell just by looking at her. Maybe she might occasionally be mistaken for a doctor. That wouldn't be so awful. Maybe people would treat her with respect without understanding why they did so. Cocktailing was never her dream job, but then nothing else struck her as all that compelling, either. When she was young, if there was a chance to fuck up, Tania usually took it, just to see what it felt like. And the result was that she felt, after forty-seven years, that she'd lived, even if she didn't really have much to show for it.

The idea of being a hygienist was one she pursued during that year of waiting, if nothing else because it looked good on all of her adoption applications. People at the various agencies seemed to treat that with some dignity. But staring at the women trying on skirts too short by a decade, she thinks that it's all the same in the end. Just a job. Just a way to afford the things you want. Tania doesn't *want* anything anymore. She *needs* to find Natalya, if only to know that she's okay, but even that has quelled some in the intervening years as she's learned how frequently teenagers adopted out of Russia simply pick up and leave when they have a little money or the keys to the car or the PIN to their parents' ATM card.

Tania checks her watch. She agreed to meet Gordon at six thirty in front of the statue of former Palm Springs mayor Sonny Bono that graces a courtyard up the street from the casino. He asked if he could buy her a drink after work and when she told him she didn't drink anymore, which wasn't strictly true, he didn't flinch. "Then let me buy you a lamp. You must like lights, right? I know a great little lamp store. They even give you the shades and bulbs, too. It's a real deal."

"You're crazy," she said, but she agreed to meet him anyway and now was going to be late if she didn't hustle. Sundays were always sad nights for Tania, and the truth was she was likely to pop some Two-Buck Chuck in front of the TV herself, Sundays her night off of the Internet, a night away from her search. Really, it was more a habit now than anything: check the message board at LostAndFoundChildren.com to see if anyone responded to her photo of Natalya; read the listserv messages from her Yahoo group; scour every search engine, newspaper archive, and blog index on the planet for any mention of Natalya. This searching was her infinity. A bottomless hope. But she gave Sundays up after her mother told her to start weaning herself, that she had to grasp the idea that Natalya wasn't really her child, that she'd just been a child who lived with her for a time. "Think of it like a car lease," her mother said. "That's how we've approached it emotionally; she wasn't our grand-daughter, just a child who lived with our daughter."

Like a car lease. Tania knew her mother meant well, and so she tried, on Sundays, to treat Natalya's disappearance like an epi-sode of a TV show that she found particularly affecting, if only for twenty-four hours.

Up ahead, Tania sees Gordon leaning up against the Sonny Bono statue. He doesn't see her yet, so she takes a few seconds to stare at him, notices that a few of the passing tourist ladies are do-ing the same. It's late spring and the air smells like a mixture of coconut tanning oil and jacaranda blooms, and it only makes sense that Gordon has changed from his casino uniform into tan pants and a white linen button-down, but for some reason Tania is sur-prised by this, how he seems to fit in so perfectly. Even from several yards away Tania can see his tan skin through his shirt, the con-tours of his body. She wonders how old he is, thinks he's probably thirty-five, maybe thirty-eight, too young for her now, anyway. And what does she know about him? What does she know about any-body anymore?

"There you are," he says when Tania finally approaches him. He puts an arm over her shoulder in a friendly way and gives her a pat, like they're brother and sister. "I thought you were going to ditch me here with Sonny."

"You know I'm forty-seven," she says.

"How would I know that?"

"I'm just telling you," she says.

"Is today your birthday?"

"No," she says.

"Then why are we talking about it?"

"I'm not sure why you asked me out," Tania says. "What we're doing here."

Gordon exhales, and Tania realizes he's been holding his breath, that he actually seems a little nervous now that she's paying attention. "Can't people go out for a drink, Tania? Isn't that what normal people do?"

"Are we normal people? All day spent watching people fuck up their lives. Who would call that normal?"

Gordon nods, but it's clear he's not agreeing to anything, just happy to let Tania vent whatever it is she feels the need to vent. She likes that, though she is certain he's just trying to humor her. *Give him a break*, Tania thinks, *act like a person for an hour. See how it feels.*

"Where was this lamp store you were talking about? I'm in great need of track lighting."

WHAT TANIA REMEMBERS about Natalya is insignificant if looked at obliquely. She's realized this before tonight, before she saw Gordon's expression glaze over while she prattled on about the way Natalya used to sneeze every time she ate chocolate, or how Natalya's eyes were brown on some days and green on others, or how, when she's feeling particularly sentimental, she'll spray a bit of Natalya's perfume on her old pillow and set it down across the room while she's watching television or cooking something, so that she'll just get a whiff of it in the course of doing regular things and it will be like Natalya's in the other room, sitting on the floor like she used to do with her headphones on, listening to her English-language tapes.

She could blame the liquor for this sudden descent into reverie, but that would be useless. As soon as Gordon asked her, "How did you end up in Palm Springs?" she felt it all bubble out, the whole

story, from her basset Lucy dying to coming home from her overnight shift at the Mirage to find Natalya gone, along with all of her
clothes, a couple thousand dollars in cash Tania kept in her closet,
and, most disheartening, three full photo albums of pictures taken
since Natalya's arrival, the last five years erased, as if Natalya had
never existed.

How did she end up in Palm Springs? She asked herself this
question repeatedly and the answer was always the same: it wasn't
Las Vegas. Usually that sufficed, but tonight, sitting across from
Gordon, his face getting younger with every passing moment, until
she's certain he's no more than thirty-two (unless what's happened
is that with each drink she's tacked on another month to her life,
so that she's now pushing seventy), she knows that she ended up in
Palm Springs because it was the only place where she had no memories, no connections, nothing to remind her of everything lost, but
where the world itself was essentially the same. She could do her job.
She could breathe the desert air. She could listen to the dinging of
the slots, the whooping of the drunks, the crunching of ice in the
blender, the drone of mindless cocktail conversation and pretend
that her life had frozen in place, that she'd conjured the whole sad
affair. Yes, she could close her eyes inside the Chuyalla Indian Casino and imagine herself thirty, childless and disproportionate to
reality.

"I've ruined the night," Tania says. She and Gordon have been
sitting at the patio bar in front of the Hyatt for three hours. There's
a man playing acoustic guitar on a small stage a few feet away from
them, and every fifteen minutes or so he plays "Margaritaville" and
another ten tourists stop to sing along. "I didn't mean to go on like
that."

"No, it's fine," Gordon says. He reaches across the table and tries to take her hands, but she puts them in her lap before she remembers her own admonition: Be human.

"I should go home," she says, forgetting that she doesn't have a car anymore, that she'll need to call a cab or ask Gordon for a ride, since the buses stopped running hours ago. "I'll end up telling you about every boyfriend I've ever had otherwise."

Gordon doesn't smile like she thinks he will. He just stares at her. "Let me ask you something," he says eventually. "You think you'll ever find her?"

"No," Tania says, and for the first time she believes it. The truth is that no one has ever asked her this question, though of course it existed in the subtext of her life all the while—a nagging sense that her search for Natalya was what she *should* be doing, but the fact remained that if Natalya wanted to be found, if Natalya wanted Tania to find her, specifically, it would have already happened. "I may locate her at some point. But I don't think I'll ever see her again."

TANIA STARES OUT her sliding glass door as Gordon's taillights disappear down the hill, back toward Palm Springs. It's midnight and though the air has chilled, Tania feels feverish. She told Gordon, as he pulled up to her complex, that she'd invite him in but was afraid she'd caught a bug sitting outside for so long this evening. She shakes her head thinking about it, how silly she must have sounded, as if she could catch consumption from sitting outside listening to Jimmy Buffett songs on a spring night.

"It's okay," he said, and Tania sensed solace from Gordon, though the truth is that she's forgotten how to read young men. They used to be so obvious to her, but now they're just mannerisms in her peripheral. "There will be other nights. I know where you work."

She kissed him lightly on the cheek and got out of his car, didn't bother to turn and smile or even give a little wave when she got to the top step of the metal staircase that leads to her apartment, though she knew Gordon was watching her. He'd been raised well enough to wait until a woman was inside her home before driving off, but not well enough to be doing something better with his life than bartending at an Indian casino, and that alone made Tania sad for him.

Tania opens the sliding door and steps outside onto her tiny patio. She's arranged three pots of daisies around a single white plastic chair and though it doesn't seem like much, it's all she can do to keep those daisies alive. She stands against the wrought iron railing surrounding the patio and stares south toward the wind farms of Palm Springs, watches as light jumps between the spinning windmill turbines, listens for the low whine of the coyotes that often rummage in the dumpsters behind her building and who she sees lazing in the shadows on the hottest desert mornings.

She knows she gave up too much tonight, that things will be awkward with Gordon from now on, but that's okay. Nothing's permanent anymore. There's nothing that says this life has to be lived waiting for the next shame. "Natalya is not coming back," Tania says aloud, and then she says it again and again and again, until her words have lost all shape in her ears, until she feels something rise up inside of her, a sense of confidence, of lucidity, that she can't recall ever possessing. She sits down in the white plastic chair and realizes what she's feeling, after so long, after all these years, is relief.

THE SPARE

Chicago
Summer 1973

If Dark Billy Cupertine had to kill a guy, he preferred to do it up
close, with his bare hands. He didn't want to get used to it, was the
thing, and if you were popping motherfuckers in the back of the
head, maybe you could pretend it wasn't real, that the bullet did the
work, that you weren't involved, like how all these young guys from
the neighborhood talked about greasing motherfuckers in Vietnam.
Just a thing they did every day. Push a button and boom, done. You
kill a guy with your hands, you punch his teeth into his throat, you
beat his eyeballs into the back of his head, you break his windpipe
and watch him choke on his own blood? Man, that's yours.

"This would go faster if you grabbed a shovel," Germaio Moretti
said. The two of them were in a vacant lot, surrounded by a corona of
semi-built homes, that eventually would become a three-bedroom
house, Germaio chest-deep in a grave being dug for a guy named
Randall Dover, who owned a car dealership in Batavia.

Mosquitoes the size of tennis balls buzzed around them. Near
dawn and still in the nineties.

Billy said, "You kill a guy, you dig his grave. That's the rules."

"Since when?"

"Since now," Billy said. Germaio didn't really answer to Billy Cupertine, since he was cousin Ronnie's personal muscle, but Cupertines were Cupertines, and so Billy had rank. Cupertine blood ran The Family since 1896, back when it was just a crew robbing steam trains. "Plus, I'm going on vacation in the morning. I can't be showing up covered in fucking dirt."

"I'm lodging a complaint with the boss," Germaio said, not even half joking. "You know my back is shit."

Billy shook out a cigarette, lit it up, looked back across the Des Plaines River. He could see in the distance the thirty-foot-tall lights ringing Joliet Prison. His old man did three years there. Ronnie's pop, Dandy Tommy, did eighteen months. Germaio did a five-year bid, but somehow Billy had avoided spending any official time there, apart from visiting his father. Longest he'd ever been locked up was a couple months off and on in juvie, then maybe three months total in county over the years, but nothing since having a kid. Because the fact was, if he got arrested for the shit he did now, he'd be staring at life sentences if he was lucky. He told Ronnie he needed to be more careful, couldn't be doing this hands-on bullshit, that he could oversee, but he wasn't gonna be on the dirty end of this business.

Which he was largely able to do . . .

. . . save for shit like this right here.

Ronnie had inherited Dandy Tommy's used-car dealerships and was now turning them out, expanding into Detroit, thinking about maybe getting into new cars, too, hooking up with Ford, the real money in ripping people off legitimately, jacking up repair costs on Mustangs, recommending custom paint jobs on Granadas. Which meant Billy periodically had to do jobs that he found distasteful, and frankly beneath his rank, but which needed to be handled with a bit more sensitivity.

Ronnie wanted to own Randall Dover's Chrysler dealership, but Dover wasn't inclined to sell, no matter how much Ronnie offered, no matter how many veiled threats were made. Dover was one of those old-school Chicago guys who thought he was tough because he watched the Bears and knew how to stay warm in the winter, could maybe handle himself in a bar fight because he knew no one was going to pull out a gun and put one in his head, had enough money that he was always threatening to sue people, but nothing was really life-or-death to people like this asshole, it was just Business and Family and Jesus on Sundays when there wasn't Football.

So Randall Dover rolled into the Lamplighter for a drink, maybe not knowing it was a Family-affiliated bar, but probably not giving a fuck, because on top of everything else he was sixty-five years old, and no one really fucked with old guys, as a general rule. Twenty minutes later Billy got the call to grab up Germaio and see if he could talk some sense into Dover, and if not, bring the dog fucker to Ronnie. Which would have all been fine except Dover got mouthy in the backseat of Billy's Buick, talking about how he knew Germaio's mother, how they went to school together, how he was going to sue her, take her house, put her on the street, which got Germaio to pistol-whipping the cocksucker, and next thing, the fucker had a stroke or a heart attack and by the time they realized what was happening, he was limp as a dick and dark blue.

And he *still* hadn't sold his dealership.

Seemed like a dumb thing to die for, and an even dumber thing to go to prison for, Billy not inclined to spend his last days on earth staring out at this very subdivision for a fucking car dealership Ronnie coveted. The subdivision, called River View Estates, was being built to coincide with an expected expansion of the prison, Joliet the kind of town that applauded increased crime numbers elsewhere in the state, because more motherfuckers in prison meant more jobs. More jobs, more houses. More houses, more cars. More cars, more traffic cops. More traffic cops, more people in county jail. More people in county jail, a bigger county jail would be needed, which meant more jobs for union carpenters and millwrights, all of whom kicked up to The Family, the whole thing a self-perpetuating cycle.

"When is sunrise?" Germaio asked.

Billy looked at his watch. It was close to four in the morning. He told Arlene to be ready to go by ten. Everything went as planned, it would be fine. "Another ninety minutes," Billy said. He kneeled down, gave the grave a good once-over. "That motherfucker in the trunk isn't a midget, either, so get some length on this."

"He'll bend," Germaio said. He was soaking wet in his own sweat.

"Into thirds?" Billy said. Germaio was about a hundred pounds overweight, so behind his back everyone called him either Fats or Tits, but to his face, they kept quiet owing to the fact that Germaio Moretti was a fucking lunatic, the kind of guy who kicked women and pulled out snitches' tongues and pissed on hookers just for fun, or at least that was the legend. Billy didn't think Germaio did much of anything these days but pant out of his mouth like a dog, given how fat his neck was, air wheezing out of him even when he was perfectly still. Billy tried to imagine strangling him, tried to figure out how he'd get his hands around Germaio's throat, but couldn't work out the geometry, nor could he accurately calculate the amount of force needed for the job. "Another foot deep, too."

"For fuck's sake," Germaio said, but he got back to digging.

After another five minutes, Billy took a final drag from his cigarette, squeezed it out between his thumb and forefinger, stuck the butt in his pocket, took out his car keys, jingled them so Germaio would turn around. "I'm gonna back the car up," Billy said. "Keep digging."

"Eat a dick," Germaio wheezed out. Or at least that's what Billy thought he heard. It was hard to make out much of anything since Germaio was almost six feet underground and the only part of him above the dirt was the back of his fat fucking head.

The level of disrespect was higher than usual, but Billy recognized they were in a heightened situation, that Germaio was dealing with the complexities of a situation possibly beyond his limited fucking intellectual capabilities.

Not that it really mattered.

Dark Billy Cupertine was about five hours from getting out.

For the last year, he'd pinched where he could: skimmed fourteen grand from a heroin deal with the Windsor clan up north; collected on a fifty-G debt from a mark named Victor Noe, crushed his throat using only one hand, Victor so coke sick he probably did him a favor, drove his body all the way out to Devil's Kitchen Lake, way off Route 57, dumped him out, told everyone the motherfucker had skipped, then took his damn house, too; shook down some old folks in Little Ukraine, basic shit, thug shit, but whatever. He had a number in mind and after last week, he finally made it: $300K in cash, plus five guns, enough ammo to outlast most cops, stuffed in the trunk of his convertible DeVille in the garage at home, built into a contraption underneath the spare tire. He wouldn't be able to get to the guns fast, so he had one in the dash, too, but if the cops pulled him over, they'd need to pile through his wife Arlene's suitcases and his son Sal's toys, dump everything out on the side of the road to find anything incriminating.

No one was going to do that, not to someone with the last name Cupertine.

No. They'd just shoot him the face. So if someone pulled him over, well, it wouldn't get to that point. Dark Billy Cupertine was a dead man already; killing a cop on the way to his new life wouldn't matter in the long run.

But . . . well, it would be a *complication*, and Billy was in a place where complications would not do, like being party to senseless murder on his last day out, which is why when he got into the front seat of his '68 Buick Riviera, given to him right off the lot from one of Ronnie's dealerships, he rolled slowly back to the lip of the grave, made sure Germaio was right where he left him, and then slammed the gas pedal to the floor and chopped the motherfucker's head off.

BILLY DIDN'T GET back to his house until almost seven. After he located Germaio's head—it had landed where the living room would eventually be—he dumped it into the hole, followed by Randall Dover's body, then refilled the grave. By the end of the week, the grave would be covered by a foundation pour and then, eventually, an attached garage. Everyone getting attached garages these days, no one willing to walk ten feet out into the cold if they didn't have to.

He drove up 355, stopped behind a shopping center being built out in Bolingbrook, threw his shoes and jacket in a dumpster, then set it on fire, watched it for a couple minutes, made sure everything burned, headed back to his place in Alta Vista Terrace, slid into bed as Arlene was winking awake. "Give me twenty minutes," he told her, but she let him sleep until nine.

He pulled himself from bed, took a shower, got the last of the dirt and blood from under his nails, got busy packing the rest of his vacation-wear, then had a thought. He opened the top drawer of his dresser, reached behind the socks he'd left behind, found what he was looking for: brass knuckles. They were fifty years old. Maybe seventy-five. Belonged to his grandfather, Anthony Cupertine, then handed down to Billy's father, Black Jack Cupertine, and then Billy took them out of Black Jack's pocket before they put him in the ground.

Going on eleven years ago now.

A heart attack on a golf course in Tampa.

No one found Black Jack for two days; the poor fucker had collapsed in a sand trap, then sat there dead during a tropical squall. Meanwhile half of Chicago descended on Florida looking for him, everyone thinking he'd been abducted, was about to be ransomed a tooth at a time, only to have him found by a groundskeeper.

Black Jack decided to hit eighteen on his own, no bodyguards, died in fucking plaid pants.

The *indignity*.

Cupertine men had been beating the shit out of people in Chicago for a very long time, and here was Black Jack Cupertine taking his dirt nap with a golf club in his hand, a load of death shit in his plaid pants, bugs already eating his face when he was finally located. That transferred power to Black Jack's brother, Dandy Tommy, and then onto his son, Ronnie, which turned Billy Cupertine into The Spare.

Maybe if Billy had been a different kind of guy, none of this would have mattered. He could have earned a living, had a nice family, been content. But the problem with being The Spare was that there was always someone thinking about making a move, and the first move would always be to take Billy out, no use killing Ronnie if there was someone else waiting in the wings, Billy also aware that the only people who called him Dark Billy were members of his own crew.

Motherfuckers in Miami and Detroit and Memphis? They called him The Spare, big fucking jokers, each.

Fact was, though? It was true. That knowledge fucked with Billy Cupertine.

Billy slid the knuckles on, made a fist. They felt smooth. Comfortable. His son, Sal, wasn't gonna grow up to be a pussy, but Billy would be damned if he'd be out breaking legs for a living, either. He was too smart for that. Ten years old and already reading adult books, getting into his grandmother's stash of Harold Robbins, but had to act dumb around his friends, retards like Germaio's son Monte down the block, who couldn't tie his shoes until he was seven, had to get his stomach pumped after swallowing a handful of nickels. Sal could probably run the whole Family's finances right now, figure out decent investments, get everyone clean and legit. Maybe make a lawyer or a doctor or banker, help people.

What had Billy ever done? Created a network for pushing heroin. Killed maybe ten guys on his own. Twelve now. Could be more. He didn't dwell on it, because what was the use? Heroin killed more, that was sure. Made his cousin Ronnie and before that, Ronnie's father Dandy Tommy, rich. Yeah, he'd done fine, too. Had a good life, apart from living with the fear that every single day someone was going to get the drop on him. Not that the fear bothered him—it kept him sharp—rather it was the idea that it would somehow infect his wife, his kid. He'd picked this life. He'd decided to look over his shoulder in every room he entered. But having a kid changed him. Made The Spare shit more acute. Because if Billy was The Spare, what was Sal? Every day that he came home with some motherfucker's blood on his hands and he saw his son playing with his Army men, it was like getting stabbed with a dull knife.

Billy's experience, you could live with a stab wound. But then eventually, infection would get you. Eaten up from the inside.

"Are you about ready, honey?"

Billy turned around and saw Arlene standing in the doorway. She had on a sundress, her shoulders bare, a little sweater in her right hand.

"One sec," Billy said. He slipped the brass knuckles into his pocket. Once they got where they were going, he'd bury them along with every other trace of their old life. Three hundred thousand dollars wasn't a fortune. But it was enough to put some real estate between him and the rest of the Family, the plan being to get to Arizona by the end of the week. He'd decided on Sedona after watching an old Jimmy Stewart movie called *Broken Arrow* one night on WTTW. Jimmy Stewart played an ex-solider named Jeffords sent to talk Cochise into peace. He spends most of the movie staring out at the Sedona landscape and trying to figure out how to keep the U.S. military and a piss-angry Geronimo—who would have made a good capo—from wrecking a fragile détente. Hotheads on both sides would get them all killed, Cochise and Jeffords knew, so everything was a fucking negotiation, good men caught up in the mire just out of association, the red rocks watching all of it, not going anywhere, proof enough that history could outlast the foolishness of men. Billy thought Jimmy Stewart was a bit of a bitch in most cases, but he liked *Broken Arrow*, liked the message, liked how Jeffords ended up living with Cochise until he died, how the Indians in the movie weren't portrayed as animals, just people who had a code.

"Sal is already in the car," Arlene said. She was under the impression that the three of them were driving out to Lake Geneva for a week. Get out of the broiling city. They had a favorite spot they liked to go to around this time every year. Shuffleboard and mint drinks and magazines and dime-store thrillers.

First they'd drive south, all the way to Texas. Eighteen hours. He had a guy in Austin with fresh identification for them all. Billy would take care of him, get rid of his body, no witnesses, and then they'd keep moving, get to Flagstaff, another fifteen hours, put the family up in a hotel for a few days, then prospect out to Sedona, find a house.

"For how long?"

Arlene looked at her watch. "Fifteen, twenty minutes," she said. "He tried to sleep in the backseat last night. Went in to kiss him goodnight and couldn't find him. Nearly had a stroke, Billy. I thought someone took him, you know?"

This got Billy to laugh. That kid. He was like a dog. You couldn't say certain words around him or else he'd start jumping around. Once he knew there was a car trip, every day he'd ask when they were leaving, and it didn't matter the answer because he had no sense of time. Everything was right now for Sal.

"Sorry," Billy said. "I didn't expect to be out all night. One thing led to another and it was dawn."

Arlene waved him off. She knew who he was. "You're here now," she said. "And I get you to myself for the next week."

He stepped across the bedroom and kissed her lightly. She tasted like cigarettes, but not in a bad way. "The car all packed?"

"Only thing missing is you," she said.

He'd tell her once they were on the highway. Maybe she'd fight him at first—she had a sister, her mother was still alive, she had friends, a life—but the reality was that Arlene would do what Billy said. Because she didn't want to wash someone's blood off his clothes any more than he did. Not anymore.

"We gotta make one stop," Billy said.

FOR THE LAST four years, Dark Billy Cupertine and his cousin, and de facto boss, Ronnie Cupertine, had a standing date on the top floor of the IBM building being constructed between Wabash and State. At first that just meant going up a couple rickety floors to where Family-connected contractors were pouring concrete, but now it meant making a trip up fifty-two stories of anodized black aluminum to the last bit of open construction. The building was set to open by fall and already the city was hailing it as an architectural wonder, a monolith of power and money, as if Wall Street had been cut and pasted right in the middle of the broad shoulders of Chicago, the city never content to just be Chicago, always needing to compare itself to New York. A perpetual small-dick problem was how Billy thought of it, but the fact was it infected how The Family did business, too, constantly worried that some Gambino fuck was going to show up and muscle them out of their territory. His father and grandfather had built The Family into its own thing, beholden to no one, but Ronnie, he had different ideas.

He was connecting to LA and Memphis, had some Florida shit going on, plus their continued interests in Las Vegas, maybe even some offshore shit in the future, Ronnie always going on about how if The Family was going to survive Nixon, half of their muscle in a fucking jungle in Vietnam, the other half in prison, it had to treat its business like McDonald's, put up shop wherever there wasn't somebody else. It was some shit he'd read in a book somewhere. So Ronnie had The Family going into small towns and blowing up what were effectively mom-and-pop shops, digging graves in Omaha to get into the meat business, which was really just a way to get access to big rigs for moving product across state lines, greasing small-town cops to look the other way on gambling setups around college football season, which was how they were getting into the extortion game with wealthy farmers, Billy thinking it was all too much, that

McDonald's got fries and burgers right, which is why they didn't fuck with hot dogs.

All this other stuff? It was hot-dog business. It was how they were going to get caught, Billy thought. Or how Ronnie was, anyway.

"What an eyesore," Arlene said when they pulled up beside the construction entrance to 330 Wabash. Workers milled around a roach coach, sipping coffee, eating sweet rolls, bullshitting. It was just after ten thirty in the morning, but due to the heat, workers had been pounding nails since five a.m. Billy had the top down on their convertible and Arlene had her head craned back to see the top of the building.

"Yeah," Billy said. In his view, the IBM building looked like a big black thumb.

"Why does Ronnie like to meet here?"

"Only place he knows where no one is listening," Billy said.

Arlene sighed. "He thinks Eliot Ness is waiting on top of the Sears Tower with a stenographer?"

"The Sears Tower is 110 stories," Sal said from the backseat.

"That right?" Billy said. He looked at him in the rearview mirror, Sal busy with a coloring book. The Sears Tower had just opened a few months earlier, but already Sal was obsessed with it.

"That's eight stories taller than the Empire State Building," Sal said. "And fifty-eight stories taller than this will be."

Arlene had given Sal a book called *Great Skyscrapers* for Christmas and every night for the last six months, he'd read the damn thing before falling asleep. The only thing Sal didn't know was who was buried under every building. Maybe he'd become an architect? The guy who designed the IBM building had died before they even started putting rebar down and yet this fucking thumb would be here another, what? Hundred years? Two hundred? How long did skyscrapers last these days? Wouldn't that be something. A Cupertine who came to Chicago and built something that lasted for a hundred years and no one got killed because of it.

"Maybe one day we'll go to the Empire State Building," Billy said. "Would you like that?"

Sal shrugged. "I guess so."

Billy reached across Arlene and into the glove box, came out with an envelope filled with cash. It was payday, Ronnie getting his cut from the H business. Twenty-five grand that went straight into his pocket, just for being Ronnie Cupertine.

"Don't be long," Arlene said.

"I won't," he said.

"Tell Ronnie that I'll give Suzette a call when we get back," she said. Suzette was Ronnie's wife. For now, anyway. She couldn't get pregnant, so Ronnie was already looking for somewhere else to put his dick.

"Keep the car running," Billy said.

"Do you need anything else?" Arlene asked. The glove box was still open, his pistol there.

He looked into the backseat again, Sal's head down in his coloring book. Maybe this would be the last day his son ever saw Chicago. Last day as Sal Cupertine, anyway. Maybe he'd come back as an adult, with a new name, barely any memories of this time when his father was in deep with this gangster bullshit. Who would Billy be by then? He saw himself owning a bar. One of those places where you could get a decent steak and a cold beer and on weekends, they'd have a little spot out back where they'd have BBQs, so you could bring your wife and kid to your daily spot and they'd realize it wasn't some dive.

Or he'd be dead.

"No." Billy closed the glove box. "I'll be right back," he said. "Ten minutes." He gave Arlene's hand a squeeze. "Hey," Billy said, and Sal met his eyes in the rearview mirror. "Look up at the top floor. I'll wave."

RONNIE CUPERTINE WAS a couple years younger than Billy, but he was already going gray at the temples, which made him look surprisingly dignified, so Ronnie played it up, wore nice suits, spent some money on shoes, styled his hair, even when he was going to be at a construction site seven hundred feet off the ground. He was also starting to do things like donate money to cancer research, ever since his father Dandy Tommy ended up with a bum pancreas that killed him in two months.

"You got a luncheon or something today?" Billy asked when he found Ronnie on the south side of the building, done up in a blue suit, white shirt, red tie, looking like the fucking flag.

Ronnie pointed out the window, which wasn't a window yet, just a square covered in clear plastic tarp. "You ever been inside that building?" he asked.

Billy looked down at the eight-story building across the street. "The *Sun-Times*? Fuck no. Spent my entire life trying to keep my name out of that fucking thing."

"I got a meeting there today," he said, Billy thinking he sounded pretty satisfied. "I'm buying some advertising."

"You fucking crazy?"

"Full-page ad," he said. "Color. Gonna run every Sunday, starting this week. Then I'm gonna have smaller ads in Sports and Business on weekdays. Thinking I might start doing some radio, too."

"How much is that?"

Ronnie shrugged. "Way I see it," he said, "once I buy into the paper and the radio, we're partners. I think they'll see it the same way. Might be I start doing TV ads, too. That's the next thing, Billy. They'll have more room to talk about Nixon if they aren't talking about me."

"You mean *us*?"

"You know what I mean," Ronnie said. Billy was afraid he did.

"What would Dandy Tommy say?"

"Eh," Ronnie said. "He's dead. It's a new era, right?"

"Doing shit in the open," Billy said, "is gonna piss people off."

"Who? The Outfit? New York? Fuck them. Let them come at me," Ronnie said. "It's about *complicity*. The newspaper, they aren't gonna piss on me if I'm giving them twenty Gs a month. Cheaper than paying off the cops. Cleaner than moving H and no one's stiff in an alley because they OD'd on Mike Royko."

"Someone wants to write about you," Billy said, "an ad isn't gonna stop them."

"We'll see," Ronnie said. "In the meantime, you're holding the first month's rent."

Billy reached into his pocket, came out with the envelope. Ronnie flipped through the bills absently, then waved over a new guy, gave him the cash. Big Kirk they called him. He was a big white kid, but his last name was Biglione, gangsters not exactly fucking Shakespeare with the nicknames. His sister Gina was married into The Family, hooked up with some motherfuckers out in Detroit who had a bingo skim going at a bunch of retirement homes. This was Big Kirk's summer job, getting sandwiches and coffee for Ronnie, standing around, looking imposing. He was maybe eighteen. Next year at this time, Billy figured he'd either be dead or in college. Billy hoped, for his sake, college. He counted the money.

"Twenty-five," Kirk said.

Billy said to Kirk, "You ever count *my* money in front of me again, your mother will be on a fucking feeding tube."

Kirk stared blankly at Billy, like he hadn't been taught that part of algebra yet. "I'm sorry?"

"Give us a minute," Ronnie said. Kirk went and stood beside the elevator. "Give him a break. He'll learn."

"I'm serious, Ronnie," Billy said, not that it mattered. But he couldn't suddenly be a pussy on his last day. "Count my money? Some Detroit fuck? His balls even drop yet?" Billy looked back over his shoulder at Big Kirk. Kid had a crooked look on his face, like he didn't know if he should smile or scream. "Dumb motherfucker," he mumbled, but with his eyes, he tried to will the kid to leave, go downstairs, hop on the L, never come back.

"He's just doing what he thinks is right." Ronnie took a few steps, motioned Billy to follow him. "You know what's going on this floor?"

"I don't know," Billy said, "a thousand typewriters?"

"IBM has a government contract," Ronnie said. "Making computers for the CIA. Up here, it's gonna be all spooks and G-men. Want the walls soundproofed. They're building an interior room back over here." Ronnie pointed to an area on the floor marked off with red X's. Maybe twenty by twenty. "They want it to have exterior walls made of metal, covered in cement. Survive a bomb. What do you think goes in there?"

"Mr. IBM?"

Ronnie considered this. "Not a bad idea." He stopped walking once they were out of earshot from Big Kirk, looked out another plastic window. "What the fuck happened last night?" Ronnie asked quietly.

"Germaio went sideways on him." Billy shook his head at the

memory. "And then the fucker stroked out. Started shaking, frothing at the mouth, and then he was toast. Maybe a minute all in."

"So if I determine that we need to dig him up," Ronnie said, "coroner isn't gonna see a broken neck or missing fingers or anything?"

"Might be absent a couple teeth," Billy said.

"That can be explained. Anything unexplainable? A fucking wrench up his ass or something?"

"No," Billy said. But they would find Germaio. By then, it wouldn't matter. Billy would be long gone. "Broken nose, maybe. But he's gonna be under a house in about three days."

Ronnie pointed out the window. There were gray clouds hovering over the lake. "Supposed to rain for the next three days," Ronnie said. "Summer storm. Gonna be eight million percent humidity for the next week. You don't watch the news?"

"I was busy last night."

"I bet."

"We buried him deep," Billy said. "It could rain for a month, wouldn't matter."

"Point is," Ronnie said, "they ain't gonna be putting foundations down in the fucking rain. Anyone see anything?"

"Wasn't how I had it planned," Billy said. "But Germaio wouldn't listen."

"I had you there so nothing would go sideways," Ronnie said. He shook his head. "The guys respect you. And then you let something like this go down? It's a lot of fucking cleanup."

"I didn't *let* it happen," Billy said. "Motherfucker turned blue on us. Besides, what were you gonna do with him? Have fucking tea and sandwiches?"

"I wasn't gonna kill him," Ronnie said.

"Of course *you* weren't going to," Billy said. He glared at his cousin for a few seconds; then he felt something soften inside of him. What was this bullshit? Grew up together like brothers, the only sons of two of the baddest motherfuckers on the planet, playing catch in the street with Family soldiers watching them like Secret Service, trick-or-treating as gangsters—trench coats, guns, hats, the whole nine—the neighbors giving up all their candy at once. Fast-forward and no one wore costumes anymore. He reached over and took his cousin by the arm. "I'm sorry, Ron. We fucked up. Whatever it costs, take it from my end. Germaio can't afford it."

Ronnie took a deep breath, exhaled through his mouth, nodded. "Where's Germaio now?"

"I dropped him at his girlfriend's," Billy said. Germaio also had a wife and a kid. This was a lie that wouldn't last long. "Where I picked him up."

"He'd have more money if he wasn't paying for two families," Ronnie said. "What time?"

"I dunno," Billy said. "Six?" Billy heard a shuffling sound, turned and saw Kirk trailing behind them, ten feet away. *This Lurch-motherfucker.* "Sure he's home by now."

"I sent a couple guys over. They said he wasn't home. Car was still in the garage. His dumbfuck son says he hasn't seen him."

"What's his wife say?"

"Same," Ronnie said.

"He's probably scared."

Ronnie nodded. "You know how many people saw the three of you inside the Lamplighter?"

"No one would say anything," Billy said.

"Maybe not. But you dumb fucks left Dover's car there," Ronnie said. "I told Germaio to bring it back with him and he just left it sitting in the parking lot. Why would he do that?"

Shit. Germaio hadn't mentioned that. "He's not real detail oriented."

"Yeah," Ronnie said, "but you are." He stepped closer to the window, found a tiny hole in the tarp, pushed his thumb through it, an arrow of breeze shot out. "Dover's wife reported him missing this morning, and there was his fucking car, right where he left it. It's gonna cost me a lot to keep this shit quiet. More than you can afford. Which is why I'm thinking I'll just dig him up and toss him in the lake, let him wash up in a couple days, get someone to call it a suicide."

"They can figure that shit out," Billy said.

"Who?"

"The coroner," Billy said. "That's how Junior Pocotillo got sent up." Billy had gone to high school with Junior Pocotillo. A big fucking Indian kid. He'd killed some Russian mope who'd tried to jack him for his car, problem being that Junior had stolen the car in the first place. He'd strangled the guy and then tossed him in the lake, only to have him wash up the next morning. Doctors figured out pretty quickly that the body was already dead when it got tossed in the water. Billy didn't know exactly how, something about the lungs, but he'd avoided dumping bodies in water since then.

"Fine," Ronnie said. "I'll put him inside a burning car with a couple hookers. That make you happier?"

"Just leave him," Billy said. "There's a problem, I'll handle it. Free of charge."

"Oh yeah?" He cocked his head to the right. "Because isn't that your car down there?"

Billy gazed out the window. The DeVille was right where he left it. Except there was a Cadillac in front of it now. And one behind it. Another pulling up across from it.

Shit.

"Yeah. I'm out of town for the next week," Billy said. "Going to Lake Geneva."

"Oh yeah?"

"Yeah. I told you."

"Right," Ronnie said. He snapped his fingers. "Right. I remember now. You said, 'Hey, cousin, I'm gonna run out of town with a trunk full of your money.'"

Billy reached instinctively for the gun on his hip . . . but it wasn't there. Because he was out with his wife and kid. Because he was going on vacation. Because it was in his glove box. Because he wasn't thinking he was going to shoot his cousin. Not that Ronnie was holding. He didn't carry a gun. That's why he had guys like Germaio and Big Kirk. He was a businessman. Why he had guys like Billy.

"What's your plan? Canada? Mexico? Maybe join those Outfit assholes at the Salton Sea? Or you getting on a boat?"

There was no use lying about anything now. Billy had been in this position before. Except he was the one asking questions. It got to this point, it was already done.

"If it's about the money," Billy said, "you can have it."

"It's not about the money," Ronnie said. "It's about family. This is our shit right here, Billy."

"Doesn't feel that way," Billy said.

"You're running off because you're not busy enough? Because you're dissatisfied with your job? Because you put Germaio in the dirt?"

"Look," Billy said, carefully, "one day, it was gonna be you or it was gonna be me looking at a gun. I'm saving us both. One of us is gonna be dead, one of us is gonna be in prison, that's if we're lucky."

I don't want either. I've got my own family now. I'm just trying to walk away."

"Looks to me like you're running away."

"Yeah, well," Billy said, "consider this my two weeks' notice."

"I needed you, Billy." Ronnie spit on the ground. "We're getting pushed out of Vegas," he said. "Fucking government is all over us. Moles in our unions, fucking snitches up and down the line. This building is finished, you think they're gonna just throw up another skyscraper tomorrow? It'll be ten, fifteen years before we get a contract like this one. But the shit I'm doing is going to set this family up for the next twenty-five years. You were gonna be a part of that, cousin. I can't trust these fucking guys like I can trust you."

"I'm not in the car business," Billy said. "And I sure as fuck ain't in the newspaper business."

"You're a small thinker," Ronnie said. "It's not about the cars. It's not about the drugs. It's not about the books or sharking. It's about the customer. Meet the customers' need before they even know they want something. The Outfit, the Five Families, all those fucks? They're gonna be out of business in five years. We're mechanized, they're horse and buggies."

"Don't tell me more of this McDonald's shit, Ronnie," Billy said. He reached into his pocket, felt the brass knuckles there, slid them on. "I had to bury a guy this morning. Ronald McDonald isn't capping the Burger King." Billy heard the dinging of the elevator. He looked over his shoulder and saw that Big Kirk was now only five feet away. Three black guys appeared at the end of the floor. Billy didn't recognize any of them, which meant they were probably Gangster Disciples. The Family had been selling them guns for years. *Shit.*

"Thought you said you needed me?"

"I do," Ronnie said. "And you want to go. So you're gonna go."

"Four guys, Ronnie?"

"Out of respect," he said.

"There one you want me to keep alive? For the story in the *Sun-Times*?"

Ronnie smiled, but he didn't look happy. "What's in your pocket? Knife?"

"Knuckles," he said.

"Big Kirk could use some scars," Ronnie said.

Billy nodded, looked back out the window. "I wasn't snitching," he said. "Wasn't planning on it, either. You should know. I was just going to retire."

"Government would find you," Ronnie said. "I'd be surprised if you made it out of town. If I knew, they knew. Next time we saw each other would have been in court."

Billy nodded again. "You gonna let me say goodbye to my kid?" Billy thinking if he got down there, Arlene would know what was up, she'd get that gun out, give him a chance.

"Sorry," Ronnie said. "I'll take good care of him while you're gone."

"Oh, I'm coming back?"

"He won't know," Ronnie said, "until he does. And that will be that."

"This isn't the life I want for him," Billy said. "Let him just be a kid. He doesn't need to be like us. Promise me you'll give him that choice."

"I can't make that promise," Ronnie said. "I don't got a son. Maybe it would be different if I did."

"If you had a son," Billy said, "I'd already be dead."

"It'll be fast," Ronnie said.

The three Gangster Disciples were beside Big Kirk now. He

guessed all three were carrying. Judging from their bugged-out eyes, they were also coked-up. He could maybe take out one of them, pop him in the temple just right, get a lick or two at least on Big Kirk, who looked like he was carrying a load of shit in his pants, but not a gun. Still, four on one without a gun only worked in Charles Bronson movies. Billy flexed his fist closed.

He had one shot at this.

One shot to save Arlene and Sal from a life of wondering. How many people from his circle of childhood friends had Billy disappeared under similar circumstances, Family members who strayed and ended up in tiny bits, buried under a Jewel's being built in Springfield or dumped in the Poyter landfill or tossed in any convenient and deep pond? How many families did he lie to and say they'd been sent to Sicily for a job, or that they flipped and were now in the Witness Protection Program, or that they'd fled to Canada, even when he still had their skin under his nails? No. There would be no questioning of what happened to Billy Cupertine, because the end was gonna be the same. He was already dead. Ronnie had already killed him. If Billy wanted to keep his son out of this shit, the boy would need an object lesson. Sal would need to know exactly what Ronnie Cupertine did to his old man.

Billy spun toward the tarp-covered window and smashed his brass-knuckled fist through the thick plastic, slid his arm all the way down, and then did the only thing that made sense.

He jumped.

Fifty-two floors.

Took him almost six seconds to hit bottom.

Six seconds and thirty-five years.

Two years old, there were pictures of him dressed in a baby jumper that made him look like a prisoner, five years old with one of his father's unlit cigars in the corner of his mouth, ten years old he was already running errands, standing outside when the boys came over, listening to the conversations. People started calling him Dark Billy by the time he was fifteen, not because of his skin tone, but because he was a thinker and he'd get a serious look on his face, so there was Light Billy when he was just running around doing kid stuff, and Dark Billy when he was working through shit in his mind, brow furrowed. Seventeen years old he'd already killed five guys. Twenty-five he was married and brokering multimillion-dollar heroin deals, ten bodies on his sheet. Thirty and he was second in line to an empire that he'd never get and didn't want. Thirty-five and he was gonna disappear and leave his kid to wonder why his father left him. Sal would look at the IBM building every day for the rest of his life trying to figure out how his father wasn't able to walk back out, how he went in and disappeared and no one knew anything. Arlene would know. Which meant maybe Arlene would be put out too, car accident or an OD or a staged robbery, shit turns around, Arlene takes a bullet. She wouldn't go quietly, no matter the situation. But he couldn't let her think he just walked out on her.

So Billy Cupertine screamed the entire way down, made sure she paid attention to the situation.

Not because he was afraid.

No, because as he fell, Dark Billy Cupertine realized he was wrong about one thing in his life. Fear hadn't kept him sharp. It had inoculated him. And so as he tumbled through the air and his past, his wife and child staring up at him, their faces coming into view now, Sal's opened mouth about to make his own scream, his last thought was that he'd fucked this all up, from beginning to end. Except for that boy. That boy who'd grow up and would never make the same mistakes. He'd know who not to trust.

GOON NUMBER FOUR

G oon Number Four hasn't been able to take a shit since landing in Dubai—which was, when? Yesterday morning? Jet lag has him all fucked-up. He'd flown commercial, which was a bad sign. If you can afford a goon, get a private jet. Twenty-some hours with layovers and delays, and then Goon Number Seven picked him up at the airport, drove him to the Monaco Hotel, told him he'd be back in ninety minutes, so get showered, look fucking presentable, he was on the clock now. So Goon Number Four checked in, went up to his room, got out of his Adidas sweat suit, scrubbed himself raw in the shower—before he did a job, he always shaved all the hair off of his body, which made him look more menacing, but also he wasn't about leaving his DNA all over the fucking place, a trick he learned from doing some work with The Family in Chicago—changed into the black Armani suit he got at the outlet stores in Cabazon, about thirty minutes from his condo in Palm Springs.

He picked at a plate of fruit. Drank a bottle of water. Checked his email on his encrypted phone. His sister Jackie sent him a proof-of-life photo of his cocker spaniel Thor, Jackie holding up a newspaper next to Thor's head, except Jackie had photoshopped it to say *Ruff You Were Here*. Jackie was a good sister. The only family he had left. "Don't you know yet," she said when she dropped him off at the airport, five a.m., not a soul around, "if you have enough money now?"

"For what?"

"For whatever."

Now, sitting in the passenger seat of a blacked-out Suburban, a locked briefcase on his lap, two other blacked-out Suburbans riding behind him in the arrow formation, the Arabian Desert streaming by, Goon Number Four found himself contemplating what "whatever" might be, while also scanning the horizon for . . . a Starbucks, if he was being honest, or a bush. Somewhere discreet. Because it turned out, he did have enough. This could be his last real job.

"How much longer?" Number Four asked.

"Twenty klicks," Number Seven said.

Klicks. Four seriously doubted Seven had ever been military. Four did two tours in Iraq, another as contract black ops, and he wasn't saying *klicks.* "I didn't ask how far," Four said. "I asked how long."

"What's the difference?" Seven said. Definitely not military.

"The difference is the difference between time and distance," Four said.

"Speedometer is in miles," Seven said. "Now you want me to do math?"

Four looked into the rearview mirror, met eyes with Goon Number Three. This wasn't their first job together. Last time was in Peru. A fucking bloodbath on the streets of Lima. Time before that was a private-security thing. Walking around Coachella in shorts. Easy job. Making sure no one put hands on someone's daughter and her friends, ten sorority girls up from USC, each with a Tri-Delt tattoo on the small of their backs, angel wings strapped over their shoulders, all of them rolling on Molly. Not exactly storming Fallujah.

"Stay frosty," Seven said. "Two o'clock."

Four looked at two o'clock. Nothing but desert. At *eleven o'clock,* however, there was a trail of dust being kicked up from three Hummers moving at an intercept angle. This dumb fuck. He was going to get them all killed.

"Any idea what's so valuable in the case?" Three asked.

"Nope," Four said. It wasn't heavy, so it probably wasn't cash or gold bricks. These days, if something was being handed over like this, it was usually technology. Four's specialty, in situations like this, was to be the guy who walked up with the briefcase, set it down, took a step back, and mad-dogged everyone else until the case was popped. It wasn't hard work. Most of the time, everything went fine. The other 35 percent of the time, yeah, maybe he shot a guy, slit a couple throats, broke arms and legs, gouged out eyes, set fire to a mound of corpses, but that was growing rarer these days. You wanted to kill someone and had the cash to hire a bunch of goons, you also had the cash to get a decent drone.

Which made Four wonder about something. He opened up the moonroof, scanned the sky. Triton drones coasted at sixty-five thousand feet, which was basically outer space. If he was getting blown up from outer space, that's just how it was going to be.

"Close that," Seven said. "Sand makes my asthma go nuts." He took a Kleenex from the center console, blew his nose. "Intercept in four klicks."

"Easy on that klick shit," Three said. He was checking the clip on his AK. "We get out of this situation," Three said to Four, "I'm going to buy a boat, park it off the Oregon coast, and become a private detective. Find missing cats for little old ladies. What about you?"

"I'm going back to school," Goon Number Four said.

"To study what?" Goon Number Three asked.

"Whatever."

"Just don't study history," Three said. "It's just war, war, war, genocide, war. In that order." He leaned into the front seat to get a better look at the Hummers coming their way, since the windows in the back were blacked out. "This is not good. Must be a tracker in here." He tapped his earpiece. "Comms are dead."

"I scanned the case," Goon Number Four said. "It was clean." He paused. "What about art?"

"That could be cool," Three said. "Tracker is somewhere in this ride or else they would have come up behind us. No sense coming from where we can see them." He glanced at Goon Number Seven, then back at Four, motioned to the floor, so Four put the briefcase on the ground. "How far until intercept, boss?"

"Two klicks," Seven said, which is when Three put a bullet in his temple.

Goon Number Four grabbed the steering wheel. Three reached around and opened the driver's side door, shoved Seven out, the Suburban caught his body under the back tires, slowing the truck down enough for Four to slide into the driver's seat. He looked in the rearview, saw one of the trail cars thump over the body, too. Three got up next to Four, put the briefcase on his lap. "Do you draw?" Goon Number Three asked.

"Isn't art mostly on computers now?"

Three held up a finger, tapped his earpiece again. "Copy that." He turned to Four. "Hard right . . . now!" Four yanked the wheel to the right, just as a missile impacted with the Hummers, blowing them to oblivion.

IT TOOK GOON Number Four two weeks to get home, his sister picking him up at the Palm Springs airport at noon on a Tuesday. "You look like shit, Blake," Jackie said when Goon Number Four got into her car. It had been a good long time since he'd heard his name. Long enough that it sort of jarred him. "What happened to your left ear?"

He ran his fingers over the ragged stitch job he received to reattach a chunk of cartilage. "A fight."

"With what? A dog?"

"Yes."

"Did you get a rabies shot?"

"I'm clear," he said. "How's Thor, incidentally?"

"He missed you," she said. "He's at PetSmart getting pretty for you."

"Did you do that thing I asked?"

"It's in the glove box."

Blake popped open the glove box. It was filled with black and purple chips from the Indian casinos in town. He kept a great deal of his cash in casino chips these days, stashed in safe-deposit boxes. It was just easier. And portable. He needed to move a quarter of a million dollars, he didn't need to bother with a wire transfer. But that wasn't what he was looking for. "What about the other thing?" he said.

"It's in there, too, in the envelope." Blake found what he was looking for, a slim manila envelope, opened it up, dumped the information on his lap. "You'll need to get a student ID in person, but that's all of your registration materials. I couldn't get you all the classes you wanted at the times you preferred. I guess there's priority registration for returning students."

"No worries," Blake said. His sister had signed him up for classes on Mondays, Wednesdays, and Fridays at the College of the Desert, the local community college. He'd driven by the campus a thousand times, marveled at the slick glass structures they'd erected for students who couldn't get into a four-year college, never thinking he'd end up there himself. He'd taken the GED and gone right into the armed forces for twelve years, which had then dovetailed into the work he'd been doing for the last decade. The upside was that he got to travel all over the world, made a lot of money. But of late his back and knees had begun to trouble him, doctors telling him he was about five years from needing a knee replacement, needing corrective glasses to see at night. He'd had a persistent prostate infection for a month in fucking Colombia, standing in a jungle like an asshole, needing to piss every nine minutes. This goon shit had an expiration date, turned out, and there was no health or retirement plan. Fortunately, he'd invested and saved, Jackie told him to buy Facebook in 2012, since she was dating someone in the company at the time, and then he had chips around the world. Lots of chips. "What do I need to know?" he asked.

"I got you whatever was still open. Mostly general-education classes." Made sense. She'd signed him up under his name, which he supposed was fine. He had passports and birth certificates for about a dozen others. But he only had high school records as Blake Webster, since no Afghani warlord was going to check to see if one of his fake names had passed Algebra II.

He had four classes: English Composition, Western Civilizations, Math, and then something he didn't recognize.

"What's JOUR 121?"

"Oh," Jackie said, "yeah, I thought that might be fun for you. It's working at the college radio station."

"Doing what?"

"I guess learning how to be a DJ? Or maybe a talk-radio host? You could be like that asshole with all the conspiracy theories."

"Which one?"

"Yeah," Jackie said. "Him."

They came to a stoplight. On the corner was MillionAir, the private airstrip Blake often flew out of. How many times had he walked off of some sheik's Gulfstream G650 with someone else's blood still under his fingernails?

"Are you really doing this, Blake?" his sister asked. "Do I get to stop worrying about you dying?"

"I'm still going to die," Blake said, "but I'm probably not going to have to kill anyone for a while. Does that make you feel better?"

The light turned green. "A little."

THAT NEXT MONDAY, the start of spring semester, Blake showed up for his 10 a.m. class promptly at 9:30 a.m., because when you're a goon, you recon. The class was held in a classroom inside the radio station offices, located across the street from the main campus, next door to a sprawling Mormon church and a gated community called Rancho Del Sol. It looked to Blake like maybe the college had bought a house, did a light remodel, and then built a radio tower in the backyard. He'd seen a similar setup at a Sinaloa stronghold in Mexico, where the bosses ran their own private radio, TV, and Internet network, though the College of the Desert's setup wasn't nearly as nice.

There was a classroom filled with Macs on his left—Blake thought it probably used to be the garage—and then a couple studios for the DJ down the hall in what used to be the living room, dining room, and family room, the house from the seventies, back when people had family rooms. Other side of the house were faculty offices, a lounge, two bathrooms. There were emergency exits in every room. Whole place was maybe twenty-five hundred square feet and could be attacked from about twenty-nine different angles. A totally unsafe spot to conduct an op . . . but Blake guessed it was probably fine for learning.

The classroom tables were set up in a U, so Blake took a seat against the southern wall, giving him a view of all the entrances and exits. Took out his Smith & Wesson tactical pen—it was a ballpoint, but it was made of aircraft steel, the cap was sharp enough to pierce a sternum, with enough force, and/or pop out a car window, and it weighed over a pound, so if he held it in his hand and punched someone in the face, he'd collapse their skull—and a pad of paper.

And then waited.

A woman in black jeans, black boots, a black scoop-necked T-shirt, and huge black sunglasses came into the classroom in a flustered rush, dropped a book bag and a laptop on the podium at the front of the room, then spilled her Starbucks on the ground, coffee splashing all over her, the podium, the whiteboard, and, Blake was surprised to see, even the low cottage-cheese ceiling. "Shit fuck motherfuck cocksucker motherfucker," she said, and then hurried back out, returning a few moments later with a roll of paper towels, only then noticing Blake. "How long have you been sitting there?"

"Twenty-three minutes."

"So you saw that whole production?"

"Yes."

"And you didn't laugh?"

"It didn't seem funny."

"It's always funny when your professor spills coffee all over herself," she said. "It's what makes going to school worthwhile." She stood on one of the chairs. "Help me here so I don't break my neck while I clean off the ceiling." All six feet five inches and 245 pounds of Blake stood up, and the professor seemed visibly surprised. "Check that. You get up here. I'll make sure you don't break your neck."

Blake had some experience cleaning spatters of fluids off of hard-to-reach places, so it was no big deal. Back when he was starting out, he did a month working for a Latvian oil scion/two-bit gangster named Vitaly Ozoles who was constantly losing his shit and shooting someone in the face. Since Blake was the lowest goon, he'd have to drag the body out, bury it, then come back and clean the room, so he had a whole checklist, literally, that he kept in a utility closet in the warehouse that contained Vitaly's fleet of a dozen cars. This was a significantly easier job. He climbed up on the chair, took his KA-BAR knife out of his cargo pants pocket, scraped the latte-stained cottage cheese pellets off into his hand, then got down, dumped it all into the garbage.

"Thank you," she said. She extended her hand and Blake shook it. "I'm Professor Rhodes, but you can call me Dusty. That's what everyone calls me, as you probably know."

"How would I know that?"

"From the . . . radio? Dusty Roads? *The Morning Zoo* on KRIP?"

"I don't listen to the radio."

"Well, we'll fix that," Dusty said. "And what's your name?"

"Blake," he said.

"No last name?"

Blake wasn't used to giving a stranger all of his details, but he guessed she probably had a roster, anyway. "Webster. Blake Webster."

"You'll need a different name for radio," she said. "Your name makes you sound like that guy you went to high school with who still lives in the same town and is now assistant manager at Del Taco."

"I did grow up here," he said.

"Oh," she said. "What do you do for a job?"

"Goon," he said. "Assassin. Private security. Depends on the assignment."

This made Professor Rhodes laugh. "Can you imagine? What a life that would be." She gazed at Blake for a moment. "I hereby christen thee Blake Danger. How about that?"

"It's not my favorite."

"Well, Blake Danger, do me a favor, that giant knife you have there? Could you go ahead and put that away? Zip it in your book bag?"

"No problem," Blake said. He dropped the knife into his bulletproof backpack. It was made from tactical-grade Kevlar, not the crap they sold students. His pack could stop a bullet from an AK, whereas the packs they sold at Target were only good for stopping 9mm shells.

"And if you don't mind me asking," she said, "why on earth did you bring that to class?"

"In case someone tried to kill me," he said. The classroom was beginning to fill with students.

Professor Rhodes smiled. "Okay then, Blake Danger," she said. "Take your seat."

"Bro, you're swole as shit." Blake looked to his left. There was a kid, maybe nineteen, sliding into the chair beside him. He had on a Warriors jersey, a non-bulletproof backpack, shorts that hung off his ass, and flip-flops and was chewing on a straw. "You do keto?"

"No," Blake said. He didn't spend a lot of time around young people, generally, so this was going to take some getting used to. Strangers didn't usually talk to him. Blake didn't usually talk to strangers. That was his whole thing.

"Cool," the kid said. "What're you in for?"

"In?"

"Like, what do you want to do? I'm on that sports tip. I can talk for hours about any sport. Throw one at me. Anything. I got it down now where I can have a hot take for thirty seconds on any sport. My radio name is Down-to-Go. Try me."

"Jai alai," Blake said.

"The fuck is that?"

"National sport of the Basques," Blake said.

Down-to-Go just stared at him. "The fuck is a Basque?"

Before Blake could answer, Professor Rhodes got up to the podium. "Okay, everyone," she said, "welcome back. I see some familiar faces. We're going to have a fun semester, I promise. For the newbies, it's cool if you call me Dusty, since I've seen too many of you on Friday nights at the Red Dawn acting like a fool, and you've seen me, too."

This got half the class to laugh. Blake had never been in the Red Dawn before, but he knew where it was: across from the Lusty Lady Strip Club on Perez Road, an industrial section of Cathedral City. Not that he'd been in there, either, but next door to the Lusty Lady was a storage facility owned by the Mexican Mafia. The kind of place where they tied a motherfucker up before they drove him out to the desert. Red Dawn, meanwhile, was the kind of bar where eighties cover bands played on Tuesday nights, or where local rock DJs might spin their favorite eighties dance hits for people born in the 2000s. Blake didn't go out much. All the bombing he'd been around had left him with low-grade tinnitus.

"I'm not spinning there this term, so you're all safe," Professor Rhodes continued. More laughter. "All right, I'm going to pass out the syllabus and then we'll get started getting comfortable on some of the equipment, so everyone fire up your computers and load GarageBand. Down-to-Go, can you help any of the newbies with getting their mics set up? We're going to get everyone talking day one. Just like if you were coming out of a coma."

•

FOR THE FIRST six weeks of classes, Blake Danger found it fairly easy to keep up. His English composition class was pretty fun—the professor had them writing poems and short essays about their childhood, which Blake liked doing, since it reminded him of things he'd forgotten, like his third and fifth stepfathers, who were the same guy—and Western Civ was fine, except that half his class had never heard of Mesopotamia before, whereas he'd spent a decade there, blowing shit up, rebuilding it, and then blowing it back up again. Math was math. But JOUR 121 was where Blake found himself making friends and learning new things. He'd started out hating the sound of his voice, but Professor Rhodes had forced that out of him by assigning a podcast project where he interviewed people who lived in his gated community. He'd gone door-to-door with his iPhone and a mic and asked each person the same five questions—*Where were you born? What was your first job? Who was your first love? What is your first memory? What is the most beautiful thing you've ever seen?*—which he then edited into a tight package, with voice-over and sound effects.

Funny things was, it wasn't like he knew his neighbors beforehand. In fact, he'd practiced not knowing them, avoiding eye contact whenever possible, and now he had this assignment . . . and Blake was a man who took his assignments seriously, so he'd emailed the entire HOA asking for volunteers and was surprised that almost everyone wanted to talk. "There's nothing people love more than opening up about themselves," Professor Rhodes had told him early on in the process. "You won't get them to shut up now."

It was true. Blake couldn't go to the mailbox without getting drawn into a conversation about HOA politics.

The grass should be greener.

The pool should be warmer.

The short-term renters should be shot.

It was only a matter of time before Blake was put up for office, because he agreed with everyone, on everything.

He'd emailed his assignment in the night before. So when Professor Rhodes walked up to Blake that morning in Beeps Café, the shitty coffee joint on campus, and asked if she could join him, he was both nervous and excited. *Has she listened? Does she want to talk about it? Am I any good?* She was dressed in what Blake had come to realize was her uniform—the same black getup she'd worn on the first day of class—including the sunglasses, which she kept on.

"I need you to tell me something honestly," she said to Blake.

"Okay," he said. *She hated it. Dammit.* He knew it. *She's going to ask me if I even graduated high school. I'll have to tell her I took the GED.*

"I wouldn't ask this if you were one of the kids, by the way," she said. "And maybe I shouldn't be asking you, regardless, because of FERPA or HIPAA or OSHA or, I dunno, Ke$ha." She leaned toward Blake, like she was waiting for him to laugh, but Blake was feeling like that time he got interrogated by that warlord in Darfur. "Anyway. I'm not loaded up with friends in this place, so, here we are. You seem like a nice person. Are you a nice person?"

"I try to be," Blake said. "But I often fail."

"Right. That's what we should all be doing, right? Trying to be nice people." She cleared her throat. Then took off her sunglasses. "Can you tell that I have a black eye?"

Professor Rhodes's right eyeball looked like a stop sign, but the skin around it was the same color as the rest of her face, which Blake realized was a trick of makeup. Concealer, powder, enough foundation to hold the Taj Mahal.

"No," Blake said.

"Really?"

"No," Blake said again. "It's clear you have an eye injury. It's not clear that the injury extends to the rest of your face. But looking closely, I see some swelling and slight discoloration. Someone sees you, they're going to know that you hurt yourself, but they aren't going to know *how* you hurt yourself. But if you start to sweat," he drew a circle in the air around her eye, "there will be questions."

"I can't be walking around this place looking like I got into a fight," she said. "That's how adjuncts lose their jobs."

"Did someone hurt you?"

She put her sunglasses back on. "I've been taking self-defense classes," she said. "This seventeen-year-old girl who works at the yogurt shop across the street? Sprinkles? She kicked me in the face like we were in a cage match. And then I sort of . . . lost it. And then she kicked me again." Professor Rhodes shook her head. "I'm the only person who has ever taken a self-defense class and got beaten up *in the class*. Unreal, right?"

"Self-defense isn't about winning. It's about surviving. You need to learn how to fight, not how to defend yourself."

"You ever see *Play Misty for Me*? The Clint Eastwood movie about the DJ?"

"Is this one of those movies with the chimpanzee?"

Professor Rhodes thought for a moment. "No," she said. "Could be. I don't think so. Anyway. It's terrible. Clint's a DJ and he has a fling with one of his fans, she starts calling him all the time, there's another woman, blah blah blah, murder, murder, etc."

"I mostly watch documentaries."

"The point is, I'm in a situation with a stalker."

"This stalker," Blake said. "Do you know him?"

"Her," she said. "She works here."

"At the college?"

"Yes," she said, "campus security. She walked me to my car one night, then a couple nights later she shows up at Red Dawn, not a huge surprise, right? Like, small town, people hang out wherever, but then two nights after that, I'm here on campus to watch a play— *Noises Off,* which was terrible—and she sits down next to me in the auditorium. Then she starts calling in and winning contests at my other job on KRIP. Duran Duran tickets one week, Robbie Knievel tickets another week, free pizzas, whatever, just so she has a reason to show up to the station."

"She asked you out?"

"Yeah, that first night. Real casual. I didn't think anything about it. Asked if I wanted to meet up for a bite sometime and I was like, Yeah, sure, sometime. It was late and I wanted to go home. Then she's at Red Dawn and she's like, How about tonight? And it's loud, so I can't quite figure out what's happening, so I say, Sure, yes, later. I get off work, it's three a.m., I'm dead, and she's sitting on the hood of my car, waiting for me. Just a real creeper vibe, so I went back inside, had one of the bartenders walk me out, and I guess that pissed her off. So now I just see her everywhere, but she doesn't actually speak to me. Which is creepy, yes?"

"Have you talked to the university about this?"

"Do you know what I get paid for teaching here? Fifty bucks an hour. That's a hundred and fifty bucks a class. That's it. I go to HR and complain about a campus security guard stalking me by, you know, following me around campus, you know what they're going to say? She's doing her job. And then fall semester will roll around and I'll be out of a job for causing problems and then I'll be replaced by that twerp from KDZT. *Mike on the Mic in the Morning*? You know him?"

"No."

"It doesn't matter," she said. "So now I'm in self-defense classes and Buffy the Yogurt Slayer kicked my ass. I might burn down Sprinkles."

"Don't do that," Blake said.

"Yeah, that would be obvious. Can you do that for me?"

Blake considered this. "It will take me some time," he said. "Tell me about this stalker. Does she have a name?"

"Annie Levy. And she's not a campus cop. She's just, like, a woman on a bike with a flashlight."

"Okay," Blake said. "That's a problem I could solve for you."

"In addition to burning down Sprinkles?"

"Yes."

Professor Rhodes cocked her head at Blake. "That would be inappropriate," she said. "Since you're my student."

"Situation like this," Blake said, "rules of engagement are fungible."

"Say you took care of this problem. What would that entail, exactly?"

"Well," Blake said, "I could either kill this person, hobble them permanently, or encourage their behavior to change by suggesting that I might kill or hobble them."

"Uh-huh," she said. "And what would this cost me?"

"Cost you? Nothing."

"I'd want to pay," she said, "for ethical reasons."

"If I killed this woman," Blake said, "that would be more than you could afford. And I don't typically kill women. Hobbling, we could negotiate a price. Payment plan if need be. A stern talking-to, I'd call that $500."

"Would you take that on a Starbucks gift card?"

"Money is money," Blake said. "I understand you'd probably be worried about a trace on it, so yes, a gift card would be fine."

Professor Rhodes sipped her coffee. Took a deep breath. Sat back in her seat. Let out a chuckle. "Can you imagine? If only it were all so easy," she said. "Anyway. Thanks for listening, Blake Danger. It's probably nothing. Just an annoyance to deal with."

"Do you really only get $150 per class?" Blake asked after a while.

"Yep," Professor Rhodes said. "I mean, it's fine. It's my side gig. I'm not working at Red Dawn this semester, because of this whole stalker shit. Plus, I got super tired of running into students there. Now that weed is legal, it's less fun to get high in the bathroom and then watch your students attempt to get their mack on to old New Wave songs."

"If teaching pays so little," Blake said, "why do it?"

"It's not about the money," she said. "It's a calling. I love to teach. Simple as that."

"I don't get it."

"There's not something you love to do?"

"No," he said.

"How is that possible? You just sit at home in the dark all day? There must be something."

Fact was, he did like sitting in the dark. If his tinnitus was bothering him, he'd sit in his living room, lights turned down, white noise machine droning in the background, Thor on his lap, reading on his Kindle. Blake thought for a bit. "Walking my dog," he said. "I like watching him see the world."

"Well," Professor Rhodes said, "then maybe you should start a dog-walking service. Imagine how much joy you would get from that."

"How does one *imagine* joy?" Blake said.

"You see, not to be overly personal? But this is what I hate about people." She took down the rest of her coffee. "I wouldn't feel right existing only for myself. I have zero money. I have a job playing music for a living at a radio station whose signal is literally thirty-five square miles. But they let me play what I want, which is pretty cool, right? Because maybe you'll hear a cool song and buy a record and some starving artist somewhere makes a buck. And then I teach a couple classes and maybe I get some kid who has no idea she has any talent and I'm the first person, ever, to tell her that she does. And then she maybe goes to a four-year college, gets a degree, wins a Pulitzer Prize. I don't know. Whatever. Just gets a decent job that makes her happy. If I played a small role in that? I can imagine joy from that. Even if I only get $150 a class."

"I've offended you."

"No," she said. "If you really feel that way, then you need to make some changes, Blake Danger. That's my advice to you, as your teacher. It should be easy to imagine joy."

"My line of work," Blake said, "it's often about making other people feel good. But I don't get a lot out of it."

"What is it you do, exactly? You told me once."

"I'm a goon," he said.

"Is that how you think of yourself?"

"It's what I am."

"We all feel that way sometimes," she said. "I'm not trying to tell you how to live, Blake Danger, I'm just telling you how I live. Maybe you just need to figure out a way to give back, even if it's not in the scope of your job."

This made sense to Blake. "Is that my assignment?"

"It's your *mission*," she said. "I want graphs and tables and all that. Keep a list. Update it daily. Extra credit if it becomes a super-cool podcast." Professor Rhodes pulled out her phone, checked the time. "Oh, shit, we're going to be late. Can I tell you something?"

"You can."

"I don't want you to take this the wrong way," she said, "but I listened to your homework in the car coming over here, and I think you could do this professionally." She grabbed up her book bag. "Oh, shit," she said again, but quietly this time. "Don't raise a fuss, but my stalker is pretending to peruse the pastries."

"Where? On a watch face."

"Does it matter if it's a.m. or p.m.?"

"No," Blake said.

"Three o'clock."

Blake looked to his right. There was a woman in a security uniform with her back to Blake. She was about five foot six, long black hair tied into a sensible work ponytail, flashlight on her belt. If Blake had to make a threat assessment, he'd say she was more likely to poison Ms. Rhodes than shoot her. "Next couple days," he said, "only drink bottled water. And never leave it unattended."

ANNIE LEVY LIVED in a second-floor apartment a mile from College of the Desert. The complex was behind a gate, which meant absolutely nothing to Blake or anyone else who wanted to do some bad shit. A gate made the people inside feel safe. It merely told criminals that they'd need to hop a fence if they wanted whatever they were after, so after Blake followed Annie home, he parked his car at the Whole Foods a block away and then slid over the block-wall fence.

Blake was dressed as unintimidating as possible. Tan cargo shorts, a blue T-shirt, a white Nike sweat-wicking golf hat, a fanny pack, his encrypted iPhone set to record. That he had zip ties, a blackjack, and a Sig in the fanny pack would be of some concern if a cop or a security guard searched him, but Blake didn't see that happening.

A cop or security guard might stop him. But no one was searching him.

Blake made his way up the stairs to Annie's place, nodded at a man walking down. He was in his early sixties and dressed in a ratty white tuxedo jacket, a bow tie loose around his shirt collar. So many people around Palm Springs wore cheap tuxedos for their jobs at restaurants that Blake thought it made the value of black tie worthless these days, except in places like Monte Carlo, where people followed certain fashion rules. Blake had tuxedos in storage around the world, because he was too big to get a rental, so he had one in Paris, one in Phnom Penh, one in Brisbane, one in São Paulo, one in New York, one in Chicago, one at home. Being a goon meant not worrying about whether or not you had a tux.

"Pardon me," Blake said to the man, who was now at the bottom of the stairs, Blake on the landing outside Annie's door, "can I ask you something."

"You just did," he said, like he was the first guy to ever say that.

"Does your job give you joy?"

"Do I look happy?"

"Not really."

"And I'm already ten minutes late," he said.

"Would you be interested in six lightly used tuxedos? You'd need to get them tailored."

"Yeah," the man said, "leave them and an envelope filled with cash at my door, Mr. Bond."

Easy enough.

Blake waited for the man to drive off before knocking on Annie's door.

"Who is it?" she said. Blake could tell she was staring at him through the peephole. Different situation, he'd shove his Smith & Wesson tactical pen through the hole, come out with her eye.

"You don't know me," he said.

"Why are you at my door?"

"I'm here to talk to you about stalking Professor Rhodes."

Silence.

"You're freaking her out," Blake said. "You'll be surprised to learn she doesn't want to go out with you. In fact, it's the opposite. She's training for the moment when she can break your arm, or leg, or skull. Personally, I think breaking your pelvis would make more of a statement, but Professor Rhodes is a pacifist."

Silence.

"I've been training her. Take a good look at me. I look familiar because you saw me with Professor Rhodes today."

Silence.

"What I want to tell you, Annie, is that your behavior is *your* choice. Professor Rhodes's reaction to your behavior is *her* choice. And she has chosen to hurt you until such time as your behavior stops. If you understand this, knock once on your door."

Silence.

And then . . .

Knock.

"Good," Blake said. "I understand you're worried about your job now. You should be. You should quit." Blake unzipped his fanny pack and took out a stack of purple chips from the Spa Casino in Palm Springs, waved the stack in front of the peephole. "You should also move. This is $5,000 in chips, which is double your take-home salary for a month. This should give you some breathing room as you start your new life. You have one week. Knock if you understand what this gift entails."

Knock.

"Good," Blake said again. He set the chips down on her welcome mat. "Now, I assume you've dialed 911, that would be smart of you, but you have not yet hit send, so I'm going to leave. If you ever bother Professor Rhodes again, I will take that money back in blood. You don't need to knock if you understand that, because, Annie, I hope you are the kind of person who does not understand such a thing. Now. Before I go. I want you to tell me something. What do you think of when you imagine joy?"

"I don't understand," Annie said.

"Yes, you do," Blake said. "Think."

"Okay," she said. Blake could hear the fear in her voice. That was good. "Monument Valley. The vastness of it all. I like standing in the vastness. I don't worry about anything."

"Good," Blake said. "Move there. Never come back. If this is all to your liking, knock for thirty seconds."

Knock. Knock. Knock . . .

Blake was already back over the wall by the time Annie was done knocking. Still, he sat in his car and watched the place for the rest of the night, waiting for the police to show up. They never did.

When he got home, Blake plugged his iPhone into his laptop, ran it through decryption software to extract the audio, listened to the playback. It was a little muddled, but he could fix it in GarageBand. He closed the file. Clicked over to a map of the Coachella Valley, found where Sprinkles was located.

There was an Arby's on one side of it, a dry cleaner on the other. Well.

He'd work it out.

THE WEEK BEFORE finals, some two months later, Blake had to spend three hours helping produce Machine Gun Kelly's show, *The*

Second Amen. It was the one conservative show they had on the campus radio station. It ran on Sundays at noon, timed for folks leaving church, and it was hosted by a guy named Kelly Stevens who'd gained local fame for transitioning from being the buttoned-up weatherman on the ABC news affiliate to habitually losing congressional elections. Each week he'd have on some whack job who had a story to tell about how guns had positively affected their lives, Machine Gun Kelly eventually saying, "Well, you must have said amen to God and then amen to your gun, am I right?"

Blake's job that day was to sit across from Machine Gun, work the board, hit a shotgun sound-effect button, and then pretend to be engaged by the topic Machine Gun was discussing with his guest, all under the auspices of learning radio production. Apparently, a big part of working in radio was feigning interest.

"You were great today," Machine Gun said after he'd finished interviewing a chef from the Marriott in Indian Wells who'd personally cooked for Oliver North. "I know it probably hurts your Libtard sensibilities, but you showed some real professionalism. I had that kid Down-to-Go in the other day. That did not work. But you, you're a person who understands might makes right, I'd guess."

"I understand it," Blake said, "but that doesn't mean I adhere to it."

"You don't have to," he said. "Everyone else around you adheres to it. No one wants to piss you off, even if you're not aware of it. And so the world has probably been opened up wide for you most of your life." He looked over his shoulder and then rolled back in his chair and closed the studio door. "Off the record. I'm not your teacher now. I'm just a guy in a bar. I bet you've gotten all the pussy, money, and power you've ever wanted, am I right?"

"Were you ever my teacher?"

"What?"

"Are you employed by the college?"

"Not as a teacher, no," he said. "But I'm right, aren't I?"

"No," Blake said.

"It's natural selection. But all you beta males out there, you won't admit to it. You, you're a beta, but you present as alpha. Me, I present beta, all one hundred and sixty-five pounds of me, but I'm all the way alpha. Right? We can agree on that?"

"I agree with exactly nothing you're saying," Blake said.

"Fair. Fair. But if we're really two guys in a bar, and I've pissed you off more than I seem to have, I've got the equalizer." He lifted up his shirt and showed Blake what looked to be a shitty little .22 shoved into his khakis. That was also his thing. At the end of his show, he'd say, "Follow me on Twitter @MachineGunKellyForCongress, but don't follow too close, because I'm always packing."

"You're aware they make holsters now."

"A good guy with a gun still needs the element of surprise."

"I don't think it's legal for you to have that on a college campus, is it?"

"Is it?" Machine Gun Kelly asked.

Blake's cell phone buzzed with a new email. It was from Professor Rhodes. He'd turned in his final assignment to her. The subject said: COME SEE ME. "Are we done here?" Blake asked.

"I'd love to have you work on the show over the summer, if you're interested," Machine Gun said. "I dig your energy."

Blake came around the board and stood in front of Machine Gun Kelly. Then, in one motion, he grabbed the .22 out of Machine Gun's pants and shoved the rolling chair across the room, Machine Gun slamming into the soundproof wall with a thud. Blake popped the magazine out, put it in his pocket. Cleared the chamber.

"What the fuck!" Machine Gun Kelly said.

Blake examined the .22. It was a shitty Smith & Wesson. Two hundred bucks at Walmart. "You ever shoot this at a real person?"

"No."

"Don't ever try," Blake said. He popped the slide off the top of the gun, yanked the spring out of it, removed the barrel, dropped it all on the floor, tucked the bottom of the gun in his fanny pack. If you couldn't field strip a Smith & Wesson in fifteen seconds, your goon card could be revoked. "In my line of work, if someone flashes their gun at you, that means they are willing to kill you. Are you willing to kill me?"

"What? No."

"See, that's why a good guy with a gun is useless." Blake smiled at Machine Gun Kelly. "You ever flash your gun at me again, you'll spend the rest of your life shitting in a bag."

PROFESSOR RHODES'S FACULTY office was located in what Blake figured was probably the old laundry room, what with the tile floor and the exhaust vent in the ceiling. She was sitting at her desk with AirPods in her ears, her eyes down. Blake knocked on her door, even though it was open. She looked up, slid one of her AirPods out, set it down on her desk. Clicked something on her computer.

"Blake," she said. "Sit down." He did as he was asked. She handed him an AirPod. "Is this you I'm listening to?"

Blake slid the AirPod in. She clicked her mouse. Blake heard a mechanical voice say, "If you ever bother Professor Rhodes again, I will take that money back in blood."

"Yes," Blake said, "I applied a filter on it, for legal reasons. I have the original if you need it, for my grade."

She clicked her mouse again. "This file you submitted. This is all you?"

"Yes," Blake said. "I completed my assignment."

"There's audio of you burning down Sprinkles. Is that . . . real? Did you do that?"

"No one was hurt."

"Half of that mini-mall burned to the ground, Blake. Did you set fire to a mini-mall?"

"I made sure the dry cleaner was taken care of," he said. "The Arby's franchise was fully insured. And let's be clear. Burning down an establishment that murders cows for human consumption is not the greatest crime in American history." Blake smiled. Professor Rhodes was a vegetarian. He'd done some fieldwork on that when it became clear that there wasn't a firewall between the Arby's and Sprinkles.

"Over the course of the last two months," Professor Rhodes said, "I've received about $15,000 in poker chips. Sometimes they come in the mail. Sometimes they're in my car. Sometimes I open my purse and there's a stack of black chips in there. Am I to presume those are from you?"

"Presume? No."

"Blake," Professor Rhodes said, "there's an audio recording of what sounds like the robot from *Lost in Space* breaking into my car and filling the glove box with poker chips. Are you telling me that wasn't you?"

"I'm telling you not to presume." Blake leaned forward. "You're undercompensated. The American educational system places its value in the wrong people. Do you know that the football coach at this school earns $125,000 per year? That should be dealt with. If you want, that can be dealt with."

Professor Rhodes pushed back from her desk, got up, closed her office door. Stood against it for a moment, then sat down next to Blake, but scooted the chair back a few inches. It was something

Blake noticed people often did with him. "Is Annie . . . dead?" she whispered.

"No," Blake said.

"Because I haven't seen her."

"She's self-relocated."

"I didn't mean . . ." she began. She picked up her AirPod, twirled it between her fingers. "Your average day, you wake up, have breakfast, what happens next?"

"I'm a full-time student," he said.

"Last year at this time," she said.

"I was in Liberia."

"That's a real place?"

"Yes," Blake said.

"What were you doing there?"

"We parachuted in and then crossed into Sierra Leone," Blake said. "Took care of a problem that the United States government was reluctant to engage in."

"And that's what you do."

"Not always," Blake said. "I'm good at standing in the background, too. I also know which joints snap without making too much noise."

"And you like this job?"

"Travel started to bother me," he said. "I have ringing in my ears. My knees hurt. I have a problem in my neck." He thought for a moment. "I missed my dog. That became problematic for me, too. Made me lose focus on jobs. So. Here I am."

"Here you are," Professor Rhodes said. She reached over, clicked her mouse, Blake's altered voice came back out of the Air-Pod. *Knock for thirty seconds.* "Say I was interested in a radio job in Los Angeles. Or New York. Or even, you know, here, in town. Like, a really good job. Morning drive-time. Something like that. You could . . . help me?"

"I could," Blake said, "if there was some . . . joy."

"Right," Professor Rhodes said. "Joy is important." She handed him the AirPod. "Did you find joy in this?" She clicked play again.

Blake listened for a moment. He'd never get used to the sound of his own voice, even altered as it was here. He was narrating the destruction of Sprinkles. Talking about how to make a Molotov cocktail with longer-burning accelerants. It wasn't *This American Life* quality, but then he wasn't hoping to be on NPR. But the production! He'd put in music, done some artful editing, really amped up the tension, which was largely missing in the actual job. He'd simply walked up, tossed the cocktail through the window, watched it all burn to the ground from a camera he'd buried in a shrub the night before.

Took the fire department eleven minutes to get there. It was, in total, an extremely pleasurable listening experience.

All those years, his job was to be silent, and now he was up front, making things happen, not waiting for someone else to order him into action. He wasn't just the guy behind the action anymore. He was the action man now.

"I did find joy in this," he said. He didn't have to imagine it.

"Then we should talk more," Professor Rhodes said, "about how we can help each other."

THE LAST GOOD MAN

They disappeared during the coldest winter on record. There was no special episode of *Dateline*. No jogger stumbled on a human skull. Instead, it was Scotch Thompson's bird dog Roxanne who came running down Yeach Mountain, three days before Christmas, with a human hand in her mouth. And just like that, James Klein and his family were found.

"Damndest thing I ever seen," Lyle, my deputy, said. "All of them stacked up like Lincoln Logs. Like they were put down gentle. Terrible, terrible thing." We were sitting in the front seat of my cruiser sipping coffee, both of us too old to be picking at the bones of an entire family but resigned to doing it anyway. "You think it was someone from out of town, Morris?"

"Hard to say," I said. "It's been over a year, you know, it could have been anybody."

James Klein, his wife, Missy, and their twin sons, Andy and Tyler, fell off the earth sometime before November 12, 1998. Fred Lipton came over that day to borrow back his wrench set but all he found was an empty house and a very hungry cat.

"You think it was some kinda drug thing, don't you?" Lyle said, but I didn't respond. "You always thought Klein was involved in something, I know, but I thought they were good people."

"I don't know what I think anymore, Lyle," I said. A team of forensic specialists from the capital was coming down the side of the mountain, and I spotted Miller Descent out in front, his hands filled with plastic evidence bags. I'd worked with Miller before and knew this wasn't a good sign. Roxanne the collie had stumbled onto a shallow grave filled with four bodies, along with many of their limbs. The twins, Andy and Tyler, were missing their feet. James and Missy were without hands.

Miller motioned me out of the cruiser. "Lotta shit up there," he said. Miller was a tall man, his face sharp and angular, with long green eyes. He had a look about him that said he couldn't be shocked anymore, that the world was too sour of a place. "Like some kinda damned ritual took place. Animal bones are mixed up in that grave, I think. Need to get an anthropologist up here to be sure, which is gonna be hard with the holidays, but it looks like dog bones mostly. Maybe a cat or two. Snow pack kept those bodies pretty fresh."

"Jesus," I said. "What's the medical examiner say?"

Miller screwed his face up into a knot, his nose almost even with his eyes. "Can I be honest with you, Sheriff Drew?"

"Sure, Miller."

"Your ME about threw up when she saw all them bodies," he said. "You know, I was in Desert Storm, so this doesn't mean so much to me. You might want to have them cut up by some more patient people upstate."

"I'll keep that in mind," I said. I'd been in Korea and Vietnam. I still didn't want to see whatever was up there.

Miller smiled and scratched at something on his neck. "Anyway," he said. "You still playing softball in that beer league?"

I never knew how to handle Miller Descent. He could be holding a human head in one hand and a Coors in the other and it wouldn't faze him.

"Not this year," I said.

"Too bad," he said, and he shuffled his way back up Yeach.

I DIDN'T GET home that night until well past ten o'clock. I brewed myself a pot of coffee and sat at the kitchen table looking over notes I'd written when the Kleins first disappeared, plus the new photos shot up on the mountain. Since my second wife, Margaret, died, I'd taken to staying up late at night; I'd read or watch TV or go over old cases, anything to keep me from crawling into that lonely bed. The holidays, I barely slept. I'd sit in the kitchen, remembering the smell of pork roast, the kind with raisins and cranberries, which Margaret used to cook on Christmas Eve. Or I'd think about how we used to wake up early on Christmas morning and unwrap presents, Margaret always getting me things I didn't know I wanted—one year, that was a kite, and every day after work for six months, I'd come home and fly it, like I was eight. Or how she cried at the Christmas cards I made for her, every year. I carved them out of birch, turning a small plank of wood into a full holiday scene, which I'd then paint. It would take me a few months to do it, but I found it relaxing and it was better than getting her a sweater or something she'd leave behind on a plane. She'd see the plank of wood and she'd just tilt her head back and start sobbing, wiping at her eyes with the back of her hand, always ruining her makeup. "This is so silly," she'd say, "I'm a grown woman." Her last Christmas, she was already dropped so low by the stroke that all I had time to carve for her was a single Christmas tree topped with a golden star against a blue sky. She'd stare at it for hours.

But that night, my trouble was not with the memory of a woman who I loved for the last thirty years of my life, or of my first wife, Katharine, whose death at the Salton Sea still haunted me, but for a family I had barely known.

The Kleins moved into Granite City during the fall of 1995. James Klein was a pharmacist, so when he and his wife purchased Dickey Fine's Rexall Drug Store downtown, everyone figured it was going to be a good match. Dickey had gotten old, and going to him for a prescription was often more dangerous than just fighting whatever ailment you had with faith and good humor.

James and Missy were in the store together most days. James wore a starched white lab coat even though it wasn't really required. It inspired confidence in the people, I think, to get their drugs from someone who looked like a doctor. Missy always looked radiant standing behind the counter chatting up the townspeople and, when skiing season started, the tourists who'd come in for directions or cold medicine.

All that to say I never trusted them. I'd known the family only casually, but well enough to discern they were hiding something. James sported a diploma from Harvard and Missy looked like the type of woman best suited for clambakes at Pebble Beach. They were not small-town people—they drove a gold Lexus and a convertible Jaguar—and Granite City is a small town. I never had cause to investigate the Kleins, never even pulled them over for speeding, but I aimed to at some point just so that I could look James in the eye when I had the upper hand, when my authority might cause his veneer to smudge. That chance didn't come.

I picked up a photo from the gravesite and there was James Klein's face staring up at me. Miller was right: the bodies had been well preserved. The skin on James's face was tight and tugged at the bones. His eyes had vanished but I could still picture the way they narrowed whenever he saw me.

His body was faceup, arms flung to either side. He was draped on top of his wife, hands chopped from his arms, wearing his now-drab gray lab coat. Shards of bone jutted from underneath his sleeves, and I thought that whoever had done this to him had taken great pains to make him suffer.

For a long time I stared at James Klein and wondered what it would be like to know that you were about to die. Andy and Tyler, the twins, must have understood all too well that their time on earth was ending before it had a chance to begin. They were only twelve.

I stood up, stretched my arms above my head, and paced in the kitchen while I tried to gather my thoughts. After the family disappeared, I'd searched their home with Deputy Nixon and Deputy Person. We hadn't found any forced entry or signs of a struggle, but we did find bundles of cash hidden in nearly every crevice of the house. All told, there was close to half a million dollars stashed in shoeboxes, suitcases, and file cabinets. The money was tested for trace residues of cocaine, heroin, and marijuana but came up empty. The serial numbers didn't come up from any recent stings in the region. There's no law against keeping a mountain of cash in your home.

For almost three months, we searched for the Klein family. In time, though, winter dropped in full force and even James Klein's own mother and father returned to their hometown. I told them not to worry, that we would find their son and his wife and their twin grandsons, but I knew that they were dead. I knew because there was $500,000 sitting in my office unclaimed, not even by the Kleins' next of kin, and no man alive would leave that kind of money on purpose. And so, as the months drifted away and my thoughts of the Klein family withered and died in my mind, I figured that one day when I was retired someone would find them somewhere.

"Dammit," I said, sitting back down at the kitchen table. My eyes fixed on a pair of pale blue Nikes, unattached to legs, pointing out from the bottom of the grave. I wanted to sit there and just cry for those boys but I knew it wouldn't do any of us any good.

I GOT TO the medical examiner's office late that next morning, figuring I didn't need to see her slicing and dicing. Turned out I was right on time. The ME, a young kid named Lizzie DiGiangreco, had been working in Granite City for just over a year. Her father, Dr. Louis DiGiangreco, had been ME in Granite City for a lifetime and had practically trained Lizzie from birth. She went to medical school back east and then moved home after her father died at sixty-four from heart failure. I was one of Louis's pallbearers, and I remember watching Lizzie stiffen at the site of her father in his open casket. I knew that her profession had not been a pleasant choice for her, but that she was duty bound.

Lizzie greeted me with a handshake just outside the door to her lab.

"Glad you could make it, Sheriff," Lizzie said, only half sarcastically.

"Miller said you were a little queasy up on Yeach," I said. "I can get someone else to do this, if you want."

Lizzie made a clicking sound in her throat, a tendency of her father's when he'd been about to get very angry, and then exhaled deeply. "I don't like to see kids like that," she said. "Maybe Miller is used to it, but I'm not."

"Understandable," I said, and then followed her into the lab.

The four bodies were covered with black plastic blankets and lined up across the length of the room. Lizzie's assistant—what they call a diener—a man who went by his last name, Hawkins, was busy gathering up the tools they would need. I'd watched a lot of autopsies in my thirty-five years as sheriff in Granite City, but it never got any easier. Hawkins had been Lizzie's father's assistant too, so he knew what I'd need to make it through the next few hours.

"There's a tub of Vicks behind you in that cabinet, Sheriff," Hawkins said. "These folks ain't gonna smell so fresh."

Lizzie glared at Hawkins, but she knew he didn't mean any harm. Hawkins could probably perform an autopsy just as well as she could, and Lord knows he never went to medical school.

Hawkins pulled back the first blanket and there was James Klein's naked, handless body.

"Where'd you put the hands, Hawkins?" Lizzie asked.

"I got 'em in the jar by the back sink," he said. "You want them now?"

"No," she said. "But make sure not to cross them up with Mrs. Klein's."

"She thinks I don't know how to do my job," Hawkins said to me, not unhappily. I'd gone to high school with Hawkins's older brother, Ralph. They were one of the few African American families in town for many years, which had been a hard life, I'm sure. Ralph ended up working for the sheriff's department when I was gone to California, but a few months after I got back, he put a gun in his mouth while sitting in the front seat of his cruiser. No note. No warning. One day he was Deputy Ralph Hawkins, the next day he was diner gossip. Hawkins was a few years younger than his brother but was already working in the examiner's office. Lizzie's father told me Hawkins even embalmed his brother, getting him right for his funeral. As right as he could. "Tell her I've never made a mistake, Sheriff, will you?"

"Never heard of an instance," I said, but Lizzie was already onto the business at hand.

She sliced James Klein with a Y incision, starting from his

shoulder, across his chest, around his navel, and down through the pelvis using a scalpel. The room filled with a smell like raw lamb.

For the next two hours, Lizzie spoke quietly and clinically into a tape recorder, noting the condition of James Klein's vital organs as she examined and weighed them. I had to leave the room only twice: when Hawkins sifted through the intestines and when Lizzie and Hawkins peeled back James Klein's scalp and removed his brain.

After they'd removed all of James Klein's vital organs, his corpse sat opened on the examining table: his trunk resembled the hull of a ship under construction. Both Lizzie and Hawkins were covered in blood and tissue.

"Well," Hawkins said to me, "he's dead all right."

"Why don't you get a cup of coffee, Hawkins," Lizzie said. "The sheriff and I need to go over a few things before we sew up."

Hawkins stripped off his gloves and hung up his apron. Washed his hands. "You know," he said, "I used to bowl with Mr. Klein. He was terrible. Couldn't score a hundred, not once. Gutter balls were his specialty." He dried his hands and wiped off his face with a paper towel. "But every week, he'd be out there, giving it a shot. Boys were terrible, too." He shook his head. "Never did meet his wife, until today. You want something, Doc? It's on me."

"No, thanks," she said, and when he was gone, she started back up. "Off the record, because I'll need to look at the tox screens and some of the neuro X-rays, but I'd say the cause of death for Mr. Klein was suffocation plus blood loss from his hands being chopped off."

"Suffocation?"

"Look here," Lizzie said, pointing at James Klein's lungs. "He had severe hemorrhaging, probably caused by inhaling so much dirt, and there's bruising along the back of his neck. See that?"

There was a dark purple bruise along the base of James Klein's neck, but what was odd was the shape of the bruise. It was a pattern of small squares.

"What do you make of those marks?"

"Probably the bottom of a work boot or hiking boot," Lizzie said. "Like someone was standing on his neck, pushing his face into the dirt, while they cut off his hands."

"Using his head for leverage," I said, not as a question, and not really to Lizzie, but to myself. Said it because I had to hear myself say it.

Lizzie nodded and I saw that she was looking over my shoulder at the bodies of the two boys. "Yeah," she said finally, her gaze averted back to James Klein, "that's probably what happened."

"All right," I said. "How long will it take you to finish the rest?"

Lizzie exhaled so that her bangs fluttered in the air for a moment. "About two hours for each of them."

"Okay," I said. "The families are flying in this afternoon. Can you get me something preliminary on paper tonight?"

"I'll try," Lizzie said, and then both of us were silent for a minute. "I didn't know Hawkins bowled," she said.

"He's a good man," I said. "You should get to know him."

"I've tried not to," Lizzie said, "in case I decide to leave. If there's some distance between me and everyone else, maybe it will make it an easier decision."

"Leaving doesn't stop this from being your home, Lizzie."

"I barely recognize this place anymore," she said.

"I miss your dad," I said, because at that moment I really did. We'd been good friends for many years, and when he died I knew that the old school in Granite City was getting close to recess time. "He was a complicated person. I don't know if he was much of a father."

"He did what he could."

"Well, I'm sure proud of the way you've stuck around here, and I know he would be, too. But if you go, you go."

Before Lizzie could reply, Hawkins walked in with two cups of coffee. When I left, they were dumping James Klein's internal organs back into his body in no particular order.

JUST AFTER NOON, a helicopter containing James Klein's mother and father, plus Missy Klein's mother, a Mrs. Pellet, landed on the football field at Granite City High School. Lyle and I were there waiting for it.

"I'm real sorry about this," I said to Mrs. Klein when I shook her hand.

"You said you'd find him," she said.

Before I could answer Mrs. Klein, before I could tell her that we'd found him just as I knew we would, her husband placed a hand on her shoulder and directed her away from me.

"This is a hard time for her," he said, and then he too was gone, squiring his wife into the back of a rented Aerostar we'd brought for them. Mr. Klein wore a houndstooth sport coat that hung off his shoulders like a dead vine and a pair of expensive sunglasses. I knew behind those tinted glasses were the eyes of a man without hope. I'd seen that look on the face of every man who'd lost a son.

Lyle helped Missy's mother off the helicopter and I could tell that, like Mr. Klein, she was face-to-face with the dead end of life. She was older than I'd remembered her from the months she'd spent in town, but I guess waiting for bad news would do that to you.

We drove the three of them to the Best Western on Central, none of us speaking until we arrived there. The lobby was filled with a dozen gingerbread houses, each sponsored by different businesses in town: The Pizza Cookery. B. Barker & Sons, Accountants. The Paulson Mortuary and Home of Peace & Tranquility. Even Shake's Bar had a house, which tilted ever so slightly to the left. Somewhere, Burl Ives was singing "Rudolph the Red-Nosed Reindeer" over tinny speakers.

"When do we get to see them?" Mr. Klein asked. We were waiting for the elevator to take the Kleins and Mrs. Pellet up to their rooms.

"Tomorrow, I'd guess," I said. "Or after the holiday."

"We'll want to bury them in Connecticut," Mr. Klein said, and Mrs. Pellet nodded in agreement. "Tomorrow is the last day of Hanukkah. I'd like to spend it with my son."

"The medical examiner still needs to finish getting some information though."

"For what?" Mr. Klein said. He reached over and pressed the elevator button twice, even though it was already lit. "So that we can be told my son suffered? I don't need to know any more to understand that he's gone. That all of them are gone."

"It's an investigation into an unnatural death," I said. We'd told both families that their loved ones had been found, though not the condition of their bodies. Foul play, we'd told them, was suspected. "There are procedures that must be followed. I'm sorry if you have to stay here one minute longer than you want to, but this is my job, and I'm planning on doing it."

"Sheriff Drew," Mr. Klein said, "do you have any children?"

"I don't."

"I know my son was a criminal," Mr. Klein said. "My wife and I have reconciled that much. He was a drug addict and probably a pretty good one, if you want to know. He was also a gifted liar. I am sure he made enemies in many parts of the world or else why would he come to a place like this?" Mr. Klein swallowed, and it seemed then that he'd come to some fine point in his mind, as if he'd figured out a troubling problem that had always been just within reach. "So, you see, Sheriff, I don't need to know who did what. I don't need that kind of element in my life. I'd prefer to think that my son was the decent person he pretended to be."

"I'll keep that in mind," I said.

"Sheriff," Mrs. Pellet said, her voice soft and tired, "I just want to bring my baby home. Whoever killed her, if anyone did, is gone. If you haven't found who did this yet, you never will."

"SHE'S RIGHT, YOU know," Lyle said as we walked back to the van. "They're both right, sort of. We went through every lead we had on this case over a year ago, Morris."

"We've got bodies covered in forensic evidence sitting on Lizzie's table," I said.

"You ran every fingerprint and strand of hair we found in that house," Lyle said. "And the answer was nothing. Whatever Miller pulled off of Yeach, after all this time, you think any of it would even be admissible? You know how many people hunt on that mountain? Hike? Just dick around?"

"But there's all kinds of new technology, Lyle," I said. "Every single day, something new comes online. We move too fast, we're gonna be digging those bodies back up in a couple years. That what you want?"

"Morris," Lyle said, "nobody cares about these people but their parents. Listen to yourself." Lyle reached into his pocket and pulled out a pack of Lucky Strikes and lit one. I'd known Lyle for half my life and he'd always been someone I could depend on. He wasn't what you'd call book smart, but he knew things instinctively like no one I'd ever known, before or since. "Tell you what," he said, smoke drifting out of his nose in smooth wisps of gray. "I get cable just like you. I see all those forensic shows on Discovery and I think they're fantastic. I'm glad the cops in LA are solving crimes from the 1950s using space-shuttle technology. But you know what, Morris? *This ain't LA.*"

"If those were your kids," I said, "wouldn't you want the truth?"

"My kids barely speak to me. I'd need to deal with that truth, first."

We got into the van but I didn't start it right away. "You remember Milton Stairs?"

"Of course. Killed the Claxson girl."

"That's right," I said. I pointed at the Best Western. "His father's hardware store used to be right there. My daddy used to go in there two, three times a week, just to bullshit. You know he never stepped foot in the place again?"

"Well," Lyle said, "you nearly killed Milton when you arrested him, as I recall. Probably made things tense between him and old-man Stairs."

"I guess so," I said. I started the van up. "You know Milton is still alive?"

"No kidding?"

"Up for parole in two years."

"You gonna go speak?"

"I already got my suit picked out," I said. "He's been in a wheelchair all this time. Eating through a tube in his stomach. And he's been doing it *in prison*. Not just wandering around free."

"I hear you," Lyle said. "I do. Now turn on the heater before they find us frozen, too."

"The twins didn't deserve to end up like that," I said. I started the engine, and, in a few seconds, hot air was blowing in my face, making my skin tingle. "Don't they deserve justice?"

"Everyone deserves justice, Morris," Lyle said. "But also, people deserve grace."

He was right, of course, which made it all the more difficult to take.

I WAS SITTING at the counter of Lolly's Diner eating meatloaf and reading the autopsies of the Klein family when Miller Descent walked in and sat down next to me. It was near nine o'clock.

"Lyle said you might be here," Miller said.

"Just reading about that family," I said, holding up the autopsy report. "And trying to swallow some food. Can hardly do either."

"We've got Bonnie's family staying with us for Christmas," Miller said, "so I've been eating my mother-in-law's food all week. You never had so much nutmeg in your life." Miller chuckled and then paused. "I wanna ask you something, Sheriff," he said cautiously, "and I don't want to offend you in any way by asking it."

"That's a tough order." Lolly came by to refill my coffee cup, and Miller asked if he could have a slice of apple pie. "Well," I said when Lolly left, "spit it out."

"Do you think maybe you should turn this case over to someone else?" Miller said.

"That doesn't sound like a question, Miller," I said. "It sounds like a request."

"Assistant DA upstate saw some of the crime-scene pictures," Miller said. "I probably shouldn't have shown him a damn thing, but you know how favors work around up there, right, Sheriff?"

"I guess."

Miller took a napkin from the caddy and wiped his face.

It was 36 degrees outside and he was sweating. "A person dies on Yeach, animals find them pretty quick," he said. "Way the bodies looked, he thinks maybe they were moved. Could be someone had them in a freezer or something then hauled them up there now."

"That what *you* think?"

"Me? I don't know," Miller said. In the years I'd worked with him, I'd never heard him sound unequivocal. "A local probably wouldn't take the chance. But someone from out of town? Hell. I don't know. But the assistant DA, he thinks this is something the Brawton police, maybe the homicide unit they got out there, should get involved with, or at least maybe a more . . ." Miller trailed off when Lolly dropped his pie off. "Hell," he said again. It was the only curse word I'd ever heard him utter. And every time he said it, it seemed like an actual declaration. That he was in hell. "You know what I'm trying to say here, right? Talk to the family, let them know it's an option."

What he was trying to say was that there was some glamour to this case: *A wealthy young family found murdered in the ski hamlet downstate. Five hundred thousand dollars sitting in an evidence room gathering dust.* And glamour means an assistant DA upstate becomes DA, or mayor, or worse—a congressman.

I also think Miller was trying to say that I didn't have a chance in hell of finding the killer and that maybe I should let the blame fall on somebody upstairs.

"Yeah," I said. "I understand."

Miller ate his slice of pie, never once asking to see the autopsy file wedged between us. Eventually, Lolly went over to the six-foot artificial Christmas tree she kept by the front door and unplugged it, clicked off the battery-powered menorah over by the cash register, started to sweep up the strands of silver and gold tinsel that had fallen onto the floor.

"All right then," Miller said, standing to leave, his plate cleaned.

"You know," I said, "there's nutmeg in apple pie, too."

"Yeah," Miller said, zipping up his down jacket, "I figured that out."

"Don't you want to know how they died, Miller?"

Miller stuffed his hands into his pockets and sort of bowed, biting his bottom lip until it looked painful, and then shook his head. "This is what I know about these things," he said. "There ain't a cause or an effect once they've started to rot and such. They're dead and they're not coming back. If they were meant to still be alive, if God wanted them here right now, then God dammit, they'd be here. Time's up, that's all."

"You're wrong," I said, suddenly angry with Miller, angry with the DA who wanted a big-city detective to run this case, angry with my wife Margaret for dying three years ago and leaving me alone, angry for those dead boys . . . and haunted by all the bodies I'd seen, all the lives I couldn't save, all the trouble I'd been party to. How many men had I killed in my life? How many people had I hurt? All in the name of some law, words on a page that could be erased and replaced by some president or king or sheriff, whoever had the power to do the work, in the moment it needed to be done. Too often, that was me. And for what? "There is cause and effect, Miller. People don't just punch in and punch out. Kids died up there, Miller. *Kids*. You can't apply your mumbo jumbo to them. No one deserves that. This isn't about rotting bodies and old bones. You can't just toss a blanket over every body you see and pretend that they aren't *someone*. Do you know that, Miller? Do you know?"

Miller frowned at me. "Acute hemorrhaging of the lungs, an occlusion of the blood vessels around the eyes and face, suggesting suffocation. General failure of the major organs due to severe blood loss and the ensuing shock," Miller said. The words tumbled out of his mouth like he was reading from a textbook. "Wounds consistent with a number of drug-related murders in a hundred different towns that aren't Granite City. I'm sorry, Sheriff," he said. "I really am." He put out his hand, but I didn't take it, so he shrugged, put it back in his pocket, and started toward the door. "Have a Merry Christmas, Morris. Take the day off. It would do you some good."

I watched Miller climb into his car—a beat-up El Camino that had a bright-green wreath on its front grill—and drive off. I knew that I didn't want to end up like Miller Descent: a hard man unable to shake the horrors from his mind. I also knew that I was halfway there and closing the gap. So, with an envelope filled with the pictures of a dissected family in my hand, I left Lolly's Diner and headed home, where I knew what I had to do, and where I knew I would not sleep.

IT WAS COLD and overcast the next morning, Yeach Mountain lost behind a thicket of low, gray clouds. A light mist of rain fell as I drove through downtown Granite City toward the station. The streets, slick with moisture, refracted the glow from the strings of golden bulbs that were hung on the light posts each year by the Soroptimists and 4-H. I saw my dead wife Margaret duck into the yarn store on Porter, saw her coming from Biddle's Flowers with a bundle of poinsettias, watched her make a call from the phone booth out front of the library, let her cross in front of me on Ninth Street, a ream of wrapping paper tucked under her arm. You live in a town long enough, the past, the present, it all occupies the same space.

But when I walked into the station, all I saw were Mr. and Mrs. Klein and Mrs. Pellet sitting in the lobby. And I thought, seeing Mr. Klein in his black slacks and yellow V-neck sweater, everything about him out of place in my station, that maybe my time in Granite City was coming to a close, that I couldn't bear to see despair in people's faces anymore. That, most of all, I couldn't keep on thinking about the daily rituals that still call to people even in their times of need: the soft pleat ironed down Mrs. Klein's pant leg, the way Mrs. Pellet had put on a nice dress and gold earrings.

"Been waiting long?" I asked.

"No," Mr. Klein said. His voice was low and I decided that he probably wasn't long for this place either. "Didn't get much in the way of rest last night."

"I've got the autopsies for your son's family," I said. "You can read 'em if you want to."

Mrs. Klein let out a short sob and squeezed her husband's arm. Mr. Klein kissed her on the forehead and patted her hand. "Did he suffer, Sheriff?" Mrs. Klein asked.

"No," I said. "Looks like hypothermia."

"What about my Missy?" Mrs. Pellet asked. "And the kids; what about the kids?"

"The same," I said. "Best guess is they went hiking and the storm hit. Probably thought they could just wait it out. Which is why we found them together. Or they simply got lost. But lost together. I do believe there is some grace in that." A look of relief passed over their faces, and though I believe they each knew that their children and grandchildren had died terribly, that in fact they'd been butchered, I had helped them in some way. Had eased something in them for at least a moment.

Lyle walked out and tapped me on the shoulder. "Dr. DiGiangreco called for you," he said. "Needs you to call her right away."

I told the families to wait for just a little bit longer and I'd get the bodies of their loved ones released. Lyle followed me back to my office.

"What the hell's going on out there?" Lyle said. "I thought I heard you tell them their family died of hypothermia?"

"I did," I said.

"Morris," Lyle said, "their damn hands and feet were cut off!"

"Were they?" I said. "I hadn't heard."

"Lizzie said some DA called her," Lyle said. "You aware of that?"

I opened the door to my office and let Lyle stand in the hall. "How about you take today off and drive down and see your daughter," I said. "Shoot, take the whole week off. Fly out to California and see your son. When was the last time you spent the holidays with your kids?"

"I ain't just showing up at their doorstep dressed like Santa," Lyle said.

"Well, try calling. See what happens."

Lyle squinted at me and rolled his tongue against his cheek. "I hope you know what you're doing," he said.

LIZZIE ANSWERED ON the first ring. "They're all wrapped up and ready to go," she said.

"How do they look?" I asked.

I heard Lizzie sigh on the other end of the line. "I had to use fishing line to sew the boys' feet back on; Hawkins had some thirty-five-pound test that worked great," she said. "It should hold."

"I appreciate this, Lizzie," I said. "More than you'll ever know."

"What do you want me to do about this DA who keeps calling?"

"Tell him to call me if he has any questions," I said. "The family hasn't asked for anything, and it's not his case."

"You've got all the paperwork there?" Lizzie asked.

"Right in front of me," I said. "I'll sign off on it and get you a copy."

"Would my dad have done this?" Lizzie asked.

"I don't know," I said. "I don't know if you should have."

"Hawkins said that if there was a problem, he'd take the blame," Lizzie said. "Said that's how it's always worked here. 'Let the shit roll downhill' were his exact words."

My recollections of Lizzie's father had grown muddy in my mind—my memories colored more for what I wished were true than what actually was. We'd worked together for a long while, and time spares no one.

"Tell Hawkins I won't forget this," I said.

"Sheriff," Lizzie said, "can I ask you a question?"

"Sure."

"Why'd you come back here all those years ago? The whole world was open to you."

I knew that Lizzie had some sense of my history. That I'd fought in Korea, had spent a time as an advisor in Vietnam, had done a turn working for Claxson Oil after I nearly murdered Milton Stairs, spending those ruined years at the Salton Sea, making mistakes I'd spend the rest of my life trying to rectify, though I never did, though I never will.

"The world had turned acrid," I said. "I was hoping I'd find some peace in Granite City."

"Did that work?"

"I found a woman I loved," I said, "and for a long time, Lizzie, that was enough. But now I don't know."

AFTER WE HUNG up, I pulled out a piece of letterhead and scratched out a three-sentence letter of resignation. I held it in my hands and ran my fingers over every word, every period. I'd been the sheriff of Granite City for thirty-five years, and in that time, I'd tried to change the course of my life. In Korea, I'd killed hundreds of men. And then the SOP changed. Kill them all. Kill everyone in sight. And I did that. I did that. Men. Women. Children. I was the gun. By the time I ended up at the Salton Sea, I barely recognized myself most mornings, each day there a week of misery, until it all came burning down on me, chasing me back home.

Before Korea, I'd never broken the law. Hadn't even had a sip of liquor before I was of age. And since, I have spent my life trying to undo the past, attempting to do the legitimate thing, like not beating the men who hit their wives, because the law for too long said we couldn't hold them. The law certainly said we couldn't take a blackjack to their Achilles, which is what I wanted desperately to do, to see these men limp the rest of their lives, to know they'd never be able to get away from me. Instead, I would gather evidence. I would wait for the next misdemeanor and tack on a battery charge, bring it up to felony, and hope that they resisted arrest. Like Gina Morrow's ex-husband, Wayne, who still manages the Ben Franklin on E. Laurelhurst, and who is missing the pinky toe on his right foot because he chose to run when I showed up with handcuffs. He doesn't run anymore.

I'd followed the letter of the law, no matter my opinion of it. What good did it do? The bad people were always going to win. Once they reached the top, worse people would come to topple them. The last good man was no better than his desire for revenge. God himself was spiteful. We can't ask more of our own kind, can we? Couldn't I have lied to Gina Morrow and told her that Wayne had been in a car accident, that he'd been burned alive, instead of letting him live in her house for months after the first call I received? How easy it would have been to stage Wayne's demise. Couldn't I have done that to every man who put a hand on a woman? I could have. I could have cleaned this world of a few dirty spots.

But Margaret, she would have smelled the violence on me. She would have tasted the mendacity. Never did there exist a woman borne out of more kindness and propriety. If she knew the man I was capable of becoming, again, she would have walked out the door and never come back.

And so, there I was with my letter of resignation in my hand and an autopsy report on my desk. Both documents were lies. Inside the autopsy report, Dr. Lizzie DiGiangreco, whose dead father I had carried to his grave, stated that all four members of the Klein family had died of exposure and acute hypothermia. She further stated that all members of the family were fully intact—that all hands and feet were connected. An accidental death, no note of foul play.

In my official report, typed the night previous on my old Olivetti, I stated that it was my belief that the Klein family had succumbed during the night of November 11, 1998. The almanac noted November 11, 1998, as being the coldest day of the month during what became the coldest winter in record. Over a foot of snow fell that night.

Case closed.

SNOW FELL IN Granite City the night I quit, too. It was Christmas Eve, and though the roads were slippery and runny, I called Lyle and asked him to meet me at Shake's Bar. We sat for a long time in a small booth sipping beer and eating stale nuts, an old Johnny Mathis Christmas song bleating out of the tape player Zep, the bartender, pulled out on special occasions. That next day I'd recommend to the mayor that Lyle be named interim sheriff, a post he would eventually keep for three years until he died from emphysema.

"You know what, Morris," Lyle said, "I've been thinking a lot about just closing up shop and moving to Hawaii. You know I was stationed out there, right?"

"Yeah," I said.

"In those days, I raised a lot of hell," Lyle said. He had a faraway look in his eyes, and I thought maybe inside his head he was on liberty in Maui. "I don't regret it, though. We all had to sow our oats at some point. Make bad decisions and then just close those chapters and move on."

"I have so much regret," I said. "I've loved two women in my life, Lyle, and both of them are dead now. From day one, I've tried to follow orders. Somewhere along the way, I think I lost sight of what that meant. Even when right was wrong. What has it gotten me?"

"Respect."

"They gonna put that on my tombstone? *Here rests a guy people respected.*"

"That wouldn't be so bad, when you think about it." Lyle took a final pull from his beer, then coughed wetly. "You did right by everyone, Morris," he said. "By everyone." He slid out of the booth, tugged on a knit cap and gloves. "I called my kids, like you said. Daughter told me I was about five years too late."

"Keep calling," I said.

"Yeah, well," Lyle said. "The thing of it is, Morris, nights like this? You know, it's arbitrary. Holidays? What are we celebrating? I don't believe in God, and finding those kids up there on Yeach, that didn't make it any better. I mean, what are we celebrating?"

"That we made it through," I said.

Lyle considered that for a moment. "I shouldn't have to be

told to call my kids. I shouldn't even have been at work today." He shook his head. "My dad was a cop. And you know what he did on Christmas Eve?"

"No."

"Nothing. He did nothing at all. He was just my dad. I don't know how that got misplaced in me."

"Go home, Lyle," I said. "You're drunk." Which wasn't true.

"I will," he said. He zipped his coat up to the neck. Took a long look out the window to the empty boulevard, then adjusted his cap, so that it rested just above his eyebrows. "I thought I'd just take a drive through the streets. Make sure no one's stuck in the snow. You could die from the cold out there tonight."

I knew that he had seen my report, had seen Lizzie's autopsy report, and that he didn't care. Or, rather, that he cared a great deal, but that he knew I'd made a judgment call not based on the nuts and bolts of the law, but on how people feel inside. I would let the Kleins and Mrs. Pellet have their sad truth, even if it wasn't reality. I would give them that dignity.

"I'll come with you," I said.

PILGRIMS

The drive from Palm Springs to the Woods Detention Center just south of Castaic usually takes Tania a bit over three hours, mostly because she refuses to speed. She was always eager to see Don, her husband of less than one year, but there was something about breaking the law to see her incarcerated husband that didn't seem logical. Of all the choices she was forced to make in her life, Tania figured putting her car on cruise control three miles beneath the speed limit was the easiest to make. And besides, it was one less thing to concentrate on, which was good since Tania liked to listen to audio books while driving. Fifty-seven years she'd been alive, but it was only in the last three that she'd found the comfort of literature, though she understood that her predilection toward spy novels didn't exactly make her feel intellectually invigorated. It occurred to her a few weeks ago that she'd be wise to pick up some nonfiction titles, too, see if she might learn something to tell Don about during those weekly moments when conversation halted and both of them realized how little they knew about each other.

So today, on a Saturday in January, Tania listens to a book about the Pilgrims' first winter. When she took it out from the library, the librarian said, "You understand that this is eighteen hours, right?"

"No," Tania said. "Is that a problem?"

The librarian, a woman named Crystal that Tania sometimes

saw playing slots at the Indian casino where she cocktailed, but who never seemed to recognize Tania in either place, shrugged. "It's just that you might not finish it in time."

"For what?"

"The due date," the librarian said. "You could get the digital version instead."

"I already know how it ends," Tania said, but she checked out the book, too, so she could read it if she started to fall behind. "And I like having the physical CD. Makes me feel like I've accomplished something when it pops out of the player."

As she winds up the last miles of I-5 toward the prison, Tania has begun to wonder if she really does know how it all ends. She's only three CDs in and everything seems insurmountable. The cold. The disease. And worst of all, the fear. Cold and disease were knowns; it was the unknown that trapped the Pilgrims. In the three hours she's driven from the low desert, through the Inland Empire, the San Fernando Valley, and now up into the Santa Clarita Valley, the Pilgrims have crossed the Atlantic and found themselves in a land that seems intent on ruining them. How much more could they possibly take?

Tania passes the exit for Magic Mountain, an amusement park she's never visited and hadn't even heard of before moving to California nearly twenty years ago. That it's only a mile from one of the state's largest prisons is surely an unplanned irony, but even still Don has told her that at night he can hear kids screaming on the roller coasters and every now and then the wind picks up the scent of churros and hot dogs and cotton candy so that there are days when he's on the yard that he can smell what life used to be.

It saddens Tania to hear Don talk like that, not because she feels he's been wrongly imprisoned, because she doesn't, but because she doesn't believe Don's life ever consisted of those things. It's just another tiny lie, one of thousands he's told in his life, and if she really wanted to know the truth of it, if he'd ever tasted a churro, ever rode a roller coaster, she could certainly ask him. Avoidance, she's learned, is not something Don is good at, and with thirty years to think about what that means, he's proved to be especially forthcoming when pressed. Lying now is moot. It's easier for Tania not to ask. It's easier to have that connection, even if it's false.

The exit for Woods comes up quickly on the right. The sign says it's a mile off, but Tania is sure it's much less than that; she always means to set her odometer to find out exactly but is usually so flustered in her attempt not to miss her turnoff that she forgets. Today she's too busy listening to an excerpt from one of William Bradford's journals and has to slide across three lanes of traffic at the last moment, a trail of honking horns at her back.

When she was learning to drive, Tania's father told her never to honk her horn on the freeway unless she had to warn someone that they were about to hit her. Honking your horn because someone had bad manners was useless, her father told her, and it might lead someone else to slam on their brakes or swerve and that could cause an accident. "Better to just let stupid people be stupid and maybe they'll kill one another off," he told her.

It was funny how often her father would creep up on her these days. He lived in the Robeson Home now, an assisted living facility in Spokane, and had since her mother died two years ago. Tania last saw him at Christmastime. Her sister Justine offered to buy her a ticket and to pay for everything ("We'll have a sister's weekend," Justine said, as if they'd had such things when they were kids), and though at first Tania felt like she should be offended by this, she accepted. Her sister was a good person. She knew that. Married for thirty-two years, two children who were now adults, a home in Walnut Creek with a long driveway, a birch tree in the front yard, and, Tania finally understood, regrets of her own, even if Tania didn't know what those regrets were.

All these years they'd led different lives—Tania a cocktail waitress, first in Reno, then in Las Vegas, and finally in Palm Springs; Justine a wife, a mother, and then, when her kids were in middle school, she got her law degree, so now she was also a lawyer, just like her husband, Mark—but they came from the same place, the same people. Justine probably thought this trip might get them closer together, and maybe it had—they now talked nearly every day—or it could have been from necessity: neither wanted to visit their father alone. Growing up, their father was paranoid and angry, afraid always of what might happen next, his entire life a series of presumptions about what he might do in worst-case scenarios. Maybe that's why he, too, always read spy novels, Tania realizes now. The difference, Tania knows, is that not everything is a conspiracy. Some things are just bad.

Since her mother died, Tania had made it a point to call her father at least every couple of weeks. They'd talk for a few minutes about mundane things—she hadn't even told him about Don, figuring that it wasn't information he needed to have—and then she'd hang up feeling like she'd done what was right. She loved her father, had loved her mother, too, and knew that both had spent the better part of their lives worried about her. It was a shapeless truth that only seemed to find its way to Tania after Natalya, the child Tania adopted from Russia, had disappeared in 2001. *Disappeared* wasn't really the right explanation for those events; Natalya had likely run away, probably back to Russia, though Tania has never learned that definitively. She'd been gone so long—nineteen years. Gone was gone, and it was then that Tania understood the responsibility that existed between parents and children, the unspoken contract that they'd be *there*, even when they were gone. Her mother was dead, but she was still alive in memory, still a temporal truth, just as her father was, sitting in an assisted living facility but for the most part an inactive concern. He'd been her father and now he was this man in Spokane who sounded like her father but who didn't have any real responsibility to her anymore.

But when Tania saw her father at the Robeson Home she was struck immediately by how happy he seemed. He greeted Tania and her sister in the foyer to the home dressed in a red V-neck sweater, tan pants, and smart-looking loafers, as if he was just back from the country club and not spending his days in a facility meant to hide the dead end at the bottom of the road. He proudly took Tania and Justine around the facility to meet his friends, the facility's administrators, the cooks, even the woman who came in and took out his trash every day. "We all just love having Stu around here," one of the cooks said. "Your father makes everyone feel good."

That afternoon they went to the Sizzler for lunch and Justine spent most of the meal talking about her kids, which was fine.

"Do you remember how we used to come here with your mother?" Stu said after a while. He'd been listening intently to Justine, but Tania could tell something was bothering him and had been since the cook had told them how well-liked he was. "It wasn't a Sizzler then, was it?"

"No," Tania said. "It was a Sambo's."

"Right, right," Stu said. He'd worked his entire life in the restaurant-supply business, even owned a fleet of refrigerated meat trucks for a time in the nineties, and when Tania was a kid he generally refused to dine out; the mere sight of a ramekin sometimes enough to throw him into a rage about some perceived workplace injustice. "She used to love their pancakes, didn't she?"

"I don't remember," Justine said.

"How can you not remember?" Stu said. He was suddenly so surprised, so animated, that Tania found herself shrinking in her seat, like she had as a child when he'd make some announcement about, say, the likelihood that the Russians would nuke them all to death sometime in the next decade. It wasn't fear she felt sitting across from him at the Sizzler, not like when she was a kid, but rather it was a feeling closer to shame. She'd forgotten, too, or maybe she never knew, what foods her mother liked. It seemed a silly thing to commit to memory in the space of an entire life, but at that moment it filled her with an uncommon sadness: How could she not know what made her mother happy?

"It's so long ago," Justine said. "I guess I've replaced it with other things."

Stu nodded once, as if Justine had confirmed something important to him, and his energy seemed to wane. "I don't ask this to be sappy," he said, "and I don't ask this because I feel like I'm going to die tomorrow or something—because I want you both to know I feel good these days, I really do—but I guess I just need to know if you think I was a good father."

"Of course," Justine said immediately, but Tania didn't say a word because she didn't really know and figured she wouldn't know until he, like her mother, was gone.

"Tania?" he said. There was a queer half smile on his face that Tania remembered from her childhood.

"What does *good* mean?" Tania said. "You were our father. I think that was enough."

"I don't think I was, particularly," he said. "And that's okay. I want you to know that I think it's okay; that's important to me. I'm not angry about it anymore, because for a long time I was, you know. Even while it was happening. Your mother ever tell you I went on vacations by myself?"

"No," Tania said, though it made sense to her in retrospect.

"It was wrong of me," he said.

"What exactly are you confessing to?" Justine said.

"Nothing," he said. "I want you to have the freedom to not remember me well. To not feel guilt about it. That's all."

"This is a pointless exercise, Dad," Justine said. "Can't we just have a nice lunch?"

"I was scared of you," Tania said to her father. "But I'm not anymore."

"I'm happy to hear that, Tania," he said.

"Only took me fifty years," she said.

THERE ARE ALWAYS barefoot women walking up the steep road leading to the prison. Today was no different. The closest bus stop is half a mile from the front gates of the facility, across the street from Castle Rock Elementary and adjacent to a mini-mall with a Starbucks and a Cold Stone Creamery and a check-cashing place. Tania figures this must be a security precaution, can't have some runaway inmate able to hop on a city bus right at the front gates of the prison, so there were always these women in tight dresses and miniskirts taking off their spiked heels and walking barefoot or, occasionally, in house slippers up to where the road levels off about two hundred yards from the gate.

Used to be Tania would stop and pick up a couple girls on her way, but she doesn't bother anymore. Tania can't stand to hear their stories. Their men were always innocent. Their men were done in by bad cops or snitches or the system, whatever that meant. No one ever guilty of anything.

At the flashing red light midway up the road—at the intersection that leads off to the Jay-Reigh Honor Rancho, a dairy farm operated by the minimum-security inmates—Tania spots a familiar face standing at the crosswalk in a leopard-print miniskirt. She can't remember her name—Carol? Or maybe it was Susan?—only that her husband is a rapist. Tania had given her a ride once and then spent the better part of an afternoon processing through the visitation sections with her, sharing small talk about the weather, the smell of the prison, about how so many of the other women were girls, really, just kids and what a shame that was.

Tania had liked her well enough—they were both about the same age—until she'd gotten around to asking what her husband was in for. "Oh," Carol-or-Susan said, "he's in for rape. But it's not like he's a rapist. It's not like that. It's not like he was out in a park waiting for some girl."

"What's it like then?" Tania asked.

"He drove a truck, you know, so I knew what that life was like, and I understood that sometimes, you know, he might get a girl. Anyway, he picked one up in King City and I guess they got high or whatever," she said. She waved her hand dismissively, as if it was just one of those things that happens all the time in the course of a marriage. "I guess you could say he touched a woman in a way that was inappropriate. It all got blown out of proportion. And here we are."

"Do you even hear yourself?" Tania said.

"My husband is a decent man," she said. "Just like your husband is, I'm sure."

"I don't have that delusion," Tania said. "But I have the hope he can become one."

"Then what are you doing here?"

It was a question Tania had asked herself at many different points in her life, so when this woman posed it to her she began to laugh. Who the hell knew? She'd worked her entire life bringing people drinks and along the way had adopted a child who ran away from her, and here she was, going to visit her incarcerated husband. A man she'd only kissed once, on the day of their marriage.

At some point, Tania thinks as she goes through the stoplight, maybe you stop asking yourself about *what* and *how* and maybe begin focusing on *why*. Maybe that's what she can learn from the book she's listening to. The poor Pilgrims dying every day in the shadow of Plymouth Rock, their lives consigned to history, must have asked themselves that same thing. Every day they got further away from the life they'd known. Every day they got closer to dying or maybe they got closer to really living, though she didn't suppose the Pilgrims were applying that kind of Oprah shit to their lives back then. All that, but at least they had the *why* down.

There's a lineup of cars waiting at the front gate of the prison, so Tania slows to a stop about a hundred yards away. Sometimes, if Tania is lucky, the guard will recognize her and just wave her through, though that's pretty rare. Rules are rules and Tania can respect that. Today, she's about ten cars back, which could mean five minutes or an hour, depending on who happens to be in the cars. So many of the people coming to visit have priors and they need to be smart about who gets inside, which strikes Tania as funny in only the barest sense. You spend your free time at a prison and weird things start to strike you as amusing.

At first, she and Don traded letters for the better part of six months after she'd seen a photo of him in another cocktail girl's order book. Tania cocktailed at the Chuyalla Indian Casino with

Britney for years but barely knew her, just as she barely knew anyone she worked with. You work at a casino long enough, you realize
everything there is transitive, including interpersonal relationships,
and so if you're smart, Tania reasoned, you just came in and did
your job and made your friends elsewhere, which Tania had done
for over a decade. No sense getting too connected to other people
who've made the same mistakes you have.

Britney wasn't even thirty, but Tania knew she had a ten-year-
old boy, who had some developmental problem that the casino's
health insurance didn't cover. The health insurance problem was a
constant source of Britney's running break-room chatter with the
other girls. She was always telling them that soon as she got her AA
from College of the Desert, the local junior college, she was going to
find a better job at a place that gave a damn about its employees, but
in all the years Tania heard this patter she'd never once seen the girl
with a textbook. She wondered if Britney even had her GED.

But that afternoon, as they stood next to each other at the bar
waiting for their orders to be filled, Tania couldn't help but notice
the photo Britney had in her order book. Britney had laminated it,
so the photo picked up the lights circling around them, but it was
also wider than Britney's book, so the edges of the photo had become jagged and Britney picked absently at the wrinkles of plastic.

"He's handsome," Tania said, though in truth he was just average, the kind of guy you'd pass on the street and never imagine what
his life might be like, but he had a smile that appealed to her.

"That's my brother Don," Britney said.

"Oh?" Tania said, because she didn't know the proper response
to Britney's answer. After Natalya ran away, she'd learned how
hard it was to explain to people things like photos and pillows and
what might otherwise be considered silly trinkets. Other people's

keepsakes . . . that was land she didn't cross into. It was usually just easier, and better manners, to say, *Oh?*

"He's in prison."

"What did he do?"

"Something went wrong in Kettleman," Britney said with a nervous half laugh, and for the first time in the years that she'd worked with her, Tania saw something more in the girl than the compendium of complaints she heard her mutter each day. Britney was someone's sister and that someone was in jail.

"Oh," Tania said.

Gordon, the bartender, put Tania's and Britney's drinks onto their trays and then gave Tania's wrist a playful pinch. They'd gone out on a date once, a million years ago, and though it hadn't gone well, he still casually flirted with her, though Tania knew he was now sleeping with a Korean blackjack dealer named Sang.

"Well, okay, sweetheart," Tania said. She picked up her tray and examined the drinks against her order. They were all there. "It's not my business."

"No, no," Britney said. She reached out and put her hand on Tania's arm. "Hold up for a sec."

Used to be a lot of the girls came to Tania for advice, but that time had passed once word got around that Tania had her own problems. Gordon was probably to blame for that, which was okay. He was the only person at the casino she'd told about her daughter, and though she regretted telling him, it had released a burden from her. So even when she heard Britney going on about her health insurance and her kid, she didn't bother to interject with whatever wisdom she might have. Problems weren't solved in the break room; they were just examined in minute detail and then left on the floor.

"We used to say that to each other back when we were kids,"

Britney said. "Kettleman is this place . . . I think it's from a Western we saw. I don't even know anymore. It just meant that a bad thing had happened in the past. You know, some unspeakable horribleness?"

"I do," Tania said.

"So whenever anyone asks about him, I think about that. This one time he broke the kitchen table—I don't even remember how, only that one of the legs was gone—and so mom comes home and she's like losing her mind, because we didn't have a bunch of money and no one expects to have to go out and buy a new kitchen table, right? So he just tells her, totally straight-faced, that something went wrong in Kettleman. And you know, what could she say?"

"You just laugh in that case," Tania said.

"That's right, that's right," Britney said. "I guess I didn't realize it then, because I was like nine. But I understand now, because what can you do? You can't unbreak the leg. I mean, that's what parenting is, isn't it?"

"Most of the time," Tania said. "What I recall, anyway."

"I'm sorry," Britney said, "I didn't mean to bring that up."

"It's okay," Tania said. "I had a daughter and now I don't. I can't unbreak that leg, either."

Britney nodded once and then looked over her shoulder, back at the tables filled with gamblers waiting for their drinks. "I should drop these off," she said.

"What did he do, Britney?"

"Killed someone in his car," she said.

"Was he drunk?"

"No," she said, "just doing someone else's bidding. He's pretty much been a fuck-up his entire life."

"You don't go from being a fuck-up to killing a person," Tania said.

"Maybe not most people," Britney said. "He's my brother and I love him, but he wasn't ever a good person until he confessed. That's something, right? Does that seem stupid to you?"

"He killed someone," Tania said.

"What kind of lesson is that?"

"None at all."

Britney nodded again, liked she'd reached a conclusion she hadn't expected. "I don't know. Your adopted daughter, she ran away?"

"Yes," Tania said.

"What did you do to her?"

"Nothing," Tania said, though that wasn't true. She'd brought her from Russia to Las Vegas. She'd changed her entire life without ever asking her consent. "She didn't want to be here. I tried and failed to keep her. If she has a better life now, that makes me happy."

"Does it really?"

"It has to," Tania said.

"What I don't understand," Britney said, "is how my brother and me, we grow up in the same house, same values, and he's this one kind of person, the kind who hurts people. And I'm this entire other kind of person. Maybe you don't know it, because we aren't friends or anything, but I'm a very caring person."

It was Tania's experience that if you had to convince someone of a certain fact, the opposite of that fact was probably true, but she didn't feel that way about Britney and it surprised her. "I'm sure you are," Tania said.

"You know I got a kid?"

"A boy, right?"

"His name is Trevor. But here's the thing. Trevor loves his uncle like crazy. They used to roll around like puppies together, just real playful with each other, and now my brother is in prison and I will not take Trevor to see him. I told him Don got a job in China. I feel a lot of shame for that."

Britney's eyes welled up and Tania knew that the right thing to do was to set her tray down and hug the woman, take her in her arms and tell her that everything would be okay, that her life didn't need to be paralyzed by the choices she'd made, that her brother had made his own choices and they were the worst possible ones, and that if Britney were smart she'd just excise him from her life and move on, stop looking for other ways her life could be fucked up by other people.

Instead, Tania stood there and watched Britney collect herself. "I'm sorry," Britney said eventually. "You're just real easy to talk to."

"You don't need to share this stuff with me," Tania said.

"I know that," she said. "I'm a grown woman, Tania."

They were both silent for a moment and Tania reached over and took the photo of Don out of Britney's order book. "You have the same chin as your brother," Tania said.

"Would you like to write him a letter?" Britney asked.

THE WAITING AREA inside Woods isn't the best place to read. The fluorescent lights flicker intermittently. There's always someone crying. It smells like a mixture of body wash, sweat, and coffee with a dash of whatever the blue fluid is that the janitors (who are actually trustees) use to periodically spray down the seats and mop up the floors. But Tania knows that if she just sits watching Fox News on the lone television suspended from the ceiling that she'll be in no mood to chat with Don. It's not the news itself, but rather the realization that dawns on Tania whenever she watches that the world is moving way too fast now, that there are so many things happening at once it's impossible to keep up anymore. *What aren't they report-ing? Who is being left behind? Do I need to worry about these sick people in China?* How is she to know what is important and what can be ignored when everything is told in that same voice that says: *The end is coming, there is no chance for anyone, run for the hills, unless they are on fire, in which case stay in your house, unless the floodwaters have reached your door.* They should say, *Stay in bed and keep the covers over your head*, and just be done with it.

So instead Tania reads her book about the Pilgrims. The experi-ence is entirely different than hearing it over her car speakers. There are copies of letters and diary entries the Pilgrims wrote reproduced in the book, and Tania finds herself fascinated by their handwriting. It's nearly impossible to read—their cursive is a thing of art, really, all flowing lines and sharp points, and the few words she can de-cipher are spelled oddly—but what interests Tania is that she can see certain points of pressure in the handwriting, places where the writer pressed harder than usual with their pen and ink pooled, or places where they seemed to pause and the ink dotted out incremen-tally between words.

But it's the white space that captivates her, the spaces in between paragraphs, specifically. Nearly four hundred years later, Tania can see where these people stopped to think. What happened in that white space? How much time elapsed between paragraphs? Was it the next moment or the next morning?

The woman sitting beside her in the waiting area was maybe nineteen. She had a tattoo of a cat's claw on her neck, and she wore a plain white top with no bra and kept asking other women to borrow things—a pen, a piece of paper, lipstick—that she had no real use for, but the asking would get her involved in a conversation for a few minutes, to the point that Tania now knew pretty much all she needed to know about the woman: she was there to visit her boy-friend Andre, who was doing five for burglary, but she was pretty sure he'd get out early on account of his good behavior, because he was pretty much innocent and thus was trying to keep it real clean in lockup. She'd asked Tania thirty minutes ago what she was read-ing about and Tania said, "The Pilgrims."

And the woman said, "That come with Columbus?"

And Tania said, "Yes," because she didn't want to have to tell her she was wrong. It just wasn't worth it.

"I learned about that in fourth grade," the woman said. "What I never understood? Why anyone would want to come to this busted-up place back then."

"They wanted freedom," Tania said.

"Yeah, that's what they said in fourth grade, but I'll tell you one thing, nothing free about freezing to death. Them and the Donner Party. That's crazy, you ask me. I'd stay home by the fire and be happy. You got a Kleenex I could borrow?"

The woman had been quiet for the last several minutes, but her words still reverberated. When was the last time Tania had been happy? Her wedding day was happy, but it ended so quickly, and then she was back on the freeway headed for the desert and each mile she drove turned the ceremony into a memory that became more diffuse with each passing city. Had she just married prisoner number 1892K075, a man who couldn't possibly love her, a man she couldn't possibly love? There was a bouquet of roses on the passenger seat and a simple silver band on her finger, a stack of paperwork in a manila folder in the backseat that included a receipt for the deposit she'd made into Don's commissary account at the prison—$300— so he could treat himself and his boys to some snacks for the next month.

She'd paid nearly $50,000 to adopt Natalya from Russia all those years ago, Tania recalls. The deflated price of love. Everything is in recession. It took Tania several months to become happy about life with Natalya, to learn to love her child, and by then she didn't even realize she was happy, she just knew that she'd survived the unknowable process of motherhood and come out the other side feeling . . . right. That was all. She felt right. When Natalya left, that feeling went with her. Don had filled up some of that space, if only because she knew he wasn't going anywhere.

"You're Tania Hobbes, right?" the woman beside her says suddenly.

"Yes," she says, though she'd never legally changed her name, though she told him she had. "How'd you know that?"

"I remember you from a few weeks back," she says. "You were reading a book about spies, so I bought it at Target."

"Did we talk?"

"No," the woman says, "I just was looking at you and thought you looked pretty put together, so I made a point to remember your name when they called it."

"Did you read the book?"

"Tried to," she says, "but it didn't make any sense. Bunch of people running around talking about conspiracies and shit. And I was like, you kill someone, you don't need to have the president behind it to make it dramatic, you know? People getting killed is people getting killed no matter who calls the shot."

"I believe that, too," Tania says, and then she tells the woman something she's never told anyone, not her coworkers, but of course they know because of Britney, not even her sister, though her sister could find out easily enough. "My husband killed someone."

"Yeah? How come?"

"I don't really know," Tania says.

"You didn't ask him?"

"No," Tania says. "It happened before I knew him."

"You seem like a nice lady," the woman says, "but you need to dump that man of yours. He makes you guilty by association."

"What about you? Are you guilty of whatever your boyfriend did?"

"I am," she says. "And so here I am, just like you, every weekend, doing my time."

IT'S FOUR IN the afternoon when Tania finally gets called in to see Don, which means she only has thirty minutes to spend with him today instead of the normal hour. She's led into the visiting area by a female guard named Sherry that she's met a few times, and who she once saw eating at the Chipotle down the road in Valencia. It was a little bit like being a kid and seeing your kindergarten teacher at Safeway buying groceries. They both nodded at each other but didn't speak, not that they would have had anything to talk about, really. But since then, Tania always got a nice smile out of Sherry when she saw her and even a few more minutes than was allotted, but it was closing time today, so when Sherry drops her off at cubicle #19, she tells Tania she can only let her stay until the half hour and Tania thanks her.

"Hey, darling," Don says when Tania picks up the phone on her side of the cubicle. It's what he says every time she visits, and at first Tania thought it was cute, but now she wonders if that's just what he says to women, if he's said that to every woman who's ever been on the other end of a phone line. It's the sort of thinking that can make you crazy, Tania realizes, the sort of thinking that disappears when you love a person, because you can't imagine them ever speaking intimately to anyone other than you. "How you been?"

"I've missed you," Tania says.

"Me, too," he says. "How was your week?"

"I'm reading this book," she says, "about the Pilgrims."

"Yeah?"

"You wouldn't believe," she says, and then she stops herself and for a long moment she stares at her husband and tries to imagine what he looked like when he was killing that guy in his car. What was that guy's name? She didn't know. She'd never asked. Never once had she even bothered to look at his court records. What was the use? He was guilty. He'd done it. And yet here she was, a few feet away from him, separated by bulletproof glass and guards with guns and the excuses they'd both told themselves over the years. So much weight. So much distance. So much time. Don looked interested in whatever she was going to say next, as if what she might tell him could matter compared to whatever it was he fought with inside his head. Fifty-seven years had come and gone in Tania's life and to what end? This day? This life? All this time looking for a bit of clarity and it was here, in a prison, all the time. "You wouldn't believe," Tania says again, "what they went through to survive."

MAZEL

Tuesday nights, Kristy Levine liked to drink at a cop bar on Sahara called Pour Decisions. Even when she was working undercover, she could pop in there for a sip and no one looked at her twice. She'd been with the FBI for a decade, first working domestic terrorism and now organized crime, the last five years in Las Vegas, which turned out to be a pretty active place to be these days, the beginning of 2001. She'd been in seven gunfights, maybe a dozen physical altercations, and had come away with nothing worse than a broken toe. Which was ironic, because Kristy Levine had just found out she was about to die.

It was a rare small-cell cancer in her lungs. She'd already had a tumor the size of her thumbnail removed over the holidays, telling exactly nobody at her office, had flown to Cedars in LA to get it done, but now was staring down three months of chemo and a prognosis that said she had anywhere between six months and fifteen years to live, depending on whether she chose to listen to her oncologist or the message boards online. Her oncologist, who looked barely old enough to park her car, suggested she should get her affairs in order. The message board on AOL said she should apply for that master's she'd always wanted, because real life was just starting!

So she called her twin brother, Len. Cried with him for ten

minutes before they tried to figure out a way to end the call. He was a Marine. Their whole family was either military or law enforcement. Weird for a Jewish family, but her dad had said from day one that they weren't "hide in the attic" Jews, they were "fight in the streets" Jews. Dad and Mom were both gone already, so it was left to Kristy and Len to fight the invaders, wherever, whenever. And she'd planned to go into HR, then tell the senior special agent what was what, get herself onto medical leave . . . which she knew she'd never come back from, because once the bureau knew you were ill, you may as well be dead, working on a desk until you wanted to die.

So she decided to wait.

"Hey, Secret Agent," the bartender said. Her name was Sarah. "Haven't seen you in forever."

"I went home for Christmas," Kristy said. Not that she celebrated Christmas. She celebrated Hanukkah, but it was easier to just say what everyone else said. It was part of her training. Leave no impression.

"Where's home?"

"Oh," Kristy said, "up north." Kristy had run into Sarah a few times in the real world, Las Vegas not that big of a town if you lived there. The last time was at Gold's Gym, Sarah working the elliptical machine for an hour. They'd had a conversation in the parking lot afterward, Sarah asking her if she was Metro or what, and Kristy told her she worked for the government, that was it. Ever since, she was "Secret Agent."

"Like Minnesota?"

"Washington State."

"I'd love to go to Seattle," Sarah said. "Have you ever been?"

"A thousand times." She'd actually worked in the field office up there for six months.

"I have this dumb idea," Sarah said, "that I'd go there and become an EMT."

"Have you taken the classes?"

"No," Sarah said. "See? It's a dumb idea. I just feel like if I lived there, I'd get off my ass and do it. Here? It's too easy to make bank just doing this kind of thing." She leaned her elbows on the bar, motioned Kristy to come closer. "I'm not trying to be in your business, but you're like, legit, right? Like, a legit badass? I see you at the gym. You're like a super-fit Jodie Foster in *Silence of the Lambs*?"

"Yes," Kristy said. She wasn't really like Clarice Starling. Kristy had done deep-cover shit before getting on the organized-crime task force. But whatever. It was close enough.

"Could I do what you do?"

"How old are you?"

"Twenty-eight," Sarah said.

"No," Kristy said. "You're too late." Kristy had done eight years of Naval Intelligence before she ended up in the FBI. "But you could be a cop."

Sarah laughed. "I'd still have to move," she said. She pointed vaguely around the room. There were maybe two dozen cops in various stages of inebriation and bad judgment already in the place. "I know too many secrets." She popped up from her elbows. "Anyway. Sorry. I just see you in here sometimes and think, now that's a person who knows who she is. I'd like to be like that."

"I don't, really," Kristy said. Fact was, last several weeks, she felt like a person wearing a Kristy Levine Halloween costume, everything hot and sticky around her eyes, her face a thick plastic mask, her breathing for shit, her vision clouded. Not sleeping wasn't helping. Because the thing was, she knew the truth: she was dying. Six months, five years, fifteen, twenty, all that mattered now was there was something inside of her trying to take her out, and it didn't matter what medical miracles were out there, you didn't survive cancer, you persevered through it, until such time as you did not. It was the wreck of the Levine family. Her mother died of uterine cancer. Her father spinal cancer. Both had grown up in Pasco, downwind from the Hanford nuclear plant in Eastern Washington. Neither died with a speck of self-respect left.

Kristy Levine was not going out like that. She'd even started going to Temple Beth Israel, up the street from her condo in Summerlin. Tomorrow, she had an appointment to walk the cemetery with the rabbi, find her happily-ever-after home, while she waited for the resurrection. Or whatever Jews believed in. She hadn't gotten that far in the Torah.

"Well," Sarah said, then poured Kristy a glass of Johnnie Walker Black, even though Kristy hadn't ordered it, "you fake it better than all these assholes."

HOW DO YOU dress to pick out your final resting place? Kristy opted for jeans and a black sweater, the same necklace she'd been wearing since her sixteenth birthday, a pair of white Chuck Taylors. Can you bring your dog with you? Kristy decided yes and put a leash on her black-and-white cocker spaniel, Bingbing. What about your gun? Kristy never went anywhere without her gun. When she pulled up in front of Temple Beth Israel, however, and saw Rabbi David Cohen standing out front holding a tiny red notebook and wearing a tailored black suit with a silk handkerchief in his breast pocket, she had second thoughts about the gun. Because the rabbi looked . . . concerned. Which is when Kristy realized Rabbi Cohen probably understood what might compel someone who'd been attending his temple for only a few months to suddenly inquire about a cemetery plot. Why anyone would, for that matter.

But wasn't that the job of a rabbi? To take on the weight of your concerns? To receive your pain and reflect it back in hope? To meet a dying thirty-six-year-old on a Wednesday morning in Las Vegas and show her the fanciest dirt he could offer? And she was so worried that some mob button man might walk up behind her and put one in her ear that she needed her nine? What did it matter? She was already dead.

So Kristy parked, took her gun from her ankle holster, slid it into the glove box before Rabbi Cohen made it to her car. She rolled down her window.

"Do you mind if I bring my dog?" Kristy asked.

"Of course not," Rabbi Cohen said. He put his hand through the window, let Bingbing sniff him. "How old is he?"

"Nine or ten," Kristy said. She got out, let Bingbing bound out after her. "The vet thinks he could be as old as eleven. I got him from that shelter over on Charleston. I've only had him for six months. I just can't imagine who would give up an old dog." Not that she was surprised by how many awful people there are in this world.

"You never know how bad someone else's life has been, what causes them to make decisions we might think are deplorable, but which, to them, are the only reasonable options." Rabbi Cohen stared at her for a moment. He had brown eyes with flecks of green in them, a thick beard, and she saw that he had unusual scarring around his eyes, like maybe he'd been in a fire as a child. Maybe he'd fallen from something. His face had the quality of a jigsaw puzzle with a few pieces jammed into the wrong spots, like she used to do when she was a kid, too frustrated to make it all work out right. "So," he continued, "instead we should celebrate the mazel that brought you to Bingbing."

"Well," she said, "that is an optimistic worldview, Rabbi."

"You have a choice in this life," he said, simply.

For the next twenty minutes, while they walked through the first phase of the cemetery, beyond the founding members of the temple who'd already slipped this life—the Lippincotts, the Goldblatts, the Siegels, the other Siegels, the other-other Siegels, the Winers, the Wolfs, and a seemingly endless line of Kales—Rabbi Cohen told her about the various pricing options. He started at $2,300 for a single plot with a standard stone—in what looked to Kristy to be an already pretty busy part of town, as it were, three crews of men shoveling dirt at various spots in the field, a backhoe at each spot, which might explain the cost, since it looked like an expensive operation—and up to $10,000 for a more elaborate plot in a more desirable location.

"What does that mean?" Kristy asked.

"Have you ever been to the penthouse of the Bellagio?" Rabbi Cohen asked.

"No," she said. "Have you?"

Rabbi Cohen smiled. Or tried to. He had a weird mouth, Kristy saw. It was like half of it worked as it should, and the other half seemed lost in thought and had to be reminded to act. "No," he said. "But I'm told it's like no other place in the hotel and has a view of the entire valley." They walked up a slight rise, which knocked out most of Kristy's breath, to a portion of the cemetery that was as yet undisturbed by the dead. Red Rock Canyon loomed around them, casting everything in a peaceful amber shadow . . . until you turned and were assaulted by the nearby sprawl of sand-colored homes and, farther away, the jutting spire of the Stratosphere, along with a nice view of half of humanity landing at and launching from McCarran. "Welcome to the Bellagio," he said.

"Those houses feel very close to us," Kristy said. "If I got in early, could pick I which direction I wanted to face?"

"Of course."

"Because the idea of spending a million years staring at Southwest planes isn't terribly appetizing, Rabbi."

Rabbi Cohen marked something in his notebook. "Very well," he said. "Canyon-facing it is."

"I'll need to find $10,000 first," she said.

"Can I ask you the impertinent question?" Rabbi Cohen said, but then he didn't. He just waited for her. It was a method she often used when interrogating people.

"Six months," Kristy said. She told him about the rare cancer. About her prognosis. About her brother, the only person in her life, really. And she didn't know where, exactly, he was. The kind of work he did in the Marines was the kind of work one didn't talk about.

"I see," Rabbi Cohen said. "Do you have life insurance?"

"The bureau gives me $203,000 in death benefits," she said.

"The bureau?" When Kristy didn't respond, Rabbi David Cohen said, "What you tell me is confidential, Kristy. I'm your rabbi."

She was allowed to tell people she was an FBI agent. Only the covert parts of her job were classified. But in Las Vegas, where half the people were about an inch away from a RICO charge, it was like telling someone in East Germany that you worked for the Stasi. "I'm an FBI agent," she said.

"I hope I'm not under investigation," he said.

"Are you in the Mafia?"

"Mafia doesn't exist."

"Then you'll be fine," she said. She looked back toward the Strip. "Do I even want to be buried here? Who would come to visit me?"

"I would come," he said.

"My brother is a Marine," she said. "He's never been here. He's one of those guys who gets dropped into a country, does his job, and gets pulled back out. I don't see him making a special point to come and leave flowers."

"I told you," Rabbi Cohen said, "I will come."

"You know what's crazy? $203,000 is the standard life insurance. If someone murders me, I'll get an extra $100,000. I know a lot of married agents who don't tell their spouses about that. But does that make any sense to you?"

"It doesn't," Rabbi Cohen said. He wrote something else in his notebook. "Hopefully it won't come to that."

"What's the difference?"

"I'm sorry?"

"I just . . ." Kristy stopped herself. For some reason, she didn't feel comfortable talking about this in front of Bingbing. She reached down and unclipped the leash from Bingbing's collar. "Do you mind if I let him run around? He's been cooped up in the yard." Rabbi Cohen told her he did not mind. "Go ahead, Bingbing." Kristy patted Bingbing on his butt, but he just stood there, looking at her. "Go ahead," she repeated, but he didn't move.

Rabbi Cohen got down on one knee, in that nice suit of his, and put a hand on top of Bingbing 's head—he had huge hands, his knuckles covered in a latticework of tiny white scars, Kristy thinking maybe he'd been a boxer in a previous life, or maybe he just liked punching trees on the weekends—and stroked the length of her dog's body, came back up and scratched inside his ears, then pressed his face against Bingbing's, rubbing his check against the dog's cheek. Rabbi Cohen stood and Bingbing trotted off toward a murder of crows in the distance, near where two generations of Ulins were lined up like dominoes.

"What happened there?" Kristy said.

"The smell here," Rabbi Cohen said, "is highly disconcerting to dogs. It's on me, constantly, so I thought Bingbing might be reassured if he knew it wasn't something to fear. That it could be on a living thing, too."

Rabbi Cohen had an unusual voice. In it, she detected a hint of the Midwest. But there was also something maddeningly precise in his diction, as if every word he said was constructed in his mouth for the most profound effect. She supposed it was something religious figures were taught. It gave him the presence of thoughtfulness even when he probably didn't give a shit.

"Where are you from?" she asked.

"All over," he said. "My father was military."

"Not a lot of Jews in the military," she said.

"I would have gone," he said, "but I felt called to the Torah."

"I'm a terrible Jew, Rabbi. I've been to shul ten times in my life and it's all been in the last two months. How does that position me for whatever comes next?"

"For all the toil of our lives," Rabbi Cohen said, "the only thing we carry into eternity are the fruits of our noble deeds."

"What if I'm not a very noble person?"

"Is that true?"

"I've killed."

"More than once?"

When she was in Naval Intelligence, she'd overseen some dark ops overseas. Probably dozens of people died because of her work. As an FBI agent, she'd killed two men, popped quite a few others.

She wanted to feel bad, in light of where she was in this life, but the plain fact was that she didn't. "I don't know how many," she said. And she was suddenly exhausted. Physically. Mentally. Nothing seemed like reality anymore. She spied a bench shaded beneath a blooming honey locust, so she walked over and sat down, made sure she was still in Bingbing's field of vision.

Rabbi Cohen sat down beside her. "There has always been something terrible coming for you, Kristy." He tried that smile again. This time it actually seemed to take. "Intellectually, you must know that. Your story has already been written. All of our stories have. So tell me what you're *really* scared of. Not what you fear."

For the entirety of her thirty-six years, Kristy Levine had avoided giving almost anyone access to her interior life. Not even Len really knew her . . . and they were once the same person. Her last boyfriend, a lawyer named Seth she met in a chat room for Las Vegas Jewish singles, broke up with her for that very reason, telling her he never felt like she allowed him into her life, even though they lived together for three months.

"I'm scared that I will kill myself," she said. "And I'm scared that I might put myself into a situation where someone else might kill me. One to the back of the head sounds so much better than three months of chemo followed by three months of slow death."

"Don't invite that into your life."

"It is my life," Kristy said, and then she just let it all out. How she'd spent her entire career chasing down the worst-case scenarios, first in the Navy, and then in the FBI. How her days in Las Vegas were spent digging into the worst tendencies of people and how the banality of evil had crusted her over with cynicism and anger and how this fucking thing inside of her was probably growing out of that very cynicism and anger, because she'd never smoked a day in her life, had never taken anything stronger than a drink. How she ran fifty miles a week at the gym, how she hadn't had a cheeseburger since Reagan was president. How she had let bad people die so that she could lock worse people up. How her own morality had become fungible the longer she'd worked in law enforcement. How her singular focus, for her entire life, was to never be in the attic, while her body was slowly burying her in the basement.

Rabbi Cohen retrieved a small packet of Kleenex from his pocket and handed it to her. She hadn't even realized she was crying. "Tell me," he said. "What month were you born?"

"May," she said.

"Ahhh," he said, as if that solved everything. "Talmud tells us whoever is born under Mars will be a shedder of blood, be it surgeon or assassin. So it was fated. You can't blame yourself for decisions made by God."

"I don't believe that," she said.

"You don't have to," he said, "for it to still be true." He waited a moment, as though he were contemplating an equation, then said, "Do you know of Bennie Savone?"

"I could pick him from a lineup. If he wasn't already in prison."

"I don't know about all that," Rabbi Cohen said, in a way that made Kristy think he did know about *all that*. It was impossible that he didn't. Kristy hadn't worked the case, but Savone had ended up getting nicked on a conspiracy charge and was busy playing spades at a federal prison upstate. He'd been on the front page of the *Review-Journal* for a month. The words *mob* and *boss* always appeared before his name. "He and his wife, who is Jewish, funded the initial expansion of this cemetery."

That was also well-known. Bennie Savone was married to the daughter of Rabbi Cy Kales, the founder of Temple Beth Israel. Kristy had seen the signs for Savone Construction every time she'd come to temple, had watched the construction foremen pulling away from the work site—they were building a full high school adjacent to the temple—in black-on-black Lincolns, which was not normal. She'd even thought she might run a few plates . . . but then decided, no. She wouldn't go looking for malfeasance in her off-hours. That's how it was in Las Vegas. Everyone on the hustle, everyone OG in something.

"It's good to fund things you're interested in," Kristy said.

"I know you're trying to be amusing. And I appreciate the effort. But let me tell you: This bench you're sitting on, all the benches you might encounter on these grounds, they were paid for by his family. Do I think Mr. Savone pays for all of this because he loves the Jewish people? Well, he loves his wife. He loves his children. But he is not Jewish; he will never be Jewish. Even if he were to convert, he couldn't possibly know what it feels like to truly care about our people." He lifted his chin, as if to point to the cemetery staff across the way, digging a plot. "And certainly not our dead. That is genetic. A link to thousands of years of trauma. That exists in you." Rabbi Cohen squeezed her elbow, to get his point across, and her entire arm went numb, all the way up to her shoulder. "My advice to you is this, Kristy. Cling to the good. That is what the Talmud tells us. Release yourself of the regrets and the anger."

Bingbing came loping back toward them. He had something in his mouth, which Kristy couldn't quite make out until he dropped it at her feet and ran off.

A crow.

Minus its head.

She'd never let Bingbing kiss her ever again.

"Oh my god," Kristy said. "He's never killed anything before. I'm sorry."

"No, no, don't be ludicrous." Rabbi David Cohen took the silk handkerchief from his breast pocket and draped it over the bird's body. "It's his nature."

A WEEK LATER, Kristy was sitting at her desk, changing the beneficiaries on her insurance policy—she decided she'd leave Temple Beth Israel $50,000 for some benches that weren't bought with blood money—when there was a knock on her open door. She found Senior Special Agent Lee Poremba in her doorway. He ran the organized-crime task force in Chicago, which meant he spent about a third of his time in Las Vegas, the tendrils of both The Family and The Outfit still poking into the strip clubs in town, less so the casinos, since all those were run by multinational hotel companies. And the ones run by individuals like Sheldon Adelson and Steve Wynn might have been ripping people off on video Caribbean Stud, but they were doing it legally, and nobody was getting tossed in Lake Mead for their troubles.

"You have a minute?" Poremba asked.

"One sec," she said. She saved her changes, sent it off. Just like that, her afterlife was settled. She'd already put down $1,000 to secure her room in the Bellagio's penthouse, as it were. She closed her computer. "You in town to pick up Moe Green? Word is he and Fredo are up to no good."

"The Corleones were supposed to be a New York family," Poremba said.

"Secret?" Kristy said, "I've never seen any of the films."

Poremba closed the door, sat down across from her. Kristy didn't know Poremba well but whenever he was in town, he stopped to pick her brain about what was happening on the streets, since Kristy ended up doing a lot of surveillance work. He said, "You're not well."

"I just don't like mob movies."

"No," Poremba said. "I mean you're sick."

"Just getting over something," she said. Truth was, she'd lost seven pounds in the last week.

"This morning," Poremba said, "we rode the elevator together."

"We did?"

"I was behind you."

"Okay," Kristy said. She was out of it this morning. The chemo made her brain feel like a hive of bees.

"You live alone." It wasn't a question.

"I have a dog," Kristy said.

"You have a bald spot in the back of your head," Poremba said.

Her first impulse was to reach back and feel for it, but that would be a tell. If you know something isn't true, you wouldn't even bother to check. She'd been taught that by an agent not so different than Poremba, in an interrogation class at Quantico. So she said, "I'm sure it was just the light in the elevator." She'd had two chemo appointments already. Her hair wasn't supposed to start falling out for another week, though she'd proactively purchased two wigs. They both made her look like Barbie's friend Skipper.

Poremba said, "Look at your desk."

She did. Strands of her sandy-blond hair were littered across every surface.

"You want to talk about it?" Poremba asked. "Friend to friend."

"Are we friends?"

"Even if we're not," Poremba said, "you look like you could use one."

"I'm dying," Kristy said.

"Immediately?"

"Eventually."

"You're in good company, then," Poremba said. It was the kind of thing agents said to one another. The black humor of the job was that something bad was coming for everyone. Prepare for every day like it might be your last on the job, your last on the planet, too. Just like Rabbi Cohen told her.

"Well," she said, "I've got my own LLC at this point."

Poremba said, "How long?" She told him her prognosis, the senior special agent never breaking eye contact with her as she put it all down. When she finished, he said, "What are you still doing working?"

"What else am I going to do?" she said. "Play slots at the Frontier all day?"

Poremba said, "It was me, I'd travel."

"I have to go to the infusion center twice a week."

"When that's over."

"When that's over," she said, "if I'm lucky, it will be radiation. And when that's over, it'll be too late."

Poremba thought on that. "Stop wearing dark colors," he said. "Your hair stands out against the fabric."

"I'm not going to keep it much longer," Kristy said.

"You have someone," Poremba said, "to do it for you?"

"I have friends," she said, but that wasn't true. Rabbi Cohen told her about a support group through Temple Beth Israel. She was going to look into that. They gave rides, took care of meals, all that. The temple paid for all of it. Maybe someone in the group had clippers. "Don't worry about me."

"You don't make it easy." He pulled a cassette tape from his jacket pocket, set it on Kristy's desk. Poremba said, "Reason I'm here, you showed up on a wire."

"What?"

"We had ears on a house that backs up to the cemetery at Temple Beth Israel," Poremba said. "We got you and your rabbi talking. Pinged on Bennie Savone." He pointed at the tape. "That's the only copy."

She doubted that. "What is Chicago doing running an op on a cemetery in Summerlin?"

"We weren't," he said. Kristy knew how that worked. Get a subpoena to wire a house when your real target might just so happen to walk by it in public, where the assumption of privacy is much harder to prove.

"That conversation with my rabbi is privileged," she said, "no matter where I am."

"Fortunately, you're not being investigated for anything."

"I'm talking about my job," she said. "Isn't that why we're having this conversation?"

"I'm not here to ruin your life," Poremba said. "I'm here to help you keep it together, if that's what you want."

"Why would you do that?"

"Why wouldn't I?"

Kristy picked up the tape, turned it over in her hand. "How much did you catch?"

"A couple minutes," he said. "Enough to know you were buying a plot. Had to run some background, make sure you weren't being extorted or something, weren't about to dirt nap yourself to get out of a problem. You came back clean, so I wanted to check on you. So here we are."

"So you already knew I was sick." She ran her hand through her hair, out of habit. Loose strands came tumbling out. *Shit.* "What were you listening for?"

"I was working a hunch on the disappearance of Sal Cupertine and the murder of Jeff Hopper. You familiar with that case?" She told him she was. Cupertine was a hit man known as the Rain Man who'd been piling bodies for The Family for fifteen years. He disappeared after killing three agents in Chicago in 1998. Hopper had tracked the frozen meat truck that ferried Cupertine out of Illinois all the way to Las Vegas, including to the Barer Academy, the private school on the grounds of Temple Beth Israel . . . and then Hopper disappeared. Eventually his decapitated head turned up back in Chicago. Kristy had read the file back and forth. Everyone had. Solve that one, you could pick your assignment. Finding Hoffa would be easier. "Suffice to say, didn't pan out. And it would have been inadmissible anyway."

"So what was the use?"

"Hopper was my friend," Poremba said. "I wanted to know."

"Like we're friends?" Fucking with him a little bit.

"Hopper was an asshole," Poremba said. "But he was good FBI. He doesn't have any advocates left in the bureau. No family to speak of, either. So. It's my duty. To close the case. In my mind or on paper. Doesn't matter to me."

"Bennie Savone's small-game, if that's your worry," Kristy said.

"Half the people who work at the funeral home and cemetery have criminal records," Poremba said. "I'm not talking shoplifting. Legit hard knocks. And one of the rabbis across the street was found floating in Lake Mead. Missing key parts of his anatomy."

"Every synagogue in town has some criminal history," Kristy said.

"That's the point," Poremba said. "*History*. Temple Beth Israel hasn't been around that long. Where Bugsy Siegel got circumcised is not my concern. Metaphorically speaking."

"I hope so," Kristy said. "Look, Bennie Savone wouldn't be

tossed up with Chicago. His influence extends to the edge of Clark County. So he got guys with criminal records to dig holes. Big deal. Harvard MBAs don't typically end up gravediggers."

"You're probably right." He got up, went over to Kristy's window, looked out. The FBI office in Las Vegas was in a building on W. Lake Mead, wedged between a housing development inexplicably called The Whispering Timbers and a Dollar General store. Kristy's office had a view of the Dollar General's parking lot. It was clean and well lit and known by junkies as The Fed. You could score there pretty much 24/7. He tapped the window. "What's happening here?" Poremba said.

"See the camper-van?" Kristy asked. "Far west corner."

Poremba squinted. "Huh. Yeah."

"He's a Metro CI," she said. "They let him do his work. It's just weed." And some pills. A little coke, probably. Poremba didn't need to know that.

"How long?"

"Long as I've had this office," Kristy said. "It's a pretty safe spot. Only two killings since I've been here."

"I need to retire," Poremba said. He turned from the window, regarded Kristy with that steady gaze of his. "Listen. You encounter anything strange at that temple, give me a call, okay? Anything."

"The mayor of this city is a fully owned subsidiary of the Philadelphia crime family and you're worried about a synagogue." Kristy thought about Rabbi Cohen's knuckles, his face, how he brought up Bennie Savone at all. There was surely something off there. But you could also smoke in the grocery store and gamble in the drugstore, and Siegfried & Roy fucked with that white tiger every night. One day, something bad was going to happen. To everyone. "*Everything* is strange."

"We've got ears on the mayor's synagogue, too."

Kristy couldn't tell if Poremba was joking. He probably wasn't. She held the tape up. "I get to keep this?"

"Take it home. Put it through your shredder." He headed for the door but stopped before opening it. "And listen. Don't come back to work. If you want, I'll tell your boss you're doing undercover for me. Whatever you need."

"You hardly know me."

Poremba shrugged. "Your rabbi," he said. "He gave you good advice. Cling to the good. Nothing here is good, Kristy. Every part of what we do is the worst. The very worst. Disavail yourself of it."

"Wait," Kristy said. He was halfway through the door. She got up from behind her desk. "Show me where the bald spot is."

KRISTY COULDN'T SLEEP that night. The steroids they gave her after chemo were keeping the nausea at bay, but they also had her body and mind running a constant treadmill. So, at 3 a.m., she put a leash on Bingbing, put her nine on her ankle, and walked out her front door. She lived in a condo complex called The Allegro. It was a mile down the road from Temple Beth Israel, so fifteen minutes later, she and Bingbing slid through a gap in the chained-off front gate and made their way to Kristy's forever home. Both stood panting atop the rise where her grave would be. It was cold outside, barely 45 degrees, but Kristy was clammy with sweat and Bingbing's tongue lolled out to one side. Six months ago, she was running marathons for fun; now she could barely walk a mile.

This was life. For now.

Tomorrow would be different. She was going to do the right thing and take a medical leave. And then she was going to contact Len and tell him she needed him. That she was alone and needed someone familiar with her. She wanted to see his face to remind her of her own, because already she was changing.

She tied Bingbing to the leg of the bench and for a few minutes they both sat there, catching their breath, staring out at the lights of the Strip. Her years living in Las Vegas, she'd never played a single hand of blackjack, hadn't put a quarter in a slot, hadn't looked at a roulette wheel. She prided herself on being no one's sucker. And yet, since getting her diagnosis, she was plagued by the idea that she should empty her bank account and put it all on red, as a test of her ability to beat the odds. Though of course, she'd never do that. Because what if she won? She wouldn't be able to handle the notion that her entire life had been a series of lucky breaks and not the result of hard work. Luck is *Them* not finding you in the attic. Hard work is fighting *Them* in the street.

She tipped her head back and stared into the sky, hoping she'd see some stars, like back home in Washington, but even all the way out here, in the shadow of the Red Rocks, there was too much light pollution. All she could make out was the moon, which was no comfort. Stars had a much more compelling story. They were proof that dead things could still be remembered.

A breeze blew down off the Red Rocks. It smelled like damp creosote, but this time of night—of morning—everything did, sprinklers at golf courses and gated communities and parks and cemeteries across the valley timed to go off between 3 and 4 a.m. By the time the sun came up, every blade of grass and desert shrub would glisten, another level to the sheen of surrealism that everyone took for granted here. In Washington, dew existed. In Las Vegas, it was manufactured for effect.

It was a cynical thought, Kristy recognized. It was her pulling back from the beauty of what she loved about this life, the simple pleasure of a scent. If this life was to have meaning, it had to be that. The mundane magnificence of simplicity.

The breeze swirled past her again. A chill ran down her neck, tickling the sweat there. She reached back reflexively and patted down her hair—Poremba had placed his thumb on her bald spot that afternoon, it was just above her occipital ridge—and came back with strands of hair stuck to her slick palm. *Shit.* She let the strands fall and they were picked up by the wind, whisked into the darkness. Maybe they'd become like the stars, floating out there somewhere, landing on someone, a stranger discovering months of her life in a simple strand, and they would brush her off, and she would go on, over and over again, persisting.

How she loved the feeling of the wind in her hair. Had she ever realized that prior to this morning, in this graveyard? Would she ever feel it again?

She reached down and unstrapped the holster from her ankle, set it and her nine on the bench, stood up, and did the only thing she could think of in that moment: she ran, first in circles, her arms out like wings, letting the wind cover her, feeling it in her hair, in her eyelashes, in her eyebrows, in the salt of the tears that slid from her eyes and into the corners of her mouth. And then she took off down the berm, into the darkness below, the wind pulling the hair from her face, strands blowing into eternity, her whole body tingling, her lungs straining, electrified by a feeling she'd always taken for granted.

She got to the bottom of the tiny hill—it was only a ten-foot slope, but it felt like she'd run down the face of Everest—and doubled over to catch her breath, which is when she saw a pair of black work boots. She raised up and standing there, maybe five feet away, was Rabbi David Cohen. Or she thought it was him. She couldn't see his face. He wasn't wearing a suit. Instead, he had on jeans and a black hooded sweatshirt, the hood resting lightly on his head. Behind him was a backhoe. Had she not seen that in the dark before? Or had he pulled up in it?

"What do you think you're doing here?" he said.

"I'm sorry," she said. She barely had any voice, her breath not quite back yet.

In the distance, Bingbing began to bark hysterically, like he did when there were coyotes running around outside, but Rabbi Cohen didn't even lift his head in that direction. "Are you alone?"

"How did you know I was here?" Rabbi Cohen didn't answer. Then she realized: the temple was covered in cameras. There must be CCTV cameras mounted in the trees or on top of the buildings. She exhaled through her mouth. Blinked once. Took in Rabbi Cohen standing there. Jesus, he was big. How had she never noticed that? Not that he was tall. No. That wasn't it. He had a . . . presence. It was like staring at a black hole. He was both there and not there. *I'm losing it.* He had something in his hand. A shovel.

"Are you alone?" he said again.

"Alone? I have never been more alone in my life."

"Step toward me," he said.

Kristy ran her fingers through her hair. "Do you see? I'll be gone before I'm even gone."

"Step toward me," he said again, and for some reason, Kristy did. "Are you armed?" he asked.

"Yes," she said. And in that moment, Rabbi Cohen was right in front of her, the distance between them closed from five feet to five inches, and he had hold of her arms, pinning them to her side. "No. I mean. No. I left my gun on the bench. I'm not here to harm myself. I don't think. It's not what you think."

Bingbing was howling now. Could he even see her?

Rabbi Cohen shook the hood from his head. His hair was normally combed perfectly, like he was a Republican congressman, but it was messy and loose.

She looked down at his hands. Even in the dark she could see the scars on his knuckles.

"You need to look at me," he said.

He had scars around his mouth. She hadn't noticed that before.

"You shouldn't have come here," he said.

He squeezed her arms.

Bingbing made a noise Kristy had never heard before. It sounded like he was barking inside of a blender.

A second later, the dog came snarling down the berm. Half of his leash dragged behind him. Blood pumped from his mouth and stained his chest coat red.

Jesus.

Bingbing had chewed through his leash. And lost some teeth in the process.

Rabbi Cohen stared down at the dog. "Stop making that noise," he said.

Bingbing did. The dog stood there. Waiting.

"You should have been killed tonight, Agent Levine," the rabbi said.

And then, he pulled her into his chest, and hugged her.

Softly.

"It's freezing," Rabbi Cohen said. "You're freezing." He took off his sweatshirt. "Put this on." Kristy did. "You have no immune system. Breaking into here was dangerous. You know that. Or you know that now. And so you know that you will never do it again, because Agent Levine, on the wrong night, you could die right here and no one would ever see you again. I want you to understand that. Appreciate this gift you've been given." He looked at his watch. "Sun will be up in two hours. Take your dog and go home. You need rest. And then you can decide to fight or you can give in. Which is it going to be?"

"What was it you said before," Kristy said. "About finding Bing-bing. What did you call it?"

"Mazel," Rabbi Cohen said.

"What does that mean?"

"It means fate," he said. "And luck."

"Where does it come from?"

He pointed up. "Above," he said. "Around. Wherever you find God."

"That," she said. "I'm going to look for more of that. For mazel."

Rabbi Cohen nodded, then turned around, picked up his shovel, got onto the backhoe, and drove off, leaving her there, alive among the dead, in silence, save for the fresh howling of her dog and the whispering of the wind, searching for her mazel.

PROFESSOR RAINMAKER

Professor William Cooperman hated teaching in the summer. The information was always the same no matter the season, of course, but for Cooperman it was more about the students. If you were taking Introduction to Hydrology in the middle of July, that meant you'd spent the entire year avoiding it, or had failed it in the fall and now were spending a few weeks getting the F off your record, maybe earn yourself a D and be done with it. That was the problem with students today. Here it was 2007 and no one thought that understanding how water worked on the planet was vital, never paused to consider how something as simple as sprinklers had changed the course of human development, or that eventually the world was going to turn to shit and water would be a commodity you'd kill for. Well, maybe a few people thought about those things.

Maybe at UCLA.

Or Yale. Somewhere smart kids went.

Somewhere smart people taught.

No, he thought, sitting behind his narrow desk at the front of the lecture hall, his thirty-five students midway through the fifth pop quiz he'd proffered to them in just two weeks, these students today just didn't want to fail water. His students couldn't see beyond the moment, couldn't understand that the ripples they were causing would eventually be tsunamis. Didn't matter if it was water or gasoline or not caring about their bodies, kids today just didn't grasp the enormity of the predicament.

He checked his watch. It was 2:13. Cal State Fullerton required him to hold class until precisely 2:30 each day, so that the students would get the exact amount of contact hours they needed, lest some state accreditation auditor pulling undercover duty in the class was just waiting to pounce on the college for skirting the rules. And then he had another section at 7:00, which meant his whole day was lost. Cooperman thought the administrators at the college were a bunch of fucking communists, but this slavish dedication to time really didn't jibe with his thoughts on higher education, which is perhaps why he was just a lecturer. Cooperman figured education shouldn't keep a clock. If it took five minutes to teach something, what was the use of sitting around for another hour talking about it? Especially in the summer. And on a Thursday, everyone's last day of class. It was useless, so the pop quizzes were his way of getting around that issue of talking. Invariably someone would finish the quiz before 2:30, but the social Darwinism at play in the lecture hall essentially forced them to stay seated until a reasonable point, which was usually about 2:15.

But for some reason the students were spending more and more time on the tests, as if they were thinking about each question, and the result was that class was not only going the prescribed length, sometimes it went over, and that wasn't going to work today.

Cooperman had a business meeting at the Sonic over on Lemon at 2:45 and couldn't be late. The guy he did business with, Bongo Pocotillo, wasn't real big on excuses and apologies. He said he wanted to meet at 2:45 at some crap-ass drive-in fast-food restaurant and you got there at 2:50? Might as well not show up at all. It occurred to Cooperman that working in academia and working in the illegal drug trade weren't all that different: people expected a certain level of punctuality, which he thought was a really bent business model. If any two fields demanded fluidity, it was academia and drug trafficking.

The professor stood up. "Excuse me," he said, and when that didn't elicit any response, he said, "Pencils down," and then the entire room came to a full stop. It never ceased to surprise Cooperman how conditioned students were. He could have taken a shit on his desk and no one would have noticed, but utter those two words together and it was holy sacrament. "I'm afraid I'm not feeling too well. Today, everyone gets an A on their exam. Just be sure your name is on your Blue Book when you pass it in."

There was a slight murmur in the class and immediately Cooperman knew it meant bad news. Normally, a professor says, "Everyone gets an A," and no one bothers to ask for any kind of explanation, but Cooperman had set a poor precedent on Monday. He'd asked everyone to turn in a two-page essay on what they perceived to be the most fascinating aspects of hydrology and then accidentally left the whole lot of them in the trunk of his rental Ford Fiesta, which wouldn't have been a huge problem had he not torched the rental in Mexico when it became clear he had to lose that car fast . . . subsequent to a regrettable shooting incident. After making up a suitable lie ("I'm afraid I left all of your essays at an important conference in El Paso this past weekend"), he gave them all Bs on their papers, which caused a tribal war to break out between the Good Students and the Back Row of Assclowns, like those three frat guys whose names he intentionally didn't learn, since he was pretty sure he'd seen each of them purchase weed from Bongo sometime in the last year.

Predictably, perfect-student Monica Williard raised her hand.

"Yes, Ms. Williard?"

"I'm sorry, Dr. Cooperman, but I'd like to finish my exam and get the grade I earn. I think most of us feel this way."

He liked it when she called him Dr. Cooperman. Though he wasn't a PhD, he didn't bother to correct her. A little bit of respect went a long way. All these other kids? Half of them didn't address him at all. Worse was the preponderance of adult students who'd found their way into the college after getting shit-canned from their jobs at the post office or bounced from the police force and now found themselves in GE-level courses with a bunch of kids; those students always thought they should be able to call him Will or, worse, Bill. He blamed the geology professor, James Kochel, for that particular slight, since Kochel let all the students call him Jim or Jimmy, said it was the pedagogical difference between *teaching* and *fostering* and he preferred to foster.

Monica, she had a little class. A respect for authority. He kept thinking that he should Google her name from home to see if she kept a blog, see if maybe she was harboring a small crush on him. Who could blame her?

"Yes, Monica, I understand," he said. "That makes perfect sense. So why don't we do this: Everyone, take your quizzes home with you. Complete them at your leisure and bring them back, and all of you will get the grade you've earned."

That was enough for the Back Row of Assclowns, which meant it would be enough for the Good Students, since all the Good Students really wanted was to be like the Back Row of Assclowns, the kinds of people who managed to pass their classes without any mental exertion at all. The whole school was filled with future middle managers anyway, Cooperman thought. It really was no use being like Monica Williard. Ten years from now, someone from the Back Row of Assclowns would be her boss regardless, if they weren't reality TV stars.

COOPERMAN FELT ABSURD pulling up to the Sonic in his white-on-white Escalade, but it was important to convey a positive image while doing business. It was the rap music he had to blast out of his speakers that really bothered him, particularly now that it was 2:44 and there was no sign of his associate, which made the fact that there was a middle-aged white guy dressed like a professor sitting by himself listening to The Game all the more obvious. If it was up to him, he'd have Gordon Lightfoot on. It's what his parents used to listen to on long car rides, presumably to lull him into sleep. But now, decades later, whenever he felt his pulse quickening, he found himself humming "The Wreck of the Edmund Fitzgerald."

He only listened to gangsta rap so that he could figure out what the hell people were saying to him, both in class and on the streets, and so guys like Bongo Pocotillo, who was now officially late for their appointment, wouldn't think he was a complete asshole.

It wasn't supposed to be this way. Fresh out of graduate school, Cooperman got a top-shelf research job working for Rain Dove, the sprinkler-industry equivalent of being drafted in the first round by the Dallas Cowboys. Within a year he was the big dog in the Research & Development department, but by his fifth year he was thinking about bigger possibilities. The sprinkler industry had always been about making the world green, about giving customers the impression that no matter where they lived, they were in lush surroundings; that their backyard could look like the eighteenth hole at Augusta if only they purchased the latest automatic sprinkler system. It was a successful model—one only had to visit Rain Dove's corporate offices in the middle of the Sonoran Desert of Phoenix for proof.

Nevertheless, Cooperman saw the future one night while watching a Steven Seagal movie, the one where Seagal plays an eco-warrior who, after breaking fifty wrists over the course of two hours, makes an impassioned speech to save the world from the disasters of human consumption. As far as epiphanies went, Cooperman recognized that this was one he'd probably have to keep to himself, but he realized change was coming—that if even marginal action heroes were taking time out to admonish the very people they entertained to conserve, hell, it was only a matter of time before the offices of Rain Dove would be picketed by some fringe water-conservation terrorist cell or, worse, Seagal himself. Better to be ahead of the curve.

He spent the next two years developing new technology that would *limit* the need for the expansive sprinkler systems Rain Dove was famous for. He migrated Doppler technology into existing systems to measure air moisture and barometric pressure, developed a probe that would constantly measure soil dampness, linked it all to a master program that calculated exact field capacity reports that would then decide, without any human interaction whatsoever, when the sprinklers needed to go on. Or if they ever needed to go on.

And that was the rub. Test market after test market determined that most people who were buying Rain Dove systems lived in places that needed no irrigation at all. Grass would grow and die in precisely the manner it had since the beginning of time, with or without a system, and specifically without Cooperman's vaunted RD-2001.

At the time, he had a huge house in the Sunny Hills neighborhood of Fullerton (the locals called it Pill Hill because of all the doctors who took up residence there); he and his now-ex, Dawn, were talking about having kids (which meant he'd have to cut down on his weed smoking, since their doctor said it was lowering his sperm count to dangerous levels) and seriously considering a little condo in Maui. Still, he always had the strange sense that he was living in the opening shot of a Spielberg movie, right before the aliens showed up to turn the bucolic to shit.

He shouldn't have been surprised, then, a week after the last test market showed everyone just how cataclysmic the RD-2001 would be to the sprinkler industry, to find himself out of a job. But that was his problem. He was like one of his goddamned students, never thinking about ramifications, never watching the ripples, even when his own fear kept setting off alarms.

A month later, he was out of a wife.

A year, he was living in his parents' house in Buena Park and making pro–con lists about his life, trying to figure the relative value of killing himself. His parents blasting Gordon Lightfoot during every shared meal.

Two years and he was using the RD-2001 technology to grow some of the most powerful weed in the universe.

Three years, he was supplying.

Cooperman checked his watch again. It was now 2:55. Where the fuck was Bongo? In the years they'd been doing business, Bongo had never been late for anything; in fact, Cooperman couldn't remember showing up to a meeting and not finding Bongo already shifting from foot to foot like a five-year-old needing to piss. Back in the day, when Cooperman just bought weed for his own consumption, Bongo was his connect. Now they were partners, though he never really got the sense that Bongo liked him. They didn't have much in common, of course, apart from the weed, but they'd made each other a lot of money, and because of that they often shared moments of happiness together, which Cooperman thought gave their relationship a unique value.

At 3:00, Cooperman's cell phone rang, the opening strains of "Nuthin' But a 'G' Thang" replacing his preferred rotary-dial ring tone. When he looked at the display screen and saw Bongo's digits, he felt inordinately relieved.

"You had me worried," Cooperman said when he answered.

"You wanna tell me again what the fuck happened in Mexico?"

"I thought we were meeting."

"You at Sonic?"

"Yeah."

"Then we're meeting."

"This is bullshit, Bongo," Cooperman said.

"So is shooting a motherfucker in the face," Bongo said. "Now we're even."

The problem in dealing with criminals, Cooperman had learned, was that most of them were paranoid and narcissistic, which isn't an ideal combination. Everything was a personal affront. There were only so many ways of telling someone that you weren't going to fuck them and that you respected them completely, before you started to think of ways to fuck them and disrespect them just to change the conversation. Cooperman hadn't reached that level with Bongo yet, but he recognized that his problem in Mexico was probably a subconscious manifestation of that very thing.

"Listen, Bongo," Cooperman said, "it was completely my fault. I got nervous and everything fell apart super quick. But I want you to know that I'd never fuck you, and I completely respect you and your position."

"You shot a motherfucker who couldn't even read," Bongo said. "You realize that? You killed a motherfucking illiterate."

"The failure of education isn't my problem."

"You think this is funny?"

In fact, Cooperman did think it was funny, if only in the way everything seemed off-kilter to him these days, as if each moment were separate from the next. He liked to think that he'd finally learned how to compartmentalize, finally got over his obsessive tendency to overanalyze all things, what his ex used to call his "ego-driven OCD." But the truth was that once he set something aside, he never bothered to think of it again. Cooperman realized this likely meant he was losing his mind, but in time even that got shoved aside. Like this Mexico shit. He'd driven down to Tijuana with a trunk full of his reconfigured RD-200is to sell to a contact of Bongo's, who was supposedly going to move them to some influential people connected with a prominent cartel—William couldn't remember which one, except that it wasn't the one El Chapo was in charge of, because Bongo had assured him they were a "less violent" cartel, not the guys who were beheading priests and tourists and whatnot, which made William feel better about the situation—who, if they liked the system, would bankroll an entire development program. Or at least that was the story. But when Cooperman finally met up with the contact—he was just a punk, really, maybe eighteen or nineteen, who didn't look all that different from the faux gangsters and frat boys who rolled across the Fullerton campus en route to their Freshman Comp sections—a switch flipped in Cooperman's head. He finally saw the ripples in their entirety: the cartel would take his technology, reverse engineer it, and he'd be out of a job in two months, maybe less. And what would it matter, anyway, since how much longer would weed even be illegal? This Obama guy running for president? There was no way he didn't get high. Grew up in Hawaii?

Please. This motherfucker was high as fuck as a kid, which meant it would only be a few years before some state would make it legal. Probably California. Then Washington. Oregon. And then he'd be out of the game. Halliburton and Kellogg's and Disney would be making weed, no doubt. How much longer did he have? Five years at most. This teaching shit, which he only did so he could pay off his monthly alimony, would be his entire life. Teaching Intro to Goddamned Water to a whole legion of consumers who wouldn't change anything for the better would just perpetuate the world's problems, so that in ten years, or twenty, when people were really staring at the end of things, they'd ask who was responsible for teaching these morons how to conserve, and that's when fingers would start getting pointed at the educational complex and guess what? He'd be out of a job again anyway.

Cooperman ran it all through his mind from several different angles to make sure he wasn't overreacting, examined the empirical evidence, and then shot the kid in the face.

It wasn't like it had happened without Bongo's complicity, really. Bongo had asked Cooperman months before if he wanted a gun, since Cooperman refused to have any additional security at his house, apart from the rent-a-cops who worked the gate at the Coyote Hills Country Club, and since Cooperman thought the neighbors would find it odd that a bunch of gangsters were loitering around the community pool. So he said sure, absolutely, since it sounded like the type of thing he should want, even if the idea of shooting a gun went against all of his political inclinations. Yet, once he had his handsome chrome-plated nine, Cooperman started going to the Orange County Indoor Range in Brea to shoot, and he found he liked unloading into the bodies of the various people who'd done him wrong over the years, at least metaphorically.

The problem was that Cooperman wasn't much on metaphors, and after a while he started thinking about making a trip out to Rain Dove's corporate offices in Phoenix to discuss his anger regarding his termination. It wasn't like he wanted to kill anyone, specifically, only that whenever he left the range he felt positively Republican for the first time in his life. Like the kind of guy who handled his problems versus having his problems handle him.

So when the switch flipped, Cooperman did what those leadership-structure books always advocated: he rightsized his problem.

Crazy thing, it felt pretty good. Taking the power back. All that.

"I admit my mistake, Bongo. What do you want me to do? The kid shouldn't have stepped to me. You know me. I don't G like that."

Cooperman heard Bongo sigh. It wasn't a good sound. He'd already sketched out for Bongo a general idea of how things had gone down in Mexico the day previous, substituting the moment of self-realization for a hazy recounting of the kid waving a knife in his face and trying to steal his car. He knew when he told Bongo the story the first time that it was filled with holes, so he tried to cover his tracks by saying things like, "And I'd never seen so much blood!" and "I can't sleep now, Bongo, I keep seeing that knife in my face!" and "It was all slow motion. One minute, we were sitting there in the Fiesta, the next he was jabbing a knife at me. What was I supposed to do?" Cooperman thought his mania would make Bongo realize he'd been scarred by the event, since it wasn't every day Cooperman killed somebody, and that it was therefore only reasonable things weren't lining up correctly.

"All you had to do was hand him a couple boxes. That's it. No reason for you to feel threatened in the least. It wasn't even *illegal*. And this is what you do? You make some shit up about a knife?" Bongo said. "That kid had parents, dog. Relatives. Motherfucker had an existence, you know? That shit went over five fucking borders. You think the Mexican Mafia is going to just let that shit slide?"

"I thought you said it was a cartel," William said.

"I never said that," Bongo said.

"So, are we talking MS-13? Is that the same as the Mexican Mafia?"

"Dog," Bongo said, "you are focusing on the wrong shit."

"I highly doubt MS-13 death squads are coming for me," Cooperman said, but as soon as he said it, he began to think of it as a real possibility. "This is Orange County."

"You think that matters?"

"This is America!"

"Dog, place don't matter in the least." Bongo went silent. William thought he heard a baby crying. Bongo was always having childcare problems. His wife, Lupe, was trying to be an aesthetician, so she had classes in the daytime. "They got partners in Palm Springs. They got fools doing home invasions in Las Vegas for kicks. Like, nothing jumping off on a Tuesday, let's tie up some people, kill their cat, and steal their Oxy. We ain't dealing with normal people. You feel me?"

"I can explain it."

"My cousin Peaches," Bongo said, "he paved this road for you. *You* shooting this motherfucker is like *him* shooting that motherfucker. I vouched for you. Maybe that don't mean shit at your job, but that's all we got up in this game. Word is bond, you heard that shit before?"

"I am familiar with the concept as a lyric," Cooperman said.

Bongo sighed again. It was an especially pitiful noise coming from him. He was one of those Native American guys who looked like he had some Samoan in him, his torso like a barrel, his hair always shaved close, though sometimes he grew a rat tail off the back of his head, which he then braided. He had a tattoo of his name on his stomach, which Cooperman thought he must have gotten in prison, though he didn't even know if Bongo had done any time, but who would be bored enough on the outside to get that done? Funny thing, though, was that Bongo was actually pretty easygoing. Married to Lupe since high school, had her face tatted up on his forearm. A couple kids. *Three now*, William corrected himself, with the newborn. Coached soccer. One time Cooperman even saw him at the Rockin' Taco eating with his family, and they just nodded at each other. He had some hard knocks in his employ, there was no doubt about that, but Cooperman always admired Bongo's approach to business—apart from the timing issue—which boiled down to the simple credo tattooed in Old English on the back of his thick neck: *Not To Be Played.*

"I left what I owe you in the bathroom, second stall, taped inside the toilet tank," Bongo said. "I can get you twenty-four hours to get ghost. After that, I don't know you."

"I'm just a scientist," Cooperman said.

"Nah, " Bongo said, "you a fugitive."

"I've got a job. I've got a life here," Cooperman said. "Let's be reasonable. Bongo? Bongo?" Cooperman pulled his phone from his ear to see if he'd lost the signal, but it was still four bars strong. He called Bongo back, but the phone just rang and rang, didn't even go to voicemail.

"Well, fuck you then," Cooperman said, and he set the phone down on the passenger seat. Thinking: *I'll just let it keep ringing. See how annoyed that makes him. Let him know I'm not just going to lie down. William Cooperman doesn't get played, either.*

Cooperman reached under his seat for his nine, shoved it into the front pocket of his Dockers, and got out of his Escalade. He circled around the Sonic once to make sure there wasn't a SWAT team waiting for him, and then entered the restroom. The only person inside was a Sonic carhop, still in his roller skates, washing his hands at the sink. The only sound was the running water and the ringing of a cell phone, which sounded like it was coming from inside the second stall.

"Oh," the carhop said when he saw Cooperman. "What's up, teach?"

Cooperman looked at the carhop, tried to see his face, but he was finding it hard to concentrate on anything. Bongo had been right fucking here, the entire time; probably got off watching him stew in the front seat of his car, probably thought about killing Cooperman himself. Probably should have. Christ.

"Who are you?" Cooperman said.

"Miles Key?" He said it like a question, like he wasn't sure that was his own name. "I'm in your Intro class."

"Where do you sit?"

"In the back," Miles said. "I know, it's stupid. I should sit up front. All the studies say people who sit in the front do better, but, you know how it is when you have friends in class, right?"

"Right," Cooperman said. The longer he looked at Miles, the less he seemed real, the less his words made any sense. Maybe it was that constantly ringing phone that was making everything skew oddly. Maybe it was that he could feel his nine pulling the front of his pants down, making him aware that he looked like one of those slouch-panted thugs he avoided at the mall. "Was there a big fucking gangster in here a minute ago? Maybe holding a baby?"

"I'm not sure."

"There is no 'not sure,' Miles. Either a human being meeting the description of a big fucking gangster was in here or was not in here."

"I'm not sure I know what you're talking about."

"A Native American gentleman," William said, calmly, trying another tack. "Holding a baby." Nothing. "A fucking gangster. A bad motherfucker. Did you see that? Was there a bad motherfucker taking a piss in here, while holding a crying baby? You would remember that, correct? This is for your final grade, Miles. You get this right, you get a fucking A. No more class. All summer off."

"Professor," he said, "you're kind of scaring me."

Professor. Of all the times to finally show some deference. It never failed to amaze Cooperman how often people could astonish you, because even the way Miles had said the word indicated a kind of awestruck reverence for the moment, for all the time Cooperman had put into his place of academic standing, even if the truth was that he'd put in shit for academics, it was all just the sprinklers that had brought them to this moment. Or maybe it was just confusion Cooperman heard. Either was fine with him.

Cooperman stared at Miles Key for a moment and tried to decide what to do next. His options seemed simple enough. Shoot him or let him roller skate back into his mundane life. The realization that those were his two best choices sealed the deal.

"I have to take a shit," Cooperman said. He walked over to the second stall, opened the door and closed it behind him, then waited until he heard Miles skate out the door before he dropped Bongo's ringing phone into the toilet. The cash was right where Bongo said it would be, but there wasn't much there. Maybe ten thousand. Enough to get out of town, but then what?

This whole thing was ridiculous. At his house in the Coyote Hills Country Club, where he'd lived a grand total of six months, he had another fifty, maybe more, plus his entire harvest growing in his backyard, which would net three times that much this month.

Probably closer to four. He wasn't a big mover. Cooperman had no delusions about that, he was just happy to provide a niche market, so maybe he'd been wrong thinking globally with this whole cartel thing in the first place; but he'd realized that in time, that was the ironic thing now.

Cooperman just wanted to go home, spark up a bowl, grade some papers, and forget this mess, but going home didn't seem all that prudent. He realized Bongo was trying to do him a favor, realized that Bongo could have killed him if he wanted to, could have alleviated this now-international incident without a problem, but didn't. Cooperman didn't know what to make of that, except that perhaps Bongo felt a twinge of loyalty. Another surprise. Getting out of town was a gift, but where would he go? He'd lived his entire life in Orange County, and it's not like moving to Pasadena was going to somehow change the fact that a bunch of angry cartel motherfuckers were now looking for him.

He stepped out of the stall and saw that the sink where Miles Key had been standing not five minutes before was now overflowing with water, the tile surrounding the sink a growing lake of piss-colored water. His natural inclination was to turn the faucet off and conserve the water, but then he thought about where he was standing; thought about how just up the street there used to be groves of orange trees that grew wild from the water in the soil that had, nevertheless, been ripped up and paved over; thought about the chimpanzee and gorilla that lived in a cage next to that jungle restaurant on Raymond back when he was a kid and how no one seemed to give a shit that it wasn't in the least bit natural; thought about how nothing in this place has ever lasted, how it's always been a course of destruction and concrete gentrification. And what did that produce? Nothing came out looking any better, Cooperman thought. No one had figured out a way to make the Marriott across the street from campus as pretty as the citrus trees that once lived in the same spot. No, Cooperman decided as he walked back out into the furnace of the late afternoon, the faucet still going strong behind him, no one ever recognized the ripples.

THE INDIGNITY OF teaching at Cal State Fullerton extended beyond indignant students and keeping a clock. On top of it all, William Cooperman, who'd invented the most technologically advanced piece of sprinkler machinery ever, who thought he should be held up as a paragon of conservation and awareness in this new "go green" world, who'd figured out how to grow marijuana in an environmentally sound way that actually heightened the effectiveness of the THC in ways that could probably help a lot of cancer patients (and in fact, that was what Cooperman had always thought he'd use as his alibi when he was finally busted, that he was growing a mountain of weed in his backyard as a public service to those poor souls with inoperable tumors and such), *"the* William Cooperman," as his ex used to call him, had to share an office.

It was up on the second floor of McCarthy Hall and overlooked the Quad. During the term, it wasn't such a bad view. Cooperman even sort of liked sitting at his desk and watching the students milling back and forth. As long as he didn't have to teach the students, he liked the idea of them, of their determination to learn, their enthusiasm for stupid things like baseball and basketball tournaments, their silly hunger strikes protesting fee hikes. Back in the 1970s, riot police beat the shit out of students in that quad, but now things were much more civil. Protest was just as cyclical as the tides and, in a bizarre way, it comforted Cooperman during the school year. It also made the prospect of sharing his space with *fostering* Professor

James Kochel less offensive since there was something to occupy his vision other than Kochel's collection of "family" photos, all of which were of cocker spaniels and shots of the geology professor in various biblical locales.

In the summer, however, it was just the two of them with no view to speak of, since the students who liked to protest and march and rally in the Quad typically avoided summer session. Cooperman didn't know where they went and didn't really care, but the loneliness of the campus this evening made him nervous as he walked from the faculty parking lot to McCarthy. He paused in the Quad and looked up the length of the building to see if his office light was on, and sure enough he could see Kochel moving about. Cooperman found it strangely comforting, especially since he'd left his gun in the car, figuring he'd just run upstairs, grab his laptop, maybe heist a few other laptops from open offices since they'd be easy to sell along the way, and then . . . *get ghost*. Bringing a gun onto the campus might awaken his worst traits, a likely scenario since he was supposed to be teaching another class within the hour, and that meant a few students might show up early wanting to *talk*.

He hadn't figured out where, precisely, he was going but had a vague notion that the Pacific Northwest would be a hospitable place for the world's finest weed grower, sort of liked the idea of finding himself in Eugene or Olympia or Longview or Kelso, particularly since he'd spent the last few hours liquidating his bank accounts and now had $40,000 in cash stowed in the Escalade, a couple RD-2001s, and, finally, a reason to leave. The idea of living in constant rain had a sudden and visceral appeal, and it astonished Cooperman that he hadn't thought of living in Oregon or Washington previously. He liked apples as much as oranges.

Cooperman climbed the two flights of stairs up to his office.

He was surprised by how light he felt, how clarity had lessened the weight of all this crap. It wasn't just about water anymore; it was about living a more principled life. He'd stood for one thing for a very long time, and what had it earned him? Cash, of course, but in the end no one cared that he possessed the key to saving the world. What good was being a superhero if no one respected your powers?

Proof was right in front of him, even: Professor Kochel's nameplate was above his on the little slider beside their office door. Respect was dead, so fuck it to death. *Maybe I'll get that inked on my neck in Old English*, Cooperman thought. *Fuck it to Death.*

"There you are," Kochel said when Cooperman finally opened the office door.

"Have you been looking for me?"

"Your phone has been ringing constantly. I took some messages for you." Kochel handed Cooperman a stack of Post-it Notes. The first was from Monica Williard, another was from Enterprise Rent-A-Car—a problem Cooperman hadn't quite taken care of yet—and another still that had one word on it: *Bongo.*

"What did Monica Williard want?"

"Lovely girl, isn't she? So bright."

"What did she want?" Cooperman heard a new tone entering his voice. He liked it. Thought it made him sound like the kind of guy who just might have some neck ink.

"Candidly? I think she's upset about your afternoon class."

"Did you talk to her?"

"Briefly. She indicated to me that she just wasn't satisfied in the level of teaching. It's no reflection on you, William, I'm sure."

"I'm sure."

"I've had Monica in other courses and she's just very particular," Kochel said. He had a look of smug satisfaction on his face that

Cooperman recognized as the same face he used when he talked about how his faith in Christ allowed him to see that many of the great mysteries of science were merely God's way of testing us.

"Someone named Bongo called?"

"Oh, yes, sorry," Kochel said. "That's what the name sounded like. I could barely hear him."

"He say anything?"

"It was very strange," Kochel said. "I thought maybe it was a wrong number. All he said was to tell you that he couldn't get you twenty-four anymore. I have no idea what that means. Do you?"

Cooperman looked out the window and down at the Quad, half expected to see an army of men already massed. But it was empty except for a lost seagull picking through an overflowing trash can. It was still sunny out, would be for another hour and a half, two hours, not that it probably mattered. The more frightening aspect was that Cooperman couldn't remember ever giving Bongo his office phone number.

This was not good.

"No," Cooperman said. "Must have been a wrong number."

"Anyway," Kochel said, "you should really ask for voicemail in the fall."

"I won't be here," Cooperman said. He was still looking out the window but wasn't sure what he was hoping to find. Something or someone that seemed out of place. Like a guy walking around with a MAC-10. Across the Quad, a black SUV pulled up in front of Pollak Library. A man holding a stack of paper walked out of the Performing Arts Center. A gust of wind through the breezeway picked up a Starbucks cup from the ground. What he wouldn't give for the Quad to suddenly fill with riot police.

"No?"

"I've been offered a job back in the sprinkler industry," Cooperman said.

"It really is a despicable profession, if you must know," Kochel said. "From a geological and religious standpoint, if you must know."

"Tell me about it," Cooperman said, and Kochel did, at length, somehow winding it all up in a rant that included the mainstream media, Muslims, globalism, globalists, Bill and Hilary Clinton, and the need to return to the gold standard.

The Starbucks cup hovered in the air and then fell and then was swooped up again in another gust. Wind technology. Maybe that's where he'd make his second wave.

"What time did this Bongo call?" Cooperman asked when Kochel eventually ran out of righteous steam.

"*Please* opens more doors."

Cooperman turned from the window and found Kochel staring at him in beatific glory. Why had he left his gun in the car? A dumb mistake, really. But he wasn't used to being the kind of person who was always packing, at least not on campus. "What time, Professor Kochel," Cooperman said, his voice finding an even deeper register than before, "did this fucking message come in, please, before I put your hand in the paper shredder?"

"Ten minutes ago," Kochel said. "Okay? Ten minutes ago."

"Thank you," Cooperman said. He fixed his gaze back out the window. A man got out of the backseat of the SUV in front of Pollak and walked in a semicircle, a cell phone pressed to his ear. Cooperman couldn't make out much from his vantage point but could see just from watching his body language that the guy was confused about something. It was probably nothing.

"If you want my opinion," Kochel said, as if Cooperman had just asked him a question, "you might want to look into anger management courses. Your attitude will be a real detriment in a corporate environment. Not everyone is as easygoing as I am. You get back with a bunch of MBAs and those egos, well, I'm just saying it might be a bad fit."

The man from the car was walking toward McCarthy now, his cell phone in his hand. He looked like his head was on a swivel—looking this way, that way, back behind him—and when Cooperman looked back to the library, the SUV was gone.

"I'll work on that," Cooperman said.

"I know this isn't your speed, Will, but you might also start thinking about your relationship with the Lord."

"That sounds like a good idea," Cooperman said. The man was in the middle of the Quad now, and Cooperman could finally make him out more completely. He was older—maybe fifty—and wore white slacks and a black shirt, had on wraparound black sunglasses, nice shoes. Cooperman thought he was maybe Mexican but couldn't really tell. Had Bongo mentioned a cousin?

It didn't matter. Cooperman was getting the fuck out while he still could. He grabbed his laptop, a few books that meant something to him—*Forest Hydrology* and *Groundwater Hydrology*. He tucked everything into his messenger bag while keeping an eye out the window. The man was on the move again now, his pace more brisk, his direction clear.

"And anyway," Kochel was saying, and Cooperman realized his office mate hadn't ever stopped talking, was actually quite animated about something, "what you might find out is that everything has consequences, Will."

Cooperman turned to Kochel and studied him seriously. He didn't hate Kochel, didn't really think about him on a regular basis, though he never enjoyed being around him. It wasn't only the religion that bothered him. It was Kochel's presumption that he was always right. "You know, this is all very fascinating. I'd like to learn even more about this, James. Can we continue this conversation after I get back from my car?"

Kochel brightened. "Of course, of course, I'll be right here."

Cooperman took one last look outside before he exited his office, saw that the man was now only twenty yards or so from the building, and closing fast.

Professor William Cooperman stepped out of his office and closed the door lightly behind him. No panic, no fear in the least, just a person skipping out of his office, just a person, just anyone at all. He looked down the hallway and saw that a few students were loitering down by the vending machines, another couple were lined up in front of the photocopier, two were sitting on the floor in front of his classroom reading from their textbooks. None of them bothered to look at Cooperman, so they didn't notice him slipping Professor James Kochel's nameplate out of the slider and into his messenger bag, though Cooperman did pause for a moment before exiting out the back of the building, to look at his own name. He liked how it looked on the slider by itself, thought that it looked esteemed and powerful and worthy of respect.

THE SALT

B eneath the water, beneath time, beneath yesterday, is the salt.
The paper says that another body has washed up on the
north shore of the Salton Sea, its age the provenance of anthropologists. "Washed up" is a misnomer, of course, because nothing is
flowing out of the Salton Sea this winter of interminable heat: it's
January 10, thirteen years into a century I never thought I'd see,
and the temperature hovers near 100 degrees. The Salton Sea is re-
ceding back into memory, revealing with each inch another year,
another foundation, another hand that pulls from the sand and
grasps at the dead air. Could be the bodies are from Tom Sander-
son's family plot, first swallowed by the sea in 1971, or perhaps it
is Woodrow East's girlfriend, risen up from the muck at long last,
or maybe it is my sweet Katharine, delivered back to me in rusted
bone.

I fold the newspaper and set it down on my lap. Through the
living room window I see Rebecca, my wife of seven months, prun-
ing her roses. They are supposed to be dormant by now, she told
me yesterday, and that they are alive and flowering is nothing short
of a miracle. Much is miraculous to Rebecca: we met at the cancer
treatment center in Rancho Mirage a little over a year ago, both of
us bald and withered, our lives clinging to a chemical cocktail.

"How long did they give you?" she asked.

"Nothing specific," I said. The truth was my doctor told me that I had a year, possibly less, but that at my age the script was likely to be without too many twists: I'd either live or I wouldn't. And after spending every afternoon for three months hooked to an IV, I wasn't sure if that was completely accurate. What kind of life was this that predicated itself on waiting?

"I'm already supposed to be dead," she said.

"You should buy a lottery ticket," I said.

She rummaged in her purse and pulled out a handful of stubs and handed them to me. "Pick out one you like, and if you win, we'll split it."

We live together behind a gate in Indian Wells, and our backyard abuts a golf course that my knees won't allow me to play on and that my checkbook can't afford. My yearly pension from the Granite City Sheriff's Department is more suited for the guard gate than the country club. But Rebecca comes from money, or at least her ex-husband did, and so here we are living out the bonus years together. At least Rebecca's hair has grown back.

I pick up the newspaper and try not to read the stories on the front page, the colored bar graph that details the Salton Sea's water levels from 1906 until present day, the old photos of speedboat races I can remember, the black bag that holds a human form, the telephone poles jutting out of the placid water, the quotes from environmentalists decrying the ecological disaster of California's fetid inland sea. *Almost $9.8 billion to preserve it, saving it is out of the question. If we let it go any further, all that will be left in fifty years is a toxic dust bowl, blowing disease from here to Los Angeles.* I try to read page A-3, where the local news stories are housed safely out of sight from passing tourists: *A broken water pipe has closed the Ralphs in Palm Springs. A dead body found in Joshua Tree identified* *as a missing hiker from Kansas. Free flu shots for seniors at Eisen-hower Medical Center.*

"Morris," Rebecca says. "Are you feeling all right?"

I see that Rebecca is standing only a few inches from me, worry etched on her face like sediment. "I'm fine," I say. "When did you come in?"

"I've been standing here talking to you and you haven't even looked up from the paper," she says.

"I didn't hear you," I say.

"I know that," she says. "You were talking to yourself. It would be impossible for you to hear me over your own conversation." Rebecca smiles, but I can see that she's worried.

"I'm an old man," I say.

She leans down, takes my face in her hands, and runs her thumbs along my eyes. "You're just a boy," Rebecca says, and I realize she's wiping tears from my face. "Why don't you ever talk to me about your first wife? I know living out here triggers memories. It wouldn't bother me, Morris. It would make me feel closer to you."

"That was another life," I say.

"Apparently not," she says.

"She's been gone a long time," I say, "but sometimes it just creeps back on me and it's like she's just in the other room, but I can't seem to figure out where that room is. And then I look up and my new wife is wiping tears from my face."

"I'm not your new wife," Rebecca says, standing back up. "I'm your last wife."

"You know what I mean," I say.

"Of course I do," Rebecca says.

The fact of the matter, I think after Rebecca has walked back outside, is that with each passing day I find my mind has begun to recede like the Sea, and each morning I wake up feeling like I'm younger, like time is flowing backward, that eventually I'll open my eyes and it will be 1962 again and life will feel filled with possibility. What is obvious to me, and what my neurologist confirmed a few weeks ago, but which I haven't bothered to share with Rebecca, is that my brain is shedding space; soon all that will be left is the past, my consciousness doing its best imitation of liquefaction.

I go into the bedroom and change into a pair of khaki pants, a buttoned-down shirt, and a ball cap emblazoned with the logo of our country club. In the closet, I take down the shoe box where I keep my gun and ankle holster and for a long time I just look at them both, wondering what the hell I'm thinking, what the hell I hope to prove after fifty years, what exactly I think I'll find out there by the shore of that rotting sea but ghosts and sand.

Dead is still dead.

I FIND REBECCA in the front yard. She's chatting with our next-door neighbors, Sue and Leon. Last week, Leon wandered out in the night and stood on the fifteenth fairway shouting obscenities. By the time I was able to coax him into my golf cart he'd stripped off all of his clothes and was masturbating furiously, sadly to no avail. That's the tragedy of getting old and losing your mind—that switch flips and everything that's been sitting limply beside you starts perking up again, but you can't figure out exactly how to work it. Today, he's smiling and happy and seems to have a general idea about his whereabouts but is blissfully unaware of who he is, or who any of us are.

"I can't thank you enough for the other night," Sue says when I walk up.

"It's nothing," I say.

"He was happy to do it," Rebecca says. "Anytime you need help, really, we're just right here."

"His medication . . . Well, you know how it is. You have to get it regulated. I wish you'd known him before all of this," Sue says, waving her hands dismissively, and then, just like that, she's sobbing. "Oh, it's silly. We get old, don't we, Rebecca? We just get old and next thing you know, you're gone."

Leon used to run some Fortune 500 company that made light fixtures for casinos. They called him The King of Lights, or at least that's what he told me in one of his more lucid moments. But today he's just a dim bulb and I can't help but think of how soon I'll be sitting right there next to him at the loony bin, drooling on myself and letting some orderly wipe my ass. Part of me wonders if forgetting wouldn't be so bad, if maybe I'd get a decent night of rest for the first time since the 1950s. And then another part of me wonders what it was all worth if it can just slide off the back side of my brain into nothingness. All the sorrow, all the joy, all the fear, all the hope, and in the end, you're left with blackness? It hardly seems right.

"I have to run out," I say to Rebecca once Leon and Sue have made their way back to their condo.

"I could clean up and come with you," she says. "It would just take a moment."

"Don't bother," I say. "I'm just gonna drive out to the Salton Sea. See what's going on down there. Talk a little shop."

"Morris," she says, "if I go inside and look in the closet, will I find your gun there?"

"I'm afraid not," I say.

"You're a fool to be running around with that thing."

We stand there staring at each other for a solid minute until

Rebecca turns heel and walks inside. She doesn't bother to slam the front door, which makes it worse.

TO GET TO the Salton Sea, I drove east through La Quinta and Indio and Coachella on Highway 111, even though I could have taken I-10 and arrived a little faster. The 111 used to be the only way out to the Imperial Valley, Indio the last real bit of town before the desert gave way to date groves and farmlands. Even now, the desert reclaims itself for the last twenty miles before the great mirage: a sea where no sea should be.

I'm standing on the other side of a stretch of yellow caution tape, though this isn't a crime scene, watching as a rental security officer stands guard over a patch of dirt while two young women and a man wearing one of those safari vests and a pair of ironed cargo pants brush rocks and debris away from a depression in the earth. The Salton Sea laps at the edge of the sand, the stench rising from it as thick as mustard gas. The two women and the man are all wearing medical-grade N95 face masks, but the security guard just keeps a handkerchief to his face while in the other hand he clutches a clipboard. It's not the body that smells—it's the sea, rotting with dead fish; a winter marked by avian cholera; and the aroma of hydrogen sulfide gas wafting from the depths of this vast illusion: the shimmer of this fake ocean is at eye level, giving everything a dreamy resonance. It could be now. It could be never. I might be inside of a dream.

Fifty years ago, this was roughly where Bonnie Livingston had her little bar and café. During the week, the working men would sit at the bar all night drinking the stink out of their skin, but on the weekends the LA people would drive in with their boats and water skis and, eventually, speedboats, and come into Bonnie's looking for authenticity. More often than not, they'd leave without a few teeth and, on occasion, without their girlfriends, wives, or daughters. They thought the Salt would be like an inland riviera. They thought we'd find oil and prosperity and that a city would rise from the fetid desert floor.

Forty years ago, Bonnie's bar slipped into the sea. Thirty-five years ago, Bonnie's home followed suit. Shortly thereafter Bonnie followed her bar and house, simply walking into the water with a bottle of wine in her hand, drinking big gulps all along the way. Her entire family watched her walk into the sea, bricks tied around her ankles. It wasn't a suicide, her son wrote to tell me, because she'd been dead for at least three years, but more a celebration of the Salt. Of all the things that return to it.

At some point, however, memory becomes insufficient in the face of commerce and space. These bodies that keep pulling themselves from the sea are a hindrance to something larger and more important than an old man's past: real estate.

The Chuyalla Indians intend to put a twenty-six-floor hotel and casino here and then, in five years, one hundred condos.

Never mind the chemicals that still leach from the sand, the result of World War II B-29s test-dumping dummy atomic bombs into the Sea and across the desolate sand of the surrounding beachfront. Pretending this nowhere was Hiroshima, never thinking it would become somewhere. The next dozen years, the Salton Sea was the site of hundreds of ballistic tests and war games, the scraps of bombs leaving depleted uranium thick in the ground, back before cleaning such things up was much of a priority.

I became the law here a few years later.

We were told nothing, until people kept dying.

But of course people are always dying.

The government said they cleaned it all up in the nineties, but now the people still foolish enough to try to live beside this environmental disaster are showing up with innovative cancers, endocrinological disorders, and intestinal bacteria only found in Chernobyl. Problem is the people who live out here aren't the kind of people to call their congressmen. So every few months, a twenty-five-year-old reporter from the *Desert Sun* gets a phone call and rolls out to check on the rumors and for a week or two, it's a story . . . but then Coachella starts, or the big tennis tournament in Indian Wells, or President Obama visits, and the sick and the aggrieved, a blemish to the east, are forgotten again. Which is how everyone wants it.

Nevertheless, the Chuyalla intend to fund a project that will eradicate the blight and once again tempt the folly of beachside living in the middle of the desert.

I'll be gone by then. Or at least without the ability to know the difference.

The security guard finally notices me and ambles over, his gait slow and deliberate, as if traversing the twenty feet from the body to the tape was the most difficult task of his life. "Can I help you?" he asks, not bothering to remove the handkerchief from his face. I'd guess that he's just a shade under sixty, too old for real police work, which probably makes this the perfect job for him.

"Just came down to see the excitement," I say. I open my wallet and show him my retired sheriff's card. He looks at it once, nods, and then from out of his back pocket fishes out his wallet and shows me *his* retirement card from the Yuma, Arizona, PD. His name is Ted Farmer and he then explains, as former cops are apt to do, the exact path he took from being a real cop to a rental cop. When he runs out of story, he turns his attention back to the body in the sand.

"Yep," he says, motioning his head in the direction of the grave.

"Lotta fireworks. My opinion? They should just leave the bodies where they are. No sake digging them up just to move them somewhere else." One of the female anthropologists carries a hand and wrist over to a white plastic sheet and sets them down across from another hand and wrist. "That first hand? Still had rings on it. That sorta thing messes with your head. It's dumb, I know. Lady's probably been dead fifty, one hundred years, more fertilizer than person. But still."

"In my experience," I say, "hands are pretty durable."

About two hundred yards from the shore a small aluminum boat with a screaming outboard motor trolls back and forth. I can just make out the outline of a shirtless man sitting at one end, a little boy at the other, a long fishing pole bent between them. I can hear Katharine in the whine. *You know, the water doesn't know where it is, it only knows it is beautiful. It doesn't see the ruin around it. Those are blinders I wouldn't mind wearing.*

When she passed, I gave her that.

I look now at the bones being sluiced from the ground and know, of course, that it's not Katharine. Oh, but she is here, holding my hand as we walk from Bonnie's and dip our toes into the water, the air alive with laughter behind us, music wafting through the thick summer air, Chuck Berry singing "Johnny B. Good" into eternity. Her hair is pulled back from her face and she's wearing a V-neck white T-shirt, her tanned skin darkening the fabric just slightly, a scent of vanilla lifting from her skin. It's 1962. It's 1963. It's today or it's yesterday or it's tomorrow.

"You okay, pal?" Farmer says. I look down and see that he's got a hand on my chest, steadying me. "Drifting a bit to stern there."

"Not used to the heat anymore," I say, though the truth is I feel fine. Though my perception is dipping sideways, it does not bother me. Seeing the past like a ghost is a welcome part of my new condition, and if it brings with it a few disorienting side effects, I suppose I'm willing to make the trade. Farmer fetches me an unused bucket from aside the dig, turns it over, and directs me to sit. After the horizon has straightened out, I say, "I used to be the law out here, if you can believe that."

"When was that?"

"About a million years ago," I say. "Or fifteen minutes ago."

Farmer winces noticeably, like he knows what I mean. We watch the anthropologists going about their work. It becomes clear after a while that the two young women are students—graduate students, most likely—and that the man in the funny vest is the professor. Every few minutes he gathers their attention and explains something pertaining to what they've found. At one point, he goes back to the white plastic sheet and lifts up a leg they've pried from the earth and makes sure his students have made note of an abnormality in the femur, a dent of some kind.

"You know what I think?" Farmer says. "Guys like us, we've seen too much crazy shit, our brains don't have enough room to keep it all. Pretty soon it just starts leaking out."

"You're probably right," I say.

"I guess I've seen over a hundred dead bodies," he says. "Not like this here, but people who were alive ten minutes before I got to them. Traffic accidents and such, sometimes I'd get called out on a murder, but I was mostly a low-hanging-fruit cop, if you know what I mean. I tell you, there's something about the energy surrounding a dead body, you know? Like a dog, it can just walk by, take a sniff, and keep going. Us, we got all that empathy. What I wouldn't give to not have that."

"You ever kill a guy?" I ask.

"Jesus no," he says. "I pulled my gun nine times. You?"

"I was in a war," I say. "And for a time, I wasn't a great cop." The truth was that I wasn't really a cop when I was out here. Working for Claxson gave me power, but not authority, a symbol, like a noose looking for a hangman. In Granite City, when I became sheriff, I was better. When I could be. "Comes down to it, you begin to wonder if the badge is just an excuse to be the worst kind of person."

"I'm sure you did what you had to do."

"*Had*? Maybe. Maybe. You know, Ted, you got lucky. I wish I'd never seen a gun."

The two women lift the trunk of the body up out of the dirt. There's still bits of fabric stuck to the ribcage, and my first thought is of those old pirate books I used to read as a kid, where the hero would find himself on a deserted island with just the clothed skeletons of previous plunderers lining the beach. How old was I when I read those books? Eight? Nine? I can still see my father sitting on the edge of my bed while I read aloud to him, how the dim light on my bedside table would cast a shadow across his face, so that all I could make out was his profile. He was already a sheriff, already knew about empathy, had spent a few sleepless nights on the beginnings and endings of people he'd never know, though he was only twenty-eight or twenty-nine himself. Thirty-five years he's been gone. You never stop being somebody's child, even when you can see the end of the long thread. Maybe that's really what Rebecca finds absent; it's not Katharine that calls to me in the night, even when the night is as bright as day, it's all that I've lost: my father, my mother, my brother Jack, who passed before I was even born, but whose presence I was always aware of, as if I lived a life for him, too. My second wife, Margaret, and the children we never managed to have. My younger brother Conrad, who has been absent in my life for thirty years, because Margaret had once been his girlfriend, a slight he never recovered from. How many friends of mine are gone? All of them, even if they are still alive. And here, in the winter soil of the Salton Sea, the air buttressed by an ungodly heat, I remember the ghosts of another life, still. These bodies that keep appearing could be mine.

I tell myself it's just land. My mind has ascribed emotion to a mere parcel of a planet. It's the very duplicity of existence that plays with an old man's mind, particularly when you can see regret in a tangible form alongside the spectral one that visits periodically.

"They bother looking for kin?" I ask.

"Oh, sure," Farmer says. He waves his clipboard and for the first time I notice that it's lined with names and dates and addresses. "We got some old records from back when Claxson was out here detailing where a few family plots are and such. Claxson kept pretty good record of who came and went, but this place has flooded and receded so many times, you can't be sure where these bodies are from. Back then, people died, they just dug a hole and slid them in, seems like."

"That's about right," I say.

"Anyway, we get a couple visitors a week, like yourself."

"I'm just out for a drive," I say.

"What did you say your name was?"

"Morris Drew," I say.

Farmer flips a few pages, running his finger down the lines of names, and then pauses. "I'm sorry," he says quietly.

"So am I," I say.

I DRIVE SOUTH along the beaten access road that used to run behind the marina but now is covered in ruts and divots, the pavement long since cracked and weathered away, plant life and shrubs growing between bits of blacktop. Back when Claxson Oil still believed life could take place here, they built the infrastructure to sustain a population of one hundred thousand, so beneath the desert floor there's plumbing and power lines waiting to be used, a city of coils and pipes to carry subsistence to a casino, one hundred condominiums, tourists from Japan. They'll bring in alien vegetation to gussy up the desert, just as they have outside my home on the twelfth hole; they'll install sprinklers to wash away the detritus of fifty years of emptiness. There are maybe six hundred people living permanently around the Salton Sea, Ted Farmer told me, more if you count the meth addicts and Vietnam and Gulf War vets out in Slab City, the former Marine Corps base that became a squatter's paradise.

I stop my car when I see the shell of the old Claxson barracks rising up a few hundred yards in the distance. To the east, a flock of egrets have landed on the sea, their slim bodies undulating in the water just beyond the shoreline. They've flown south for the winter but probably didn't realize they'd land in the summer. I can make out the noise from the lone boat on the water.

The barracks themselves are a Swiss cheese of mortar and drywall, to the point that even from this distance I can see the sparse traffic on Highway 86 through their walls, as if a newsreel from the future has been projected onto the past. Farmer warned me not to go into the old building, that transients, drug addicts, and illegals frequently use it for scavenging and business purposes.

It's not the barracks that I'm interested in; they merely provide a map for my memory. It's 1962 and I'm parked in my new Corvair, Katharine by my side, and we're scanning the scrub for the view she wants. It's not the topography that she cares about; it's the angle of the sun. She tells me that anyone can have a view of the mountains, anyone can have a view of the sea, but after living in the Pacific Northwest her entire life, she desired a view of the sun. She wanted a morning room that would be flooded in natural light at dawn, that would be dappled in long shadows in the afternoon, that at night would glow white from the moon. All my life I've lived in clouds, she said, I think I deserve a view of the sun. She got out of the Corvair right about *here*, I think, and she walked out into the desert, striding through the tangles of brush and sand while I watched her from the front seat. She was so terribly young, just twenty-three, but I know she felt like she'd already lived a good portion of her life out. Still, she always told me that she envied the experiences I'd had already in life, that she wished she could see Asia as I had, wished that she knew what it felt like to hold a gun with malice, because to her that was the thing about me that was most unknowable.

Late at night, she'd wake me and ask what it felt like to kill someone, to know that there was another family, somewhere in North Korea, who didn't have a father. She didn't ask this in anger, she said, only that it was the sort of thing that kept her awake at night, knowing that the man sleeping beside her, the man she loved, had killed. I'd find Katharine dead long before I was able to give her a satisfying answer. And still, when I wake in the night, I often search for her in bed, only to find Rebecca there, a woman I do love, a woman who has chosen to die with me at my least. Which is a different kind of love, a choice for near sorrow. When I did find Katharine, mere yards from where I stand, I made promises that would result in a viscous loss of self that would turn me into something foreign and angry. And when I saw Katharine last, though she was long gone, I would see her in the moonlit glow of the Salton Sea, her body slipping between my hands into the deep, murky waters.

I step out of the car and there's Katharine, her face turned to the sun, motioning for me to join her, to see what she sees. She calls out for me to hurry to the spot that will be our home. Did this happen? I'm not sure anymore, but at this moment it is true. Surrounding me are nearly a dozen old foundations, this tract of desert bifurcated by the phantom remains of paved roads and cul-de-sacs. From above, I imagine the land surrounding the old barracks must look like a petroglyph left by an ancient civilization.

I triangulate myself with the sea, the mountain, and the barracks and then close my eyes and walk forward, allowing my sense memory to guide me, to find the cement that was my home. But it's useless: I trip over a tumbleweed and nearly fall face-first into the ground. *Sweet Christ*, I think, *it's lucky I didn't break my hip.* How long would it be before anyone found me? With the heat as it is, I'd die from exposure before Rebecca noticed that we'd missed the early bird at Sherman's Deli. So instead I walk from foundation to foundation, hoping that the layout of the Claxson Oil Executive Housing Unit makes itself clear. I picture the payroll manager, Gifford Lewis, and his wife, Lois, sitting on their patio drinking lemonade, their baby frolicking between them in a playpen. I picture Jeff Morton, sitting in his backyard, strumming a guitar he didn't know how to play. I picture Sassy, the Jefferieses' cocker spaniel, running across the street to our scratch of grass, her tail wagging in a furious motion. I picture myself leaning down to pet Sassy and the way the dog would lick up the length of my arm, her tongue rough and dry from the heat and how I would step inside and get a water bowl for the dog, and that the dog would sit and wait patiently for my return and then would lap up the water in a fuss, drops of water flying from the bowl and catching hits of sun. I see Jim and Gloria Connelly, pulling away from us in their nearly empty station wagon, leaving behind every damned and ruined thing for me to fix.

I try to see the world as it was and as it is now, try to find what used to be my home, what used to be my life, try to locate the Fourth Estate of my memory: a dry reporting of fact. You lived *here.* You slept *there.* You made love and you witnessed death and you mourned and you buried your wife in the simple plot Claxson provided and allowed behind your home and you carried your wife's corpse—because that's what it was, it wasn't a body anymore, not with the dirt and the sand and absence of any kind of reality, any kind of relevance beyond what you'd emotionally ascribed to it—to the sea, because that was what she asked of you, not to allow her to rot in the desert, but to give her a perpetual view of the sun and the water, to let her float free. That is *across the way.* And you see the end of your own life, don't you? You feel the creeping dread that you've beaten that same slow poison yourself but have found another, more insidious invader. And what will you do about it, Morris Drew? Why did you bring that gun with you?

WHEN I GET back home, I find Rebecca sitting on our back patio, her eyes buried in a magazine, golf carts moving in a steady stream past her as dusk has begun to fall. She doesn't see me, so for a time I just stare at her. I imagine what she might look like with the fine lines around her eyes smooth, her gray hair blond, her skin thick and healthy instead of thin and stretched like parchment. The trauma of memory is that it never forgives you for aging. What would Katharine look like to me today? Would she be an old woman or would she be young in my eyes, always twenty-three years old? The other trauma of memory is that it can absolve you of reality if you let it, and the reality is that I've come to love other women, finally, a fact I'm not ashamed of.

"I'm home," I say.

"I know," Rebecca says, not looking up.

"I didn't know if you heard me come in," I say.

"Morris," she says, turning pages, "your footfalls have the delicacy of a jackhammer. There are no secrets between tile floors and you."

I sit down beside Rebecca and put my arm around her and pull her close. I see the young woman she must have been. I've seen photos, of course, but you never truly see someone in a photo. You see what they looked liked, but not who they were. Fear shows you all the colors in a person's skin.

I reach down and lift up my pant leg and show her my empty holster. "I almost killed myself today. I'm not proud of that, but I wanted you to know that it won't happen again."

"Jesus, Morris," she says.

"I threw that gun into the Salton Sea," I say, "even said some prayers over it. I'm not gonna let it take me from you."

I know that if I look down I'll find Rebecca crying, so I stare instead at the long shadows crawling into the bunkers on either side of the twelfth hole, at the last glimmers of sunlight that eke over the rim of the San Jacinto Mountains, at the green shards of grass that grow just beyond our patio. I watch as lights flicker on inside the condos across the fairway from us and I think that where I am now, at this very moment, with my wife beside me, with a hint of cool in the breeze that has swept by me, the smell of jasmine light on its trail, *this* is the memory I want to live out the rest of my years with. A moment of perfection when I knew a kind of contentment with who I was and what I'd tried so desperately to forget. I am not surprised when a strong gust of wind picks up from the east and I make out the faint scent of the Salt, pungent and lost and far, far away.

RAGTOWN

oesn't matter where in the world he is, February 11 rolls around,
Jacob Dmitrov gets a phone call from Las Vegas Metro Detective
Tiffany Peng. Today, he's at Odessa, his restaurant over on Paradise,
a couple blocks from the Hard Rock.

"I'm not bothering you, am I?" Detective Peng asks.

"Lunch rush won't be for another thirty minutes or so," he says.
"Didn't think I'd be hearing from you this year."

"Oh, you read the paper?"

"Every morning," Jacob says.

"Print?"

"Yeah," Jacob says. "I like to spread it out on the table while I eat
my breakfast. Read every page. Been like that my entire life."

"I wouldn't have pegged you for a guy who keeps up with the
news," she says.

"I was real sorry to hear about what went down." There'd been a
bank robbery in Summerlin. Three assholes with AR-15s and M203s,
fucking grenade launchers. *Review-Journal* said Detective Peng was
one of the first responders. It went bad. Three dead cops, a dead police dog, five dead civilians, plus two of the bank robbers. Third guy
made off with $4,000. Police were still looking for him. Way Jacob
figured, dude was probably already dead from embarrassment. Get

all those people killed for four grand? "Thing I didn't understand: Who shoots a dog?"

"Same person who shoots a cop," Detective Peng says.

"So you're still in the hospital?"

"Another week or so," she says. Jacob thinks "or so" is the more likely outcome. Every word she says sounds like it's coming from somewhere near her knees.

"Which one?"

"Sunrise. You're not thinking of coming to visit, are you?"

"Let me send over a peasant pie. Everyone loves our peasant pies."

"Gonna be a while before I'm eating solid food, Mr. Dmitrov. But maybe my brother would eat it."

"Well," he says, "when you're up and around, you come on down to Odessa and we'll do you up, okay?"

"I just may take you up on that," she says. "And Mr. Dmitrov? She would have been thirty-six today." Detective Peng coughs. Then coughs some more. When she's done, Jacob can hear her gasping for breath, but still, she hangs on the line. So Jacob says, "Where'd you get hit, if you don't mind me asking?"

"Stomach," she says, "right shoulder, right leg. Left foot. Doctors took that. Couple other places."

"What do you mean 'took that'?"

"Shooter basically blew my foot off," she says. "Doctors just finished the job."

"I'm sorry," he says. He really is. Eighteen years of phone calls. Eighteen years of Detective Peng showing up at his home, at his restaurant, once at Stateline to check the contents of his trunk, she's always been straight-up. Just doing her job. "Well, get some rest, Detective."

Detective Peng is silent but doesn't hang up. They're both waiting. "One day," she says, eventually, "you're going to wake up in a
cell, Jacob." There it is. Same as ever. But then she says, "It's me, it's
someone else, that's what's coming. Do what's right, Jacob. Jesus. Do
what's right."

"Get better now, Tiffany," Jacob says, and hangs up.

ODESSA DOESN'T EVER close. Midnight to nine a.m., everything
on the menu is under five bucks. It's been like that since Jacob's dad,
Boris, opened the place in 1980. Jacob took over in 2003, after his
dad got sent up for ten years on some RICO shit, ended up dying in
prison of pancreatitis two years short of getting out. Jacob's adjusted
the overnight menu so that it's not just food from the Old Country,
so as to get more people in the door. You can get still get borscht or
goulash or bigos, but now there's also steak and eggs, French toast,
a Monte Cristo. Plus, whatever the strippers and soldiers and cops
want. Pizza? Tacos? Peanut butter and jelly? Done. Long as no one
acts up. Odessa is neutral ground after midnight.

Which is why it wasn't so unusual to see Gang Unit Detective
Cecil Kiraly eating a plate of eggs and potatoes at 1:17 a.m. in the
bar, a week after Detective Peng's annual call. Jacob's known Kiraly
since high school. Bishop Gorman class of 1989. The two of them sat
on the bench for four years of baseball and football. Kiraly went on
to UNLV, then the academy, worked as a beat cop, did some time
in vice and homicide before settling down in the gang unit, where
the real action was. If you wanted to work murders but didn't want
to care too much about the dead, gang unit was the perfect place
to be. But the bigger issue was that it kept a local like Cecil from
arresting his friends. Get to a certain age, you don't even know the
OGs anymore.

Jacob grabbed a stool and slid in next to him.

"There he is," Kiraly says. "The Putin of Paradise Road."

"Easy with that shit," Jacob says. His cousin Svetlana, who works the bar, drops off a bottle of Stoli, two shot glasses. "You still on the clock?"

Kiraly looks at his phone. "Another forty minutes," he says, but then he turns the phone off.

Jacob pours two shots. "To the end of Western civilization," he says, and they toast.

"Putin is very popular with a certain segment of society," Kiraly says. "Maybe change the name of this place to Putin's Odessa. Bet you'd make a million."

"Guys like him are why we left." Not that Jacob has any real memory of the country. His parents got out with him in 1975, when he was four. "No one likes KGB except KGB. And anyway, Odessa is in Ukraine. Putin don't have that yet."

"Your old man know him back in the day?" Kiraly asks.

"No, of course not," Jacob says. It's like this sometimes. People think the USSR was some tiny little town where everyone knew everyone. "My pops was Militsiya. That's actual, real police. Not like you, motherfucker." Jacob pours them both another shot, but neither takes it down right away. Fact is, Jacob can't stand the taste of vodka. Makes not drinking it easy. But the cliché, he's found, makes working in his own restaurant untenable, so he's learned to tolerate it. "Spoke four fucking languages. You believe that? Read all the classics. All that time devoted to those pursuits. All to die in Lovelock, two cells down from O. J."

"You miss him?"

"Sometimes," Jacob says. The *Review-Journal* referred to his father either as "the alleged wiseguy" Boris Dmitrov or "reputed

Russian organized-crime figure" Boris Dmitrov, depending on who was writing the story. "My mom's in one of those memory homes, that's what they call them now. The one up over by the temple in Summerlin? Half the time I go to see her, she thinks I'm him. That brings it back." Svetlana drops off a bowl of cashews, Jacob's favorite. She keeps them behind the bar just for him. It gets the taste of vodka out of his mouth. "But then there's all the other shit."

"That's tough," Kiraly says. "I tell you about my parents?"

"No." Back in school, his dad had worked Metro, too. His mom was just his mom.

"You know my pops retired?"

"Yeah. Few years ago?"

"Right before the election in 2016. Since then, he was doing private security. You know, put on a suit, walk around with some rich fucker while he plays pai gow. Finally got tired of it, moved down to Sarasota. Stroked out dead on a lawn chair two weeks later. Mom drops a bottle of Ambien down her throat the next day. Both of them sixty-nine years old. Could have been a lot of life yet for both of them."

"Jesus, Cecil. When was this?"

"Six, nine months ago," he says. Had it been that long since he'd seen Cecil? Must have been. "Grief makes shit run together, you know? Maybe that was better. Get it all out of the way at once." But then tears start streaming down his face. Jacob waves Svetlana over, gets a couple napkins. "Sorry, Jacob. It's not your problem. Just sneaks up on me." Cecil shakes his head, dabs at his eyes. "Listen, I need to tell you some bad news." He wipes his face with the napkin, examines it, like he thinks he'll find blood. "Tried to get through to this without losing it." He smiles, sadly. "Detective Peng died this morning."

"I just talked to her," Jacob says. He's surprised by his own shock. And by the immediate sense of grief that has descended onto him. Just like them, Tiffany Peng grew up in Las Vegas. Father dealt blackjack at the Rio, her mom was a stenographer at the courthouse. She was two years ahead of Jacob at Bishop Gorman. Did gymnastics, debate team. They hadn't known each other well back then, but she and Kiraly got close working Metro all these years. And sometimes, when she'd call Jacob, they'd talk about old times, too. How it was. How it could be. But by the end, it was always the same: one day, Jacob, you're going to wake up in a cell. "The fuck happened? I thought she was getting better. I sent over a bunch of cookies. Shit. I just talked to her. Like, days ago."

"Infection. Turns out, fucking hospitals are the worst place to be if you've been shot half a dozen times." Kiraly clears his throat and Jacob can tell that the bad news isn't that Peng is dead. Or not the worst news. "Last couple days," he says, quietly, "Harvey B. Curran's been sitting with her."

The one constant thing in the *Review-Journal* was Harvey B. Curran. His beat was organized crime. He wrote gossip columns about the comings and goings of local wiseguys like they were fucking Kardashians. Put out glossy conspiracy-theory books about who really killed 2Pac or Ted Binion. Every couple of years, someone would try to kill him. And then he'd write another book, about who really tried to kill him.

"He can write whatever he wants about my dad," Jacob says. Fact was, it was good for business. If the article mentioned the food, even better.

"I don't think she was talking to him about your pops, " Kiraly says, leaning in close. "Tiffany only worked missing persons. Her entire career. My guess, he's gonna write some hero shit about her in the paper, not that she doesn't deserve it. Then something on the one case she never cracked. You know how he does. He came down and asked to look at the file."

"And they just let him?"

"Jacob," Kiraly said, "you know how it works."

"It's bullshit."

"So take a vacation for a couple weeks. Come back in March. By the time you're back, all anyone will care about is college basketball."

"This scenario," Jacob says, "where is it I go that doesn't make me look suspicious?"

Cecil Kiraly finished off his shot. Turned his phone back on. Gathered his jacket up. Set a twenty on the bar. "How old are you now?"

"Same as you, Cecil. Forty-eight. Why?"

"I've got twenty-five years on the job," he says. "I can walk at any time now. Got the full retirement. It was me? I'd be in San Diego. Great restaurants. Pretty girls. None of this bullshit."

"Is it gonna be you?"

"After what happened to my dad? No. Never. Or maybe tomorrow." Cecil laughed, but it didn't sound to Jacob like he meant it. "Las Vegas isn't for you anymore, Jacob. Maybe it never was. Once I'm gone, you got no one here watching your back. Consider that."

Jacob picked up the twenty, tried to hand it back to Kiraly. "It's on me."

"Keep it," he said. He looked around the restaurant, like he'd never been in it before. Nearly one thirty in the morning on a weeknight and every table was full. Cops, crooks, strippers, prostitutes, Asian tourists who didn't know where the fuck they were eating, party kids glazed from rolling all night, a couple dealers over from the Hard Rock, a couple dealers over from Naked City, too. And yet the place was mostly quiet, everyone in their phones. "I ask you something, you won't take offense?"

"I can't guarantee it."

"Was it better when the mob ran the city? Because it doesn't seem like it could get any worse."

JACOB WAITS TWO days, gets everything at the restaurant in order, and then tells everyone he's going down to Cabo to fish for marlin. Even books the trip. It's a trip he's taken before. No one will think any different, and even if they do, fuck them. Puts Svetlana in charge. Next morning, he packs up his car and heads south on Highway 95 until it meets up with the I-40, west of Needles, and then he slides down into winding back roads for another fifty miles, through what used to be known as the Buckeye Mining District.

A hundred and forty years ago, they found gold and copper here. Little towns popped up with familiar names: Cadiz. Bagdad. Siberia. Klondike. And then all the towns disappeared, along with every ounce of ore, leaving nothing but the haunted shells of industry along rutted-out roads. A twenty-foot-tall headframe. The foundation of the old mercantile. A rotted post office. A car with no tires. Tires with no car. The desert covers everything in these parts in a fine dust the color of dried marrow.

Jacob hasn't been out here in eighteen years, but as time has gone by, he's kept an eye on the region, in case someone decides to develop it, which doesn't seem likely out on the rim of the Mojave National Preserve. The only action happens when someone upstate wants to tap the aquifer that runs beneath Cadiz or when a train running on the old Southern Transcon derails and pictures come floating onto the local news of what looks like the surface of Mars.

Still, once every few weeks, Jacob taps into a VPN on his

computer and looks at the Google Earth pictures of a tiny spot called Ragtown. Google shows it as a dotted line off of Bagdad Chase Road, hard against an outcrop of volcanic rock called Swede Hill. It's all sand and creosote broken up periodically with what looks like finger scratches where primitive roads used to be, the only proof that anyone ever inhabited this place. Other than the fact that this rut of desert has a name at all.

Jacob turns his Lincoln down one of the old roads—it's demarked on either side by haphazard boulders, one of them spray-painted pink at some point, the only way Jacob remembers it at all—but thirty yards in, he comes to the grim realization that if he goes much farther, he might blow out all of his tires. There are shards of broken rock in the road, tipped-over saguaro, odd bits of ancient rusted iron strewn about.

Jacob wonders if all the junk on the road is intentional. If this is where they still take people. And then he thinks about the boulder. Would it still be pink after all this time? Is there someone who comes out here every few months with a spray can and touches it up? Makes sure none of the graves have been disturbed?

Who alive even remembers the things done to this place?

He backs up, parks the Lincoln behind the thickest row of creosote he can find. Not that it matters. He hasn't seen another car in an hour and none since getting off of I-40. If you were out here, you weren't the kind of person looking to make a new friend. Still, he takes his Glock from the glove box. Stuffs it in his waistband. It's been a long time since he's used it. Keeps it in the glove box in case someone from his past rolls up on him. So now he's always strapped. Gets out, pops the trunk, grabs the shovel he packed, and starts toward Swede Hill.

•

WHAT JACOB REMEMBERS, what plays in his mind about that day, looping, evermore: Driving his lowered Honda Civic, Jacob's got a bag of cash in the trunk, didn't count it, but it felt like $100K. Jacob's pretty familiar with how much money weighs. Jacob, he's thirty. Been running his father's errands now for over a decade. Run money here. Pick up guns there. Take a guy to an airstrip outside Elko. Drive a body to the funeral home in Summerlin. Watch to make sure that dumb motherfucker Big Leon actually kills that guy you bound up and tossed in the trunk. If Big Leon lets him go, kill both of them. Not that it ever came to that, because Big Leon, he was into violence. This is also that period of time when Jacob was abusing steroids. Shooting a cocktail in his ass. Gobbling ephedrine like Altoids so he can double-up workouts, getting swollen as shit. Takes to wearing tank tops to show off his tribal tattoos, or sweat suits because his skin always feels like it's on fire, side-effect of the steroids, and sweat-suit material doesn't rub at him. He's got these giant cysts on his back, too. Size of his fists. Boys call him OG Adidas. It's dumb, but he likes it. Makes him feel like he's on *The Sopranos.* It's 2001.

Fool.

Beside him sits his lady. Speaks about a hundred and fifty words of English. She grew up in Russia, got herself adopted by a cocktail waitress about five years ago, moved to Las Vegas. Never really took to the language. She's been working at Odessa as a hostess. Lucky for Jacob he speaks Russian, too. His mom made sure he learned the language, so he could speak to his Nana and Poppy, who were so Old Country they wanted to go back once Russia ditched that commie shit, but now they were too old, or dead, in the case of Poppy.

Baby, Jacob says in Russian, let's go get married.

Out here?

No. Later, I mean.

Don't be crazy, she says.

What? You don't love me?

This was their bit. They did it a thousand times.

Natalya stares out the window, bites on her pinky nail, a cute thing she did. Jacob loved her hands. He's got a thing about fingernails. He can't stand long nails. Or fake nails. He's got a thing about germs. Natalya kept hers super short.

My mom would freak. I don't want to hurt my mother.

You're the most expensive thing she ever bought. Piss her off, she might return you for store credit.

Natalya slaps the back of his head. She did this whenever he gave her shit about costing her mom fifty large. That's what she paid the orphanage in Tula. Natalya told Jacob all about that place. About how every dream she has still takes place there. About how she wakes up in her mother's condo at the Adagio and it takes her a few minutes to realize she's not in that orphanage, that she's replaced her dead parents with this living one, this woman who bought her, this woman who loved her before she ever knew her, and isn't that how parenting works? You don't get the chance to fall in love with a baby, either. You just love it. She did that for me, Natalya always says. I love that she did that for me. And you know, I did not deserve it at first. I was terrible to her.

You were just young, Jacob tells her.

So was my mother.

So. He'll do the right thing.

SWEDE HILL IS steeper and more difficult to climb than he remembers, so Jacob has to stop and catch his breath. Makes sure he can still see his Lincoln. What he doesn't want to do is get turned around out here. End up walking in circles, until one day a coyote takes what's left of him, piece by piece, to feed its pups. He looks for the old water tower. But it's gone. It wasn't on Google Earth, either, but Jacob thought there'd be a heap of scrap somewhere. Where would it have gone? Who would have hauled it off?

I AM NOT trying to hurt my mother, Natalya says again, in his memory.

They're in the car. Making that turn at the pink boulder.

She's a good person, she says. My grandparents. They are good, too. You will meet them one day. After you grow your hair out. And get that tattoo removed from your neck.

Up ahead, parked twenty yards off the road, beside a rust-colored ruin of a water tower, was a black Ford Explorer. There were two men standing beside it.

Who are they? Natalya asks.

My dad's friends.

If they're his friends, she says, why are we meeting them out here? There was a McDonald's in Needles, wasn't there?

More like business associates, Jacob says.

So not friends?

I know these guys. They're cool.

Why are we meeting them all the way out here? This is stupid, Jacob.

Chill.

Don't tell me 'chill,' she says. This is stupid, Jacob. Is that guy wearing a holster?

Hey, he says, we're just handing them a bag. I told you that.

And what?

And then maybe we go to Palm Springs. You wanna go to Palm

Springs? Get some sushi or something? We're halfway there. We'll have a nice dinner downtown. You know they got stars on the side-walk downtown? Like in Hollywood. But different. They got one for a chimp. It's crazy. We'll do that, all right?

In his pocket is a ring. That's why Natalya is with him this time. He's rented the house Elvis and Priscilla stayed in on their honey-moon. Had a florist fill it with red roses. A dozen in every room. Petals up the walk. Everything. He's going to do it *right*.

Why doesn't your father send a check?

Baby, Jacob says, that isn't how things work. Like how my dad gives you cash, not a paycheck? So you don't have to pay taxes? Same deal.

You could die out here. Look at this place.

"Baby," Jacob says in English, "chill."

He pulls up beside the Explorer, rolls down the window. One of the guys—Big Leon—comes up, sticks his head in, rests his arms on the windowsill. "What up, G?" he says.

"Chilling," Jacob says.

"Who's the girl?"

"My lady."

"No shit? She looks a little young, G."

"She's from Russia," Jacob says. "They make them different there."

Big Leon says, "What's your name, Shorty?" Natalya looks at Big Leon. She knows what he's saying. Even if she spoke no words of English, she'd know what he was saying.

"She don't speak much English," Jacob says.

"Convenient," Big Leon says. "Pop your trunk." Jacob does, and the other guy—goes by Pool Boy, because his name is Marco—goes around back, comes out with the bag, sets it on the front seat of the Explorer, starts unpacking it.

"You can keep the bag," Jacob says.

"You can wait a second, G."

"Come on, man," Jacob says, "it's Friday night."

"Somewhere you need to be?"

"Yeah," Jacob says. "Not out the fuck here."

Big Leon says, "Last time, it was short."

"Talk to my pops."

"I did. He says he counted it himself." Big Leon reaches into his pocket, comes out with a yellow Post-it Note. "Should be $103,261 in the bag. Is that what we're gonna find?"

Fuck me, Jacob thinks. *Fuck me to hell.* Jacob's been skimming. Not much. A couple hundred here, a couple thousand there. Counting errors. None of these guys exactly math majors, Jacob trying to get a nest egg for himself, not wanting to have to depend on his father. So if Natalya does marry him, maybe they have some cash to buy a house, down payment at least. For the last six months, he's been pinching. Dad gives him a bag, he parks over by the Krispy Kreme on Spring Mountain, counts out a few grand for himself, buys himself a coffee, a chocolate-iced cream-filled, and then stashes the rest in a safe-deposit box at the Wells Fargo next door. A couple grand meant nothing to these guys. They were all on the same team, everyone working for his father. It was his money, eventually. It would be his fucking money.

"Bro," Jacob says, "I don't have a chain-of-custody form on this shit."

Big Leon says, "What about you, Shorty? How much you think is in the bag?"

"All of it," Natalya says, Jacob surprised she even answered. "Now we go? This is bullshit."

"Oh, she talks?"

"You speak bullshit," Natalya says.

"Easy, baby," Jacob says. "We're all friends here."

"We're not friends," Big Leon says. He reaches into Jacob's car, yanks the keys from the ignition, pockets them.

"The fuck, Leon?" Jacob says.

"Just while we're counting," he says. "All of it is here, nothing to worry about."

Big Leon steps away, lights a cigarette, even though it's nearly 100 degrees outside. Natalya glares at Jacob.

Who is this fucking asshole to talk to you like that?

I told you.

What is happening?

Nothing, baby. Let me think.

He opens the glove box, to get his Glock. But it's not there. He reaches under the passenger seat. In the side pockets. Nothing. Where the fuck is his gun? It's always in his car. He's a fucking registered gun owner. It's Nevada. He's not even riding dirty.

Which means, someone took it. Only other person who has keys to his ride is his dad. Because technically, it's his dad's car.

Pool Boy has a battery-powered cash counter he's feeding bills into. Jacob has three minutes to figure this out and then the rest of his life to regret it. He just doesn't know it yet.

Jacob says, Baby, listen. We're in big trouble.

Pool Boy takes a stack of bills, feeds the machine.

I've been stealing from my dad.

What?

For us. To give us a head start.

Are you crazy?

Pool Boy takes another stack.

I don't know how short we're going to be. But when Leon comes over here, I want you to tell him you took it. They're just trying to scare us. So you say you took it. And then I'll make it right.

Jacob.

Baby. Listen to me.

Jacob.

Baby, it's going to be fine. Just do what I say, and in ten minutes, we'll be on the road.

Pool Boy whistles. Two black birds lift off into the sky.

What do I say? Natalya asks.

Let me think.

Pool Boy feeds the machine. Big Leon tosses his cigarette into a bush. A spark of flame. He kicks sand.

You say you fucked up. You say your mom is behind on her bills. You say you'll never do it again.

Pool Boy whistles again.

I won't be able to pull it off. They won't believe me.

Baby. You'll make them believe. Okay? You'll make them.

Big Leon and Pool Boy are on either side of the car, guns out. "Get the fuck out," Big Leon says.

THE SOUTH SIDE of Swede Hill descends gradually into a plateau. The last remaining ruins of Ragtown are here. A triangular foundation that Jacob thinks must have been a church, but he's not sure why he believes that. A circle of boulders surrounding what used to be a well. The bones of a house, two stone walls still standing. When he was here last, there was a shed beside the house, largely intact, somehow still upright. Back then, the house still had a chimney, too, but that's long gone. Jacob focused on the shed. The way it lolled to the right but hadn't collapsed. Tilted for one hundred years, but never fell.

It was a sign.

Jacob decided that if the shed were still alive, anything could survive out here, so they'd be fine, they'd make it out. Rationalizing his own existence based on the life span of a lean-to. It's the sort of thinking Jacob doesn't do anymore. It speaks of fate, and that's not something he believes in. Every move he's made in the last eighteen years has been a calculation.

Will this get me farther from Ragtown? If the answer is yes, then that's the move he makes.

Stop this gangster shit? Yes.

Never marry, never even get close to someone else? Yes.

Snitch out his father? Yes.

BIG LEON AND Pool Boy zip-tie their hands. Drag them up the hill. Have them kneel beside each other.

There are two shovels already up here. A roll of tarp. In the distance, Jacob sees the shed, starts his magical thinking, his bargaining.

"Anything you want to say?" Big Leon says.

Tell them, Jacob says. Jesus, Natalya, tell them.

She says nothing.

"She took the money," Jacob says.

"When?" Big Leon says.

"This morning," Jacob says. "I was sleeping. She said her mom needed money for rent. She just told me."

"How much?"

"I don't know."

"Ten thousand? Twenty?"

"Less than that."

"So either you don't know or you know it's less than that," Big Leon says. "Which is it?"

"We'll go back to Vegas and get the money. However much it is."

Why are you saying this? Natalya says. Why, Jacob? They'll kill my mother.

Be cool, he says, baby, trust me.

Big Leon steps around Jacob, so that he's standing in front of both of them. "Stop talking Russian," he says. He points his gun at Natalya. "Is he telling the truth? Did you take the money?"

Natalya turns and looks at Jacob, and he sees every age she has ever been and ever will be. He sees her as a baby, he sees her at ten, at twenty-five, at fifty, seventy-five, a ventilator breathing for her at ninety, and then she is gone, she is sand, she is ocean, she is stardust, and she is nothing.

Jacobs nods, once.

Say it. It will be fine. We'll get out of this. Say it.

Does he say this out loud? In memory, he does, but in reality, he doesn't know. God, he hopes he didn't, can't stomach the sound of him pleading with her to lie for him.

"Yes," she says. "I took the money."

Big Leon steps to one side.

Pool Boy shoots her in the back of the head.

Just like that.

JACOB STARTS DIGGING. His back is shot from being on his feet sixteen hours a day at Odessa. Many nights, he sleeps on the pull-out leather sofa in his office upstairs, had a full bathroom with a shower installed in the break room, ostensibly for the staff, but he's the only one who uses it. Keeps a closet filled with black suits and white shirts, drawers filled with underwear and socks. His house is twenty minutes away, behind twenty-foot gates, on the ninth fairway at the TPC in Summerlin. Three thousand square feet and not one of them he cares to stand in. The truth, he always wanted to tell Detective Tiffany Peng, was that he'd woken up in a cell plenty of times.

And so he digs.

All those muscles he worked so hard for? They're gone. He hasn't seen the inside of a gym in years. Steroids destroyed his tendons, turned them into dental floss, hid a degenerative problem in his neck and lower back. So every time he drives the spade into the dirt, it's like lightning through his body.

He doesn't even know if he's in the right place.

JACOB'S THIGH-DEEP IN the dirt, not sure if the grave is for him or for Natalya or for both of them, when another man shows up.

He's in a suit, holds a long black duffle bag. Shakes Big Leon's hand. Bumps fists with Pool Boy. Looks down at Jacob in the grave. Makes eye contact. Jacob recognizes him. His name is Ruben. Works at the funeral home in Summerlin. Jacob's dropped bodies off there in the past. Ruben nods at him, but that's it.

Sets his duffle bag down next to Natalya's body, which is flat on the tarp. Opens it up, starts taking out tools. A hammer. Long knives. A cordless saw. Puts on gloves. Tips Natalya over. Feels the skin on her neck.

"Can't do nothing with the organs," he says. "She's been out here too long. But I'm gonna take the legs and arms. Cool?"

"Whatever you can use," Big Leon says.

"Anything else you need?"

"You dispose of the head?"

"That's gonna be extra," Ruben says.

Pool Boy drops the bag of cash next to Ruben's feet.

Big Leon says, "We got whatever you need."

Ruben says, "All right then." He glances over at Jacob. "This the only one?"

Big Leon says, "For now."

"All right," he says. "I'm gonna need you to strip her." Big Leon and Pool Boy exchange a look. "I'm not putting my DNA on her clothes. Mr. Dmitrov knows this."

Jacob climbs out of the grave. "Get the fuck away from her," he says. "I'll do it."

THE HOLE IS four feet deep when Jacob decides he's done all he can do. He sits on the lip, digs into his pocket, pulls out the ring.

Two carats.

Princess cut.

Bought it with his own money. Nothing that he skimmed. Not that any dollar he made back then was *legit.* All of it came from some shit he was into. But when he went into Damon's Diamonds on Lake Mead and Rainbow, he put on tan slacks, a pressed white shirt. Blue jacket. Put gel in his hair. Parked in front of Organized Living, checked his reflection in their window, walked across the parking lot of the Best in the West Center, buzzed the jeweler's door, like a straight guy. Talked to the jeweler like he'd never seen diamonds, when in fact he had a drawer full of them, crusted Rolexes, stud earrings, the whole nine. Told him that his girl was twelve years younger, so he wanted to make sure the cut of the ring was classic, because the odds were, she was going to have it longer than she would have him, that there would be years when all that remained of him was the promise of the ring.

He had this vision back then that he was going out like Sonny Corleone. Become a legend. People would make movies about him.

Fool.

Sonny Corleone wasn't even real. He was just words on a page, frames of film, James Caan still fucking playmates in the grotto, never was dead, never would die.

Almost two decades lost. And here he is. Still looking for her. And she is in the dust.

Damon's Diamonds is gone. Replaced by a Men's Wearhouse. Jacob walks the racks sometimes, imagining himself. He'll buy a shirt, just so it's not weird, but in fact he's trying to capture a ghost. It's a thing he does. Visit the places he used to go when he was that guy. Champagne's on Maryland Parkway, where he'd meet his father for a drink, talk business in a place they knew wasn't bugged. Commercial Center on Sahara, where his steroid guy operated out of a sleeper van. Grape Street in Summerlin, where Natalya liked to get the chicken marsala. Hope that time will ripple, and he'll be able to stop himself, that he'll catch his own memory by the arm, will drag that boy out of his messes, and Natalya will somehow reappear beside him—thirty-six now, *My god, thirty-six!*—and this whole life will get rearranged.

But of course, that's not how it goes.

Jacob drops the ring into the hole.

It's done, he says.

The Russian thick in his mouth. He only ever dreams in the language now, never speaks it. Looping. Say it. Say it.

It's done, he says.

It's done, she says.

Gotovo.

You could die out here. Look at this place.

GANGWAY

Two weeks out of Joliet, Peaches Pocotillo gets a job delivering lost luggage for an outfit working O'Hare called Allied Baggage. This was back in the early nineties, when you could still get a job at an airport with a prison record. He'd done a year for assault after he put a guy's head through a TV. Wasn't the worst he'd ever done. Wasn't the worst he'd ever do.

First month or so on the crew, Peaches just did the work. He had to. His parole officer wanted to see him with a straight job for a few months, at least, no hanging with known accomplices, which meant he had to punch a clock. Peaches didn't mind. He had a plan for his life. This was good job experience.

Normal shift, he'd load up a company van and start making his rounds out to the neighborhoods—Wicker Park, Roscoe Village, Boystown, all those—and then to the big hotels on the Loop. The company had a contract with United, but O'Hare being the hub for half the airlines in the world, they'd pick up loose ends for a lot of the other domestic carriers, but where they made their cheddar was on the international flights. You get a bunch of pissed-off foreign tourists without any underwear, you'll pay anything to get them their shit, morning, noon, or night. Which was what Peaches thought was going down when he got the call to come in at 2 a.m., a couple nights after Christmas.

"You're using your own car tonight," MaryAnn told him when he pulled up. She stood in front of the company warehouse, three blocks north of the airport. "We're off the books. Client didn't want to wait until morning for his stuff, so we're doing a favor. I can give you twenty-five cents a mile."

"If it's a favor," Peaches said, "how about fifty?"

"This isn't a negotiation," MaryAnn said. She shifted from foot to foot. Snow fell lightly to the blacktop. Peaches spied the suitcases on either side of her. Nice ones. Tumi. Expensive bags meant expensive clothes meant expensive jewelry meant expensive medications and all that. So Peaches, he didn't say shit, until finally MaryAnn said, "Christ. I'll do thirty-five and no bitching. Pop your trunk."

Peaches wasn't down with people seeing inside his trunk, so he said, "Put it in the backseat," and MaryAnn did. MaryAnn handed him a Post-it with an address all the way out in Batavia, forty-five minutes away. "I roll up into this neighborhood at 3 a.m.," Peaches said, "they're going to call the cops."

"They're on Rome time," MaryAnn said.

"Which is what?"

"Morning. Like, champagne-brunch time."

"Their neighbors synchronize their watches?" Peaches asked. Peaches liked MaryAnn. She was around fifty and though her husband, Silas, owned the business, everyone dealt with her. The company employed maybe ten ex-cons, got some kind of tax dispensation from the state, but MaryAnn seemed to have a soft spot for guys coming out of prison. Even brought Peaches a bag lunch every day, until he got his first paycheck. It was just basic shit. Peanut butter and jelly. A bag of chips. A can of RC Cola. Nice is nice and that was nice. But still. Peaches wasn't going to have some rent-a-cop for an alarm company pull him over. That could result in a body.

"It's fine. They're expecting you. No one in Batavia has been awake for seven hours."

"You say so," Peaches said, "but I get hassled, I'm not responsible for my actions." He started to put his window up, but MaryAnn grabbed it.

"You have a good Christmas, hon? You get up to see your family?"

"No," Peaches said.

"What'd you do all day?"

"I'd planned to read," he said, "but then I got busy with a friend, who also needed a favor, it turns out." His idea was that he'd get back to his real estate textbooks over his day off, immerse himself again, get that habit back. He'd taken thirty hours of certification classes at Joliet. Did pretty well. Thought he might like to get his license. Had another sixty hours to go before he could take the test. You wanted to be a real gangster, you learned about *property*. He learned that playing Monopoly. Free parking wasn't shit. Owning Boardwalk and Park Place, that was the game.

So he was all set.

Pot of coffee.

Stack of books.

Rudolph getting bullied on the TV.

But instead he got a call from his cousin up in Kenosha about someone who needed to get got, a quick five Gs, so off he went. Peaches had been in the game since he was thirteen, had a good dozen bodies already. Just how it was. So Christmas night, he was chopping up some motherfucker and sprinkling his remains into Chain O'Lakes. Cash was coming down after the New Year and then maybe he'd enroll in some real estate classes. Kaplan had something starting February 1.

"You're a good friend," MaryAnn said. "But listen. You are always responsible for your actions. I've met a hundred boys like you. And what you think is important now is not going to seem that way if you're back in Joliet doing fifty, sixty years. Okay? Someone cares about you. Do you understand that?"

"I get fifty years," Peaches said, "I'll be doing them from the grave."

"Listen," MaryAnn said. "You come back here after the drop. I have some green bean casserole in the fridge. You take it home, okay?"

"That's real nice of you," Peaches said.

A police cruiser, running its sirens, screamed up the frontage road beside the warehouse. MaryAnn pulled away from Peaches's car, watched until the cruiser disappeared, smiled down at him. "Quick like a bunny," she said, "get it done, okay?"

"This job," Peaches said, "it's not something criminal, right? Not a bunch of cocaine in those bags, is there?"

"I wouldn't do you like that, hon."

"But don't mention it to Silas?"

"Just a side hustle," MaryAnn said, and then she stared at Peaches for five, ten, fifteen seconds, snow melting in her hair. "Fifty cents a mile, then you come back here tomorrow for your regular shift, and we're cool, okay?"

PEACHES POCOTILLO CAME from a solid criminal family. His father, Junior Pocotillo, had been running protection rackets on tribal lands and in the rural backwoods since the late 1970s. The mob hadn't touched that shit since the Green Ones got out of the meat and farming rackets in the 1930s. He'd grown up in Chicago around Family and Outfit wiseguys but set up shop in Wisconsin after getting in some trouble on a manslaughter beef. Did five years at Joliet before he flipped on some Outfit fools on *another* killing altogether. Five years was enough time to make it look like he hadn't snitched. Not that the Outfit hadn't done shit for him, so fuck them. If the old bastard were still alive—some La Raza motherfuckers had him clipped, probably hired by the Native Mob, since Junior never did clique up, and that caused understandable problems—Peaches would pull over, find a pay phone, and ask him his advice about the bags in his backseat.

Straight motherfucker would just go and do as he was told.

Straight motherfucker might not even think anything was unusual about this whole situation.

But Peaches, man, he wasn't some straight motherfucker.

After twenty minutes of circling around, thinking about the best way to handle this, Peaches pulled off the highway when he couldn't take it anymore. So he parked in front of a twenty-four-hour Jewel's, where the lighting was good, workers coming off swing shift getting their groceries, Chicago the kind of town where people still worked swing, and no one thought it was weird you're hanging around a grocery store in a jumpsuit with your name on the chest.

First bag was filled with women's clothes—a stack of St. John knits, Gucci pencil skirts and slacks, a small Gucci bag, too, a bunch of high-heeled shoes, a pair of black boots, nice, all shit Peaches recognized was pricey from periodically housing shit from the Marshall Field's on State Street—but then Peaches discovered a little pouch covered in fake pearls, unzipped it, found what he didn't know he was looking for: diamond earrings, diamond necklace, neither huge carats, but a diamond is a diamond. Tasteful gold hoops, then: a tennis bracelet, platinum, twelve diamonds, a fucking mint. Well, a junior mint. And then four other bracelets and necklaces, three sets of earrings, all of them pricey.

Whole bag could probably get him ten Gs on the streets. Those diamonds were not a fucking joke. But he wasn't going back to prison for ten Gs and anyway, they were worth fifteen times that amount, but who had $150K sitting around, waiting for some stolen ice?

So he opened the second bag.

In addition to a few men's suits—one blue, one black, one gray, all folded in a way so intricate Peaches didn't even recognize them as suits at first—and two pairs of shoes, underwear, socks, a couple polo shirts, a green sweater, undershirts, slacks, jeans, there was a combo-locked hard-side pistol case.

Size you'd use for a .357 Magnum.

Peaches picked it up, shook it, no movement. Not that he expected any. There'd be packing inside. Gun might even be in parts.

Peaches checked the airline tags. ORD to FCO. That was the airport code for O'Hare and whatever they called the airport in Rome. A week ago. A second tag, FCO to ORD, dated today, just like MaryAnn had said.

You fly to and from a foreign country with a gun, man, you really gotta have a reason for it. Who the fuck was he dealing with? The hand-written baggage tags only had the address on them. No names. Maybe it was just some dude who'd done work in Vietnam and never got used to real life again. Peaches had uncles like that. Always strapped. Fear was natural. Meant you were ready if a saber-toothed tiger leapt out at you or some shit, but anxiety, which is what made you pack a gun on vacation, that was about something else. That was not believing saber-toothed tigers were extinct.

Or it meant you were the saber-toothed tiger to someone else.

Peaches put the man's bag in the trunk, left the other in the backseat. He wasn't down to cross MaryAnn. She'd done right by him. But these bags told a story, and Peaches saw some possibilities rolling out in front of him. Maybe Peaches would tell the people at the house only one bag had been released, the other was still at the airport, he'd come back in a couple hours with it, if that was okay? There a good time? Get a clock going. That way, he'd know when they might be leaving. Get one of his boys, clean out the whole house, no worries about getting popped in the act, because if you travel with that kind of jewelry, plus a firearm, what do you keep in the house? Plus, he'd have the bag with him on the return. Someone rolled up on him beforehand, he had reason to be back, if anyone asked.

That was good. An alibi.

Peaches didn't believe in robbery as a way of life, strictly speaking, didn't think going into a bank with a gun was very smart. Opportunity cost of sticking some fool up for his Rolex was low. But a house in Batavia? A sure thing? These were the kind of people who had homeowner's insurance. A victimless crime.

Peaches went into Jewel's, bought a Hostess apple pie, ate it right there in the store. Got his mind right. Made some decisions. Could be he'd put off those real estate classes for a couple months if things unfolded right. Maybe he'd walk out of this job with a Cadillac, cash, art, jewels, shit he could move in Canada if need be, once he was able to travel. Could be he bought a house of his own with this score. Yeah, Peaches thought, maybe tonight was going to be okay.

THE DROP-OFF WAS located a few blocks west of the Fox River in a new subdivision called Lockwood Estates, the sign out front advertising three hundred homes starting at twenty-five hundred square feet. *Room for your RV! Custom Pool Lots! Plenty of Green Space!*

Yellow model-home flags hung drab off of forty-foot-tall poles, and behind them, blocks of half-constructed skeleton houses, the weather conditions inhospitable for building, Peaches thinking someone's ass was on the line for that fuck-up. But then he turned left at the bottom of Sagebrush Lane and found himself on a fully developed street of redbrick two-story starter mansions, each ringed with dead Christmas lights. Cadillacs and Lincolns and Mercedes and BMWs on the streets and driveways. Bikes and tricycles next to front doors. Nice ones. Not the peeling-red-paint bikes Peaches rode as a kid. Darkened windows covered by holiday wreaths and midnight snow . . . save for one house at the end of the block, where the Christmas lights still glowed, and the entire bottom floor was illuminated. He checked the address and his watch.

Three a.m. Right on time.

There was a black Jeep in the driveway, so Peaches parked next to it, got out with the woman's bag, looked inside: a screwdriver rammed into the ignition, a Styrofoam cup on the dash, steam rising from the coffee, a picture on the passenger seat: a man, fifty-something; a woman, twenty-something; a small white dog, fluffy-something.

The fuck?

He stepped around the Jeep and stood on the sloping front lawn of the house, looked into the panorama of lit windows. A library filled with bookcases; beyond that a kitchen surrounded by what looked like restaurant-grade appliances. Then a bedroom, double bed, that fluffy dog standing with its paws on the windowsill. The rooms of other people's homes were like a dollhouse to Peaches. He'd never own a house like this, had never spent a night in one, either, and it all looked posed . . . until he peered into the next window, and saw a den or office.

A man, standing up, back to the window, about Peaches's height.

Six foot. Big, but fit. One hundred eighty-five, two hundred pounds. Leather duster on. The man from the photo sat on a couch. Silver hair. Blue shirt opened at the collar. The standing guy, for some reason, held a lamp in his hand, the cord pulled taut from the wall.

Two men.

Shit.

Not what he was expecting.

Everything in the den looked to be leather. The man in the duster yanked the light from the wall. And then Peaches heard *bap . . . bap . . . bap.* Glock? Then another *bap.* Yeah. Glock with a silencer. It wasn't how it was in the movies. Silencers make noise. If you know what you're hearing, it's impossible not to know what you're hearing. And Peaches knew.

Shit.

Peaches was halfway back across the lawn to his car, when the rest of the house lights turned off, room by room, leaving only the Christmas lights on. The front door opened and the man in the duster walked out, gun still in his hand. If Peaches took off, he knew he'd be fucking dead. In this situation, you just assumed someone running was running to the cops. Least that was Peaches's point of view. None of that hero shit mattered, either. Some motherfucker is sprinting away from you, you shoot him in the back. So, man up. Peaches turned and faced the shooter.

The shooter said, "Who the fuck are you?"

"Whoever you need me to be," Peaches said. "You got the gun."

The shooter said, "You work for someone?"

"MaryAnn and Silas."

"The fuck is that?"

Peaches raised the bag up, so the man could see it better. "Allied Baggage."

A glimmer of recognition. "Anyone else?" Like asking if he banged, Peaches guessed.

"I rep my set," Peaches said.

"You do what to who?"

"I *represent* it," Peaches said.

"And what's *it*?"

"Four Corner Death Warriors."

"What's that? A metal band?"

"A gang," Peaches said. "In Wisconsin." It's not like the Death Warriors had Green Bay or Madison in their grip. Mostly, they were about running drugs and protection shit in the farmlands, periodically getting into it with Vice Lords and Gangster Disciples up from Chicago who wanted to move product without local sanction. "But up Joliet, I mostly worked alone."

"You shouldn't have come here," the shooter said, like they'd come to the conclusion of a dispute. "Not alone, anyway." The shooter looked down the block, like maybe he was expecting another car to roll up. "Piece of advice? Dream Warriors sounds like a metal band."

"*Death* Warriors," Peaches said. "Motherfuckers usually pay respect on it."

"You one of those guys, screams it out of the car after they shoot someone? 'Dream Warriors, motherfucker!' All that?"

"I don't drive-by," Peaches said. "That's pussy shit."

"But you got homies," the shooter said. "They do that?"

"I've seen it done," Peaches admitted.

"See. That's bad for all of us. You live through the week, stop that shit." He stepped around Peaches, still standing there holding the fucking Tumi bag like he was the help, opened the door to the Jeep, then said, "You meet Richard Speck in Joliet?"

"Seen him."

"What's that like?"

"Like seeing Godzilla or some shit," Peaches said. "But he was quiet. Kept to his own."

"Good advice," the shooter said. "Wait fifteen minutes, then call the cops, or everyone at Allied Baggage is dead."

PEACHES WAITED THIRTY minutes to call the cops, which gave him enough time to ditch some of the shit in his trunk—guns, saws, rope, tarp, that sort of thing—before coming back to the house to call 911. Just because you were a Good Samaritan didn't mean cops wouldn't run you. And sure enough, a couple hours after the first cops arrived and found the body in the living room, plus the woman tied up in a closet upstairs, unhurt, a Lincoln full of men in suits pulled up and some suit called Hopper pulled Peaches aside, took his license, then asked him to sit on the curb while he called him in. No cuffs. Nothing like that. An unusual experience in Peaches's life.

Hopper came back, still holding Peaches's license. "You're just out," he said. "And you walk into this shit. Some luck."

"No difference between luck and a curse," Peaches said. "Just depends how you look at it."

"Really now?" Hopper said. "You know who that guy inside is? The one missing his face?" Peaches shook his head. "Joey the Bishop. That name mean anything to you?"

"Nope."

"Last twenty-five, thirty years," Hopper said, "he's been fixing every college basketball game in the country."

"How'd he do that?" Peaches asked, interested now.

"Most of the time, kids are happy to brick a couple shots for money," Hopper said. "Purdue playing Southern Buttfuck

University, who really cares about the score? Who really loses, right? Higher up the food chain, say it's an NCAA tournament game, big action moving. Joey might buy off the top player on both teams. Joey really needed something good, maybe he'd blackmail a coach. Get photos of him bending over a stripper or maybe he's closeted, gets him with his boyfriend, whatever. He needs something, Joey the Bishop, he's gonna get it." Hopper paused. "Someone must have made more shots than they were supposed to, so then Joey got his."

"The fuck you telling me all this for?"

"I don't know," Hopper said. "Thought you might be interested in a less violent path."

"What about homeboy without a face?" Peaches said.

"Well, no one in Vegas gets shot anymore, for instance," Hopper said. "Gambling is practically legal everywhere. You could probably get into some minor college bullshit, take frat boys for their student loans. Victimless crime. Essentially." The coroner and two men in scrubs came out of the house, pushing a body on a gurney. And so went Joey. "The Bishop, he was old-school, though." He gave Peaches his license back. "You got somewhere out of town you can go? Lay low for a week or two if need be?"

"I'm on parole," Peaches said.

"I can help with that," Hopper said.

"How's a detective gonna help with that?"

"I'm not a detective," Hopper said. "I'm with the FBI."

"No shit?" Peaches said. He'd never met an FBI agent before. "I thought you'd be taller."

"Me too," Hopper said. "If this shooter gets caught fast, there's going to be an assumption that there was a witness. You'll want to be out of town. Just how it goes with these mob guys."

"Like Al Capone and shit?"

"Al Capone didn't own half the police force," Hopper said. "Your name is going to be on the reports. So what I'm saying, if you saw something, we can pretend you didn't. Just you and me."

Back in Joliet, Peaches had met a few of those dudes. Old ones had double-wide cells and their own TVs. Took their meals in their cells half the time. Not that they were infirm. Just how it was. Some trustee would show up with their chow, except it never looked like what Peaches was eating, the talk being they got fed from the staff cafeteria. Joliet was fucked-up. But now the fucking guy in the duster made some sense. How he didn't pop Peaches. How he talked to him like a normal guy. Those Italians guys had a code. You didn't run around killing innocent people. Peaches, he wasn't anyone's idea of innocent, but he wasn't *involved*. Dumb way of doing business, in Peaches's view, even if it had saved his life. Because now, maybe the man in the duster might need to come kill him, regardless.

"It's what I told the cops," Peaches said. "I pulled up. Door was open. Dude was missing his face. I called 911."

"You don't seem like a call-911 type," Hopper said.

"Normal situation," Peaches said, "maybe I wouldn't."

"Techs go through the house," Hopper said, "are they going to find your prints anywhere they shouldn't be?"

"I didn't even know the lady was upstairs," Peaches said. "I saw the man, made the call."

"So," Hopper said, "how'd you see the body?"

"I walked in, there he was."

"You make a habit of walking through open doors into people's homes," Hopper said, "and then down the hall, into their den?"

"Just trying to give good customer service."

Hopper smiled. "I don't give a shit about what you've done in your previous life," he said. "You're about two decades below my pay grade. I just want you to be sure of your story. I were you? I'd clique up with some soldiers with clout." He took a small spiral notepad from his back pocket, flipped through it, circled something. "You really bang with the . . . Four Corner Death Warriors?"

"Did."

"They know you're down with Allied Baggage now?" Hopper said.

"I'm on the straight."

He asked Peaches for his phone number, told him he'd call him straight away if something broke on this, then took out a business card, scrawled something on the back, gave it to Peaches. "You see anything funny, you feel like someone is watching you, whatever, you give me a call. Don't try to handle it yourself. You'll end up in a corn field."

In his life, Peaches had called the cops exactly one time.

About three hours ago now.

He didn't imagine he'd be doing it a second time.

"Ten arrests since you were fourteen. That right?"

"That juvenile shit is sealed," Peaches said.

Hopper shrugged. "That life must be getting old."

"I'm reformed."

"Yeah, that's what you keep saying." Hopper sat down on the curb next to Peaches. "Can I tell you a funny thing? Off the record?" Hopper pointed his index finger like a gun in Peaches's face. "Joey took one to his face and then there's two shots into the wall, one in the ceiling. And then he's got his hands tied in front of his body using a lamp cord, but it's still attached to the lamp. Isn't that funny?"

"Off the record?" Peaches said. Hopper nodded. "Shooting a person ain't like what you think it's gonna be like."

"True," Hopper said. "That's very true. But the guy who did this?

I'm gonna guess he was a big bastard in a leather duster," Hopper pointed his finger gun at the two-story Cape Cod on the corner, "because that's what the kid across the street saw out his window while he was up jerking off to the Sears catalogue. That guy? That guy is a professional. But he made the shooting look like it was done by someone who didn't know what he was doing. Like someone who maybe showed up in the middle of the night and saw an opportunity, then panicked. A dupe, basically. A punk."

Peaches didn't say anything, but now his mind was working. Had MaryAnn set him up? How long had she been working that game? Every fucking peanut butter and jelly sandwich another step closer to him getting framed on a murder? Peaches had a busy day ahead of him. Maybe a busy week. Could be a busy couple of months.

"We still off the record?" Peaches said eventually.

"Sure."

"You know this guy's name?"

"His boys call him the Rain Man. CI told me this guy remembers every face he's ever seen."

"You believe that?"

"Nah," Hopper said. "It's just something to scare people. Because that's pretty scary, right? You're not even sure if you remember the color of his hair and he's at home with a picture of you hanging on the wall. Still, you'd be wise not to go looking for him. Not until you're cliqued up, anyway. Like with some Navy SEALS." Hopper stood up then. "Hold on to my card. Use it as a toothpick if you need to, but don't lose it." He began to walk away.

"Hey," Peaches said, and the FBI agent stopped. Hopper wasn't a big guy, Peaches wasn't joking about that. Little bit of a gut. Nose was crooked, like he should have ducked when he was learning how to box, but instead led with his face. Must be tough to breathe out of it. "Why they call him the Bishop?"

"You never played chess?"

"Nah."

"Not even in Joliet?"

"I like to read," Peaches said.

"The bishop in chess only moves diagonally, backward and forward," Hopper said. "Plays a crooked game."

"How's that different than any of these fucks?"

"Well," Hopper said, "he was also a devout Catholic."

Once the FBI agent had disappeared back into the crowd of cops, EMTs, and neighbors, Peaches took his card out, read what was on the back: *Your Lucky Day! Get Out of Jail Half-Off.*

IT WAS AFTER 8 a.m. by the time Peaches got back to Allied Baggage.

The parking lot was empty and the doors to the luggage warehouse were chained and padlocked. Middle of the week, right after Christmas? The place should have been bustling, vans moving in and out. Airlines never worse about losing luggage than when you needed it most. Had MaryAnn called everyone and told them to stay home?

He walked around to the back, where Silas and MaryAnn kept an office in a temporary construction trailer, temporary in this case lasting maybe ten years or so, judging by how the paint had chipped off the aluminum siding. Peaches tried the door. Locked. He knocked, waited. Tried to peer into the window, but the venetian blinds were closed. He knocked again, harder, waited, then just went ahead and kicked in the door.

The office had two desks, two desktop computers with TV set–sized monitors, a fax machine, a shredder, a tan file cabinet, a small brown sofa that dipped like a *V* in the middle, probably from Silas's fat ass, a flimsy coffee table, a mini-fridge, a watercooler, a micro-wave. Nothing on the walls, apart from a calendar.

It was the mini-fridge Peaches was interested in.

He popped it open and looked inside. Two cans of RC Cola, a bunch of mustard packets, some soy sauce, that was it.

No green bean casserole to be found.

He sniffed inside, to see if he caught a whiff of it, but all he de-tected was the aroma of the BBQ sauce that was spattered like a gunshot on the back wall of the fridge.

Peaches sat down behind MaryAnn's desk, went through the drawers, only found paper clips, a stapler, scissors, and balled-up old Kleenex. The picture frames on her desk, which used to hold photos of her kids when they were babies, but who were now grown, were empty.

The kids would be easy enough to find, when the time came.

Yesterday's *Sun-Times* sports page was still open on the center of MaryAnn's desk, a full-page ad for Cupertine Luxury Sedans splayed out next to the basketball scores, a coffee mug on one cor-ner, an inch of coffee on the bottom, like MaryAnn had been in the middle of reading when she got the news and boned out. There was Ronald Cupertine dressed in his trench coat and a fedora, shooting his tommy gun through a credit report, just like in his dumb-ass TV commercials. Peaches thought that if people had any idea about what the life was really about, they wouldn't play at this shit. Wouldn't make those movies, write those books, none of it. Sure as fuck wouldn't sell cars with it. Thinking you were a gang-ster because you ripped some cartoon criminal off for your floor mats? Please. Cupertine was supposedly the head of The Family, but Peaches wasn't buying that, not with these bullshit ads and com-mercials. Like if it turned out Yosemite Sam was really an assassin.

Peaches found a Sharpie and just when he was about to black out Cupertine's teeth—a thing he'd been doing to that motherfucker in every newspaper since he was six years old—something made him stop and look at the photo. At the face staring back at him. At the shape of his jaw, his nose, the way the trench coat hung off his shoulders.

He wasn't the Rain Man, was he?

No.

Not . . . exactly. But close.

Peaches didn't have that Rain Man memory, Hopper was right about that, but he'd memorized the shooter's face. And the shooter looked a lot like this motherfucker, Ronald Cupertine. Well. Shit.

He found MaryAnn's scissors and sliced Ronald Cupertine out of the newspaper. Folded the picture in half, slipped it into his wallet, then went over to the file cabinet and yanked open the drawer marked EMPLOYEE RECORDS. It wasn't even fucking locked. These people. He flipped through the files, until he found his own. Dumped it all out. His I-9 form, driver's license, tax information, social security number, everything. Motherfuckers had access to every aspect of his life. What *didn't* they know about him? He fed it all into the shredder, watched his history turn to ribbons. Went back to the drawer and found MaryAnn's file. Flipped through. Looked at her driver license. Wrote down her address. But then something caught his attention.

He knew that MaryAnn's last name was Nicolino.

He didn't know her maiden name was Cupertine.

CUPERTINE LUXURY SEDANS was tucked between a Rolls-Royce and Aston Martin dealership on Rush Street, directly across the street from the gothic Archbishop Quigley Preparatory Seminary, on the bottom floor of the Federal Building, a fifteen-story red-brick-and-steel modernist box with a cliff-face exterior. It reminded Peaches of some of the outbuildings at Joliet. You could imagine how, if the sun hit them just right, they could make for a pretty picture. And then you got inside, and it was human despair of a hundred years. Peaches wasn't lying when he told MaryAnn he'd never be going back to prison. He wasn't ever gonna be on the even, and that meant he had to be willing to put one in his own temple if it came down to it. Which he was. Though, he had to admit, Hopper's card did make him wonder what the limits were for the kind of favors he could offer.

It was the early afternoon, so Rush Street was buzzing. Seminary students, businesspeople, shoppers, and tourists, all bundled against the wind and a drizzle of rain and snow. Everything was still done up for Christmas, but the people with bags today were all returning gifts. Except for the people inside Cupertine's dealership, who he guessed had bags of money to drop on vintage Cadillacs, Corvettes, and Lincolns. Peaches had gone home, grabbed a couple hours of sleep, showered, put on a nice pair of pants, a shirt with a collar, and an overcoat. He had two guns on his body and enough ammo to take out the Chicago Bears, Cubs, and White Sox. If the Bulls showed up, he'd have something for their ass, too.

He pushed open the double glass doors of the dealership. Marble floors. Soft music. Pretty women dressed all in black in glass offices, ten-keys on their desks, stacks of papers. A salesman talking to an older woman looking at a town car. Another salesman inspecting a Seville, popping Lemonheads into his mouth. A waiting area with leather couches. The whole showroom and office space stretched the width of the building in the shape of an *L*, and then there was an artful-looking staircase cut into the floor, leading into the basement, where Peaches figured they kept more cars and the service area.

There was a security guard in a blue sport coat sitting behind a raised, curved reception desks about nine feet from a cherry-red '68 Eldorado. He was too fat to be an off-duty cop. Too old, also. Looked like he was in his late fifties. Had bags under his eyes you could take with you on a weekend away. Nose was smashed in the middle, and he had an old flat white scar that stretched from his chin down to somewhere beneath his collar. He was still thick across the shoulders, and he had huge head. This guy was security all right. But not a guard. Peaches guessed he'd done well in the prison boxing game.

"Help you, sir?" he said when Peaches walked up. He had a gold name tag on his breast pocket. Said his name was Dom.

"Yeah," Peaches said. "I'm looking for the Rain Man."

Dom said, "You better move along." Which was not the answer you'd give if you'd never heard of the Rain Man, Peaches thought.

"Or what?"

"This is a public place," Dom said. "You got something you need to discuss? You run it up the right channel. This is the wrong channel." Calm. Cool. Not a problem. Just letting him know. "You wanna buy a car, you're in the right place. You wanna start some trouble, you're in the wrong place, son."

"I'm not your son."

"No," Dom said, "but you're somebody's son. And they probably love you. So get moving and you'll see them again."

Peaches thought about this. His father was dead. He hadn't seen his mother in ten years. He had an auntie in Green Bay. He could lose her. That would be fine. "Here's the situation," Peaches said. "I saw the Rain Man kill a guy last night. I didn't realize until afterward that I was being framed for it. Luckily, I'm not too fucking stupid, and so I am here, not in jail looking at a life bid. So. I wanna talk to someone with juice, not a fucking bitch-ass security guard too fat to stand. I'm gonna go sit on the leather sofa over there by the free coffee and donuts. When someone with some fucking juice shows up, how about we go sit in one of these nice glass offices and have a conversation, in this public place, about how I'm going to be compensated for this shit." He opened up his overcoat, showed Dom his guns. "That clear for you, granddad?"

"You don't know who you're fucking with," Dom said, wearily.

"I know exactly who I'm fucking with."

Dom sighed. He stood up. Motherfucker was about six foot eight. Hands like anvils. Peaches felt his pulse quicken, then remembered he had guns and guns don't care how tall you are.

"Have a seat. You want a Coke or something, just let one of the girls know." And then Dom disappeared down a long hallway filled with more glass-walled offices, toward the back of the building, where there were two double doors made of some dark wood, not a panel of glass to be found.

TWENTY MINUTES LATER, a black Lincoln Navigator double-parked in front of the dealership and two men got out. One big. One small. The big guy was in the passenger seat, the little guy in the back. The big guy ran about three hundred pounds and six foot three. The little guy ran about two hundred pounds and five foot six. Only the little guy walked into the showroom. The other stood outside, smoking. Watching. Dom pointed at Peaches, and the little guy walked over to him.

"You the guy?" the little one said.

"That's right."

He looked Peaches over, something like recognition dawning on him. "You Junior Pocotillo's kid?"

"Who wants to know?"

"Who wants to know? Jesus. He didn't make you smart." He motioned with his hand. "Scoot over." Peaches did, and the little guy sat down next to him. Took off his gloves. Stuffed them in his jacket pockets, then took off his jacket, laid it over the back of the sofa. Sniffed. Looked around. Like maybe he was worried someone would recognize him. "Paul Bruno. Your pops used to come into my butcher shop. You remember that? I used to give you suckers. Would have called me Bruno." Peaches had some vague recollection of this. He would have been five, six years old. "Good guy, your pops. If he'd stuck around Chicago, he wouldn't have gotten into that shit up north. Go fucking around with no backup, people get wise and realize they can problem-solve using the back of your head. Who the fuck got him? Mexicans?"

"That's the story."

"Didn't have to happen." He shook his head. "That's the thing I want to implore to you. None of this *has* to happen. You've got some choices ahead of you." He pointed to the guy outside. "That big ugly motherfucker is named Fat Monte Moretti. That mean anything to you?"

Peaches had heard of Fat Monte. He'd been breaking legs—and worse—for the Family since he was a teenager. A good career. Not exactly a model for Peaches, because Peaches didn't have his size, so he had to make up for it with smarts and the fact that he simply did not give a fuck if he had to kill a guy. Fat Monte was known to be more of a sadist. Kind of guy who'd cut your eyelids off but let you live. So Peaches said, "Yeah, I know his reputation."

"You come to his cousin's place of business and ask about the

Rain Man, only two things are gonna happen. One, they find your body. The other, they don't. But seeing as I knew your pops," Bruno said, "let's see if we can't figure out a more amenable situation. So. Tell me what happened."

The lady who'd been looking at the town car was buying it. The salesman who'd been examining the Seville had moved on to a sky-blue Corvette. Whole place was a hive of bees. Phones ringing. Service people coming up the stairs, salesmen going down. It was like watching a highly choreographed Rube Goldberg machine, the end result being some motherfucker walking out with an overpriced old car.

"C'mon, kid. You're the one showed up flashing gats and shit," Bruno said. "That's what you call 'em now? Gats?"

Fuck it. Peaches told him everything. From getting called into Allied to hearing the shooting to talking to the Rain Man to meeting the FBI agent and then kicking in the door back at Allied. Bruno listened intently. When Peaches finished, Bruno got up, went over and picked through the donuts, came over with a maple bar and a glazed old-fashioned, set them down on a napkin at the little coffee table in front of the sofa, broke off part of the maple bar, part of the old-fashioned, put them both in his mouth. Chewed with his eyes closed, Peaches watching him the whole time, trying to figure out what the fuck this guy's game was. He said he was a butcher?

"Well," Bruno said. "First thing. You're lucky to be alive. The Rain Man isn't normally the chatting type. Second thing. If he left you alive, it's not because he was trying to frame you. I promise you this. Generally speaking, the people you're talking about are not in the business of framing people. Now, maybe giving themselves a little space, sure. Creating a situation, a diversion? Sure. And so maybe that was you. But here you are. You got that G-man's card on you?"

Peaches took it out of his wallet, showed it to Bruno. He actually chuckled. "Get out of jail half-off," he said. "That's clever." Bruno looked outside at Fat Monte, now working on a cigar. "How much you want for this card? You like Cadillacs? How about that Eldorado?"

Peaches *did* like Cadillacs. But he wasn't entirely sure where this shit was going. "I lost my job today," he said. "On account of Mary-Ann and Silas Nicolino seemed to have disappeared. Cuz I guess they thought I'd either be fucking dead or in jail. Some boogeyman tried to hook a mob murder on me. And if I'm understanding things, everyone in this place is Family, am I right?"

"Not me," Bruno said.

"You're just a butcher?"

Bruno leaned forward and broke apart the donuts again, popped pieces into his mouth, took a sip of coffee. "Your pops," he said, "snitched out The Outfit. Ronnie Cupertine, if he knew you were involved, would feel real bad about this situation. MaryAnn and Silas, they don't know shit. Not exactly historians. They're cousins of cousins. Nobodies. Doing as they were told. My opinion, lack of institutional knowledge is gonna be the fucking ruin of this whole game, but that's not your problem. Your problem is that you've come to Ronnie Cupertine's place of business and thrown around a bunch of threats. So here I come, what you might think of as a middleman. I'm what's currently standing between you and Fat Monte putting you in a landfill. Maybe not today. Maybe not tomorrow. But one day. So. I'd like to not put that stress on Mr. Cupertine. He don't ever need to know you existed. So, let me ask you again. How much do you want for that FBI agent's business card so that we can all go about our lives not looking over our shoulders?"

"Fifty thousand dollars," Peaches said. "And the Eldorado." He paused. "But I want it painted blue."

Bruno nodded. "Okay. Let's do $100,000. You should have asked for a million and then negotiated. You'll learn. Now here's the other side. Chicago? That's done for you."

"I'm on parole," Peaches said. "I can't just bug out."

"We can take care of that." Turns out everybody could.

"You got that kind of juice?"

Bruno said, "This ain't some street-hustler shit."

Okay.

"How long I gotta stay away?"

"You hear Fat Monte is dead," Bruno said, "wait a year after that, in case he comes back."

Peaches said, "And if I want to come looking for the Rain Man, what then?"

"You think he gives a shit about you? Kid. Rain Man was there, he was on someone's bill. Joey the Bishop, he was big-game. You taking this shit personally is the wrong life path, my friend. You're just a tiny little piece. You're a getaway car. So don't be thinking you're important. You're not. Coulda been anyone. You got picked. It's too bad. I get that. No one likes to feel like a mark. And turns out, MaryAnn picked the wrong motherfucker. So. Let's call it $150,000. That's enough to set yourself up for a nice life up in the lakes. Maybe I can put in a word with some friends up there that your pop pissed off. Make it easier for you."

"You're scared," Peaches said.

"No," Bruno said. "I'm smart. One day, you'll learn the difference. 'Fuck the world' point of view don't make you wise."

Bruno stood up, motioned at Fat Monte. He got into the Navigator, drove off. Bruno picked up his coat, put it back on. "And that means you gotta go, but first, I'm gonna need your guns."

"I'm not giving you shit."

"Listen to me," Bruno said. "I'm gonna give you $150,000 in cash and a fucking Cadillac for a business card. You're not gonna turn around and put one in my face. You can buy more guns. I can't get another face. So either you give them to me, or Dom comes over here and turns you upside down. Maybe shakes you until you're dead. Because frankly, you pissed him off."

Peaches looked over at the reception desk. Dom had on a pair of reading glasses and was flipping through an *US Weekly*. "He don't look pissed off."

"Man's professional," Bruno said. "We got customers in here. This deal expires in five seconds."

Peaches handed him his guns, Bruno putting them in his overcoat pockets.

"Wait here," Bruno said, and then he disappeared down the hall and through the double doors.

Peaches walked over to the Eldorado. It only had forty-three thousand miles on it. If they hadn't fucked with the odometer, which he doubted. He also doubted that he'd get out of Chicago before the car blew up around him, which is why he asked for it to be painted. Give him time to get some distance, make them deliver the car to him, then let someone take a look at it, see if there was fucking TNT in the trunk. A hundred and fifty thousand dollars was a lot of money, but it wasn't fuck-you money, Peaches recognized that. But he figured he could buy some high-grade heroin with it, start making some moves up north, see if this butcher motherfucker could help get some traction with the Native Mob. Junior, he'd burned that bridge by going solo, but Peaches, he was a businessman. That FBI agent was right. He needed to clique up.

A hundred and fifty thousand dollars to not call the FBI wasn't a bad bribe, what with the car. He wasn't a snitch, anyhow.

Bruno came back, holding a duffle bag. Plopped it on the hood of the Eldorado. Unzipped it. Inside, stacks of cash. Zipped it back up.

"You got a vault down behind those doors?" Peaches asked.

"Yeah," Bruno said. "Don't spend any time thinking about housing it. You'd need to come with a tank." He put out his hand. "Give me the card." Peaches did. He thought Bruno would tear it up, but instead he carefully slipped it into his own wallet. Interesting.

"The big guy back behind those doors?" Peaches asked.

"Mr. Cupertine?"

"Yeah."

Bruno pointed at the ceiling. There were a dozen cameras. "He's everywhere. Like Santa. He'll know if you've been bad and then you'll be on a fucking list. So. Don't be bad." He waved over a salesman. The guy who'd been working on the Seville earlier. "Lemonhead," Bruno said, "this motherfucker right here? He worked for your brother down at Allied. There was a misunderstanding and so Mr. Cupertine would like him to have this car."

Lemonhead said, "I still get a commission?"

"You'll need to take that upstairs."

Lemonhead looked disappointed. He actually looked like he wanted to fuck somebody up, more specifically, so Peaches reached into his bag of money, peeled off a couple bills. "Here," he said. "My treat."

Bruno said, "He'd like it painted blue."

"Actually," Peaches said, "I changed my mind." He opened the door of the Eldorado and sat down. "I'm gonna wait right here in the front seat while you get the paperwork together. And then I'm gonna drive out the door."

Bruno put up his hands. "Whatever, kid. Lemonhead, you'll take care of this." Bruno put his hand out to Peaches. "Shake my hand," he said, and Peaches did. "You're in over your head. When you decide to come back, be ready. Until then, keep your shit tight. Don't speak on the Rain Man. Keep Ronnie Cupertine's name out of your mouth, too. We have an understanding?" Peaches said they did. "Okay," he said. He looked Peaches over one more time. "Junior Pocotillo. Forgot about that motherfucker. But you look just like him. It's actually nice to see his face. Like finding an old picture underneath the sofa." He buttoned up his coat, turned the collar up, and walked out of the showroom, into the cold of the day, disappearing among the crowd of shoppers.

"Another $500," Lemonhead said, once Paul Bruno was gone, "I'll go out and get you a decent suit to wear while you're driving the car around. Look the part."

"How about this," Peaches said, taking out another couple bills and putting them in Lemonhead's hand, "tell your sister-in-law MaryAnn I'm gonna take her up on that green bean casserole one day." Lemonhead looked confused. "She'll know what I'm talking about."

Peaches Pocotillo sat there in his Eldorado for another hour, his eyes fixed on those double doors, waiting, hoping, that Ronald Cupertine would walk out, holding his tommy gun, with the Rain Man beside him. That never did happen. He'd wait forever, if he had to, to get those motherfuckers back for thinking, even for one second, that they got one over on Peaches Pocotillo.

ACKNOWLEDGMENTS

I am deeply indebted, as ever, to the steady hand (and midnight sanity checks) of my editor Dan Smetanka. He has given me such tremendous latitude with all the books we've done together. His work on these stories made each better than I could have imagined, and I'm eager to get to work on our next project. And then the one after that, too. And of course I couldn't ask for a better team than the one behind me at Counterpoint Press, starting at the top with publisher Andy Hunter, Megan Fishmann, Rachel Fershleiser, Alyson Forbes, Nicole Caputo, Wah-Ming Chang, and the whole squad in California and New York. Thank you for taking such good care of my books. And to Barrett Briske for catching all of my mistakes.

I've been lucky to have Jennie Dunham representing my books for twenty-one years. I am so thankful for her hard work on my behalf, day in and day out. And, too, I've been lucky to have Judi Farkas representing my books to the people who make glittering pictures for just as long, which is part of why this book exists at all. I am grateful to the belief and support in my work that Angela Bromstad, David Semel, Eric Overmyer, and Amazon Studios have given me while I've written these stories. Profound gratitude, as well, to Michael Besman, for his hard work in service of the very dangerous people depicted here.

I could not have written a single word here without the support of my extraordinarily talented siblings, writers and artists each:

my brother, Lee Goldberg, and my sisters Karen Dinino and Linda Woods. We each achieved our dreams, and that we get to live them in real time, together, is an incredible gift. I am also deeply appreciative of my dear friends Rider Strong, Julia Pistell, and Maggie Downs, who each spend way too many hours with me in their earbuds, and my friends and colleagues who work with me in the Low-Residency MFA program at the University of California, Riverside, all of whom are always invited to Club 3012: Agam Patel, Mark Haskell Smith, Rob Roberge, Elizabeth Crane, David Ulin, Joshua Malkin, John Schimmel, Jill Alexander Essbaum, Anthony McCann, Mary Otis, Matthew Zapruder, Deanne Stillman, Emily Rapp Black, Mary Yukari Waters, Mickey Birnbaum, and Stephen Graham Jones.

Several of these stories have appeared, often under different titles, and each in significantly different form, in a previous publication: "The Royal Californian" in *Palm Springs Noir* (Akashic); "Palm Springs," "Professor Rainmaker," and "The Salt" in *Other Resort Cities* (Other Voices Books); "Goon Number Four" in *The Darkling Halls of Ivy* (Subterranean Press); "The Last Good Man" in *The Usual Santas* (Soho Press); "Pilgrims" in *The Rattling Wall*; "Gangway" in *Kelp Journal*. These stories have benefited from the careful work of the editors and readers who first published them, so I want to thank Barbara DeMarco-Barrett, Rob Bowman, and Eduardo Santiago; Stacy Bierlein and Gina Frangello; Lawrence Block; Juliet Grames; Michelle Franke; and David Olsen, Oliver Brennan, and Chih Wang for their hard work over all these bad words.

This project wouldn't exist without these good people and organizations, along with their moral, immoral, and tangible support and inspiration during the time I wrote these stories: Rabbi Malcolm Cohen and Stephanie Helms of Temple Sinai Las Vegas;